AGENT OF CHANGE

THE REGION TWO SERIES
BOOK FOUR

JANET WALDEN-WEST

Cover: Black Bird Book Covers

Editor: Dawn Alexander Books

Proofread By: Susan Cook

ISBN 978-1-7372190-6-4 (ebook)

ISBN 978-1-7372190-8-8 (paperback)

Contact Information: janetwaldenwest@gmail.com

CHAPTER 1

imi

"Targeting a bunch of little kids? Who does that?" Josh grumbled from the second-row seat beside mine, compulsively smoothing his palm back and forth over his sniper case in his lap. "Even for vampires, that's low."

"Demons have no decency. The more depraved their sin, the greater their enjoyment," Stavros said, scowling at the lightly populated streets and iconic double row of palm trees flashing by the SUV window. The steering wheel creaked, protesting his killer grip.

Aside from the fact that technically, vampires were humans mutated by a virus, and our adopted papá was a product of his four-hundred-year-old Christian upbringing, I agreed with him.

The virus twisted its host, amping up the parts of the brain devoted to survival, damping those associated with kinder emotions. Basically, leaving vicious, self-centered predators who enjoyed tormenting their prey.

Stavros rocketed onto a side-street. We were close to our objective, a call-out mission that'd dragged us out of bed. A group of civilian children were scheduled to leave the oceanic science museum sleepover. And a surveillance van and vampires were lying in wait.

Attacking children was ugly, a totally vamp-ish move. And the last few years' exponential increase in vampires, especially those without Masters, produced clueless newbies dumb and desperate enough to attempt feeding in a super public spot, one guaranteed to draw human law enforcement attention. Worse, the attention of older vampires, who held a rigid policy against cluing the human world in on their existence.

But something felt off.

I leaned between the front seats, catching my sister and Commanding Officer's eye, and signed, my specialty since losing my voice. "We should consider there's more going on than a pack of starving, nestless vamps."

"Children are easy prey," Vee said.

"There's desperation, and then there's suicide."

Vee glanced at the pre-dawn sky. She might be one of only two vampires able to tolerate sunlight, but she hadn't forgotten all we'd learned as cadets about new vampire's physiology, and their overwhelming biological urge to hide and sleep long before the sun rose.

She shredded a cuticle. "Specific concerns?"

I flipped the thumb drive containing my latest project over and under my fingers, burning off a little irritation, and a lot of guilt.

Stavros looked across to the passenger seat at Vee, my sister and team Commanding Officer. He was her Lieutenant, and second, but her request for input was meant for all of us. Everyone had a say, and she usually considered all feedback before making or altering a decision.

There was that part of me that always questioned whether if Josh or Stavros had brought up an issue, there would be less hesitation.

"Starvation is a powerful force," he finally said.

My fingers moved faster, the drive vanishing and reappearing in a mad dance. Eyebrow up in question, I checked with my brother, because he dang well knew what I really meant. Was this *them?* Our newest enemy, one who knew way too much about who we were and what our mission was.

"Man, we don't know if these are the vampires we're after." Josh glanced at me and put a few more inches between our spacious seats as he answered, but concern deepened his voice. "What if they're randos and instead of mind-whammying and subverting an agent, they only want kids as entertainment and the meal at one of their freaky murder-raves?"

Of everyone, Josh had the most cause for skepticism. He had been on the receiving end of my biggest mistake, one we had both barely survived. The epic error where I'd also lost my voice.

His attention settled on my hand.

I slid the drive out of sight before he asked questions, freeing my hands, and signed, "According to our contact, a generic paneled surveillance van and at least two vampires in some sort of blacked out body armor and head covering? So not basic vampires."

He grunted, grudging agreement.

There had been an uptick in vampires for the last few years, in our old Arizona Division, now in our new home in Southern California. Plus other cryptids, the natural animals with unnatural abilities and the Chameleon Effect, a trait that allowed them to basically be invisible unless you already knew what to look for, behaving out of character. Migration routes suddenly interrupted, solitary ghouls and windigos pairing up. Reclusive species not native to the Americas appearing in suburban areas.

Months earlier, we'd gotten proof, in the worst possible way, that a faction of vampires had joined forces. Thanks to our sister Liv's team's capture, we now knew that this faction was behind the cryptid weirdness. As well as being wide-spread, well-funded enough to engage in advanced genetic engineering involving the most dangerous cryptids, and had an objective that at minimum involved infiltrating the Company, the place that raised and trained us.

Company Alpha Cryptid Containment was all that stood between a clueless humanity, and cryptids.

"I've run this scenario a hundred times during the drive, and the probability rate of this being the target we're really after is sixty-four-point-four percent." I stopped signing, and nudged the tablet in my lap. They at least trusted my technical abilities as team intel specialist without reservation.

A narrow band of vampire-silver circled my sister's pupil, threatening to eclipse the brown. Stavros' infecting her had been his only option to save her after an ambush by this group. Draining another vampire as her first meal, adding the double-dose of virus DNA, allowed her to tolerate sunlight, the same as Stavros. Though if other vampires ever discovered, my sister and adopted father would have every Master vampire in the world gunning for them.

"Oversight," I signed, name-dropping my best leverage to get my point across. The only way Vee and Stavros hadn't been executed after being infected was a desperate gamble, Vee offering the team as a specialized shadow strike force, reporting to Oversight, the Company's ultimate authority.

"Hey, we've brought them experimented-on ghouls, and a metric crap ton of vampires." Josh's gaze flicking from me to studying the truck's floor-mats belied his confident statement.

Feeling like a bully, I threw our precarious position at them. "HQ and the Lab division are happy. But we haven't brought in any high-ranking members of the faction." That was Oversight's priority one.

Vee touched the back of her neck, her newest tic. The spot where a kill chip had been implanted. There was one in Stavros too, and another over Josh's heart. Waiting to be activated if Oversight ever had cause to doubt our loyalty, or effectiveness. Realistically, if we accidentally made someone nervous.

All those vampires we had hauled in had been newly infected, and Masterless. The virus had way less than a fifty-percent chance of infecting a human, and them surviving. That defect in the virus had kept vampires from overrunning humanity.

Basically, since the beginning of time, only an older vampire, where the DNA had fully matured, could attempt creating more. Yet we were *drowning* in freshies. Something major, an evolutionary mutation on a fast-forwarded scale, was occurring. Horror clogged my throat for a heartbeat, making it impossible to swallow.

Today's whole *let's race the sun in a heavily populated area and grab targets that will definitely be missed* action wasn't a tactically sound plan. Vampire rule number one was never drawing unnecessary human attention. The twitchy sensation, like bugs crawling across my skin, and the way my gut had bottomed out when I intercepted our contact's report, said there was only one reason vampires tricked out in Kevlar would risk the possible exposure so close to dawn, and the ensuing public outrage and manhunt that would rain down when an entire class of children disappeared.

The kids in that aquarium were the faction's newest lab rats.

The same gut-clenching realization flowed across the rest of the team's faces. Claws tipped out on the hand wrapped around the tablet feeding us real time data, screen cracking before Vee reasserted control over the virus DNA's alterations.

I palmed the drive from where I'd tucked it under my thigh, and slid what amounted to a super off-book free pass into anyone's system safely into my boot. Our priority was the civilians' safety.

My private secondary priority was getting inside a faction stronghold.

Lowering my window enough to catch the tang of ocean, the false dawn painted patterns on the outsides of my lids as I closed my eyes. My program would send every byte of harvested data back to my devices. I'd left a master list of my passwords and information stuck on my dresser as we'd left the compound, just in case.

Because A, I'd been waiting for the faction to show for months. It finally had, and I was executing my unsanctioned Operation Infiltrate the Vampires. And B, I was prepared, and really dang good, but there was a high probability I wouldn't survive my private mission. We faced that probability every time a call-out came, or we left for a mission, though.

Vee either didn't realize, or did but refused to acknowledge, what Liv and I had already accepted. No matter how good we were, no matter how flawless our record, if even one vampire discovered she and Stavros were sun-tolerant, Oversight would terminate us in order to avoid every Master in the Americas converging on us, and by association, the Company. If we broke any of Oversight's draconian rules, or any other agent or human discovered what my father and sister were, same result.

We had to remain indispensable to Oversight, if my siblings and father were to survive.

And if there was such a thing as a way to reverse the effects of the virus, and return Vee and Stavros to human, it would logically be found in a lab full of elite vampire scientists and researchers. That was the only true safety from Oversight, every Company agent and Instructor we'd grown up with, and the ancient Masters who had decreed day walking vampires who fed on their kind would never exist. I loved my family, but I owed them, too.

Vee would never green light my plan, partially because I was her sister and the risk was too high, and partially because of her unspoken worry that I'd botch the mission. I still hated excluding my family, and guilt as heavy as a grown ghoul weighed me down.

Without looking, I patted across my pockets, reassurance that my favorite blades were in place, then tightened the band around my topknot. Stavros cut right, and the aquarium's brightly painted murals came into view.

The building's doors opened, interior lights haloing the sleepy adults carrying supplies, while kids rushed out, most ignoring their chaperones. Excited voices rose, easily audible in the truck, children splitting off to chase each other and play. The quiet morning and our plan of removing the threat before the civilians ever woke and left the security of the museum had turned into a free for all. Josh swore and abandoned his case, his aim of setting up on the site's roof and picking off threats toast.

"We are out of time." Vee's tone was grim, the team C.O. coming out and replacing the sister.

We slammed to a stop, the camp's bus providing us protection as we bailed. Sand deposited onto the blacktop from the beach yards away crunched under my boots. We all drew weapons, keeping them pointed at the ground.

Petite, feminine, and the least threatening-seeming of us, Vee held up a badge, Homeland Security this time, and advanced on the adults. Josh slid between her and the target across the road, covering her and the civilians.

I scanned the slice of beach for anything other than sand dunes and seaweed. Parallel to me, Stavros did the same, his nostrils fluttering as he also sampled the air for the scent of our objectives.

His head snapped left at the same moment the seagrass moved ahead of us, patch rippling and sand exploding upwards. That skin-tingling rush of a new challenge swirled through me. Our intel was solid—the faction I needed was here. Grains of sand drifted down as Stavros and I split, each heading for the target, coming at them from different directions.

The screech of tires and doors slamming carried from the parking area, out of place and tearing my attention off the beach. I slowed and glanced over. Two SUVs identical to ours blocked us in. But it wasn't extra agents storming out. Not Company, anyway. These were in all black, helmets with thick, smoke gray face shields pulled down.

The faction's vampires. A double handful, aiming for the kids, Vee, and Josh.

Shots popped, children and adults screaming. On a wave of adrenalin, I spun away from whatever was waiting in the sand, running to back up the rest of the team. Stavros flashed by me. He leapt, landing on top of the bus, catching a vampire by the throat. It gave an ear-shattering wail, then the head, still shielded by the helmet, hit the ground.

I left Stavros to the other two on the roof. Vee was doing her best, pushing the herd of civilians back into the building. Getting them out of the line of fire, and stationing herself in the doorway. Creating a bottleneck where she picked off any vampires attempting to get past.

Josh's gun barked, each shot taking out a target.

The bus roof vampires hadn't been the only ones to split. A pair converged behind my brother, using the same maneuver Stavros and I had. Too close for me to risk a shot. I holstered the gun, jerking my favorite knife free instead, blade treated with a chemical compound fatal to cryptids. And sprinted, aiming for the one on the right, only steps from Josh's unprotected back.

Catching up, I kicked out, nailing it behind a knee. Not enough to down the stocky vampire. But enough that it listed, attention leaving my brother. Before it got its legs back under it, I grabbed from behind, catching the helmet strap, snapping its head back with one hand. The other slicing across its exposed throat. The vampire jerked forward. Helping me, driving my blade deeper, catching on bone. I put my all my weight on the helmet strap, hauling its body sideways, knife sawing. Bone and tendons gave with a wet crack.

I let go. Head hanging by a strip of skin, the body slumped, hitting the ground.

Claws whistled, and I ducked. Dropping and rolling over asphalt, my body armor saving me from shredding skin. Coming up in a crouch, I whipped a second blade out, the longer one from my thigh rig.

I feinted, catching the new vampire's wrist, slashing through the unprotected join between glove and uniform. Not severing it, but the creature's hand spasmed, dropping its gun, a match to our Glocks.

We circled, this one warier than the first, testing each other's defenses. I barely registered Stavros landing on the ground, tossing a body with a hole through its chest, and heading for the building. Done with his wave of attackers,

JANET WALDEN-WEST

Josh did the same, joining in to pick off the straggler vampires crowding Vee.

Finally committing, my vampire lunged. In and out, knife weaving an intricate pattern. Herding me. The bus loomed in my peripheral vision, a solid steel obstacle. Cutting off my escape route.

Close enough to his goal, the vampire rushed me. Ready to pin me against the side of the bus, and gut me.

Squatting, thigh muscles bunching, I launched up from the deep crouch, the extra bit of propulsion sending me higher. My heels hit the wide rubber tire, and I pivoted, launching back off it. Straight at the vampire under me. Knife down, I put all my velocity and weight behind my thrust. The chem-treated metal punched through the vampire's ribs.

It slashed, but stumbled, blade tip catching then skittering sideways over my thicker chest plate. I landed on it, riding it to the ground. Grunting as a flailing fist caught my jaw and sharp pain rattled my head, I angled and bone cracked, my knife sliding into its heart.

It got an arm under, but wavered, the chem hitting its bloodstream. I shoved off as it went limp, coming to my feet, and turned for my sister and the kids.

Something sharp pierced the exposed skin of my neck. I slammed elbows back, hitting body armor, getting a growl as dread blossomed. The bus seemed to waver, turning to a yellow blob, blurring into a patchwork of melting colors, black of the parking lot, green and blue of the building's artwork. I stumbled, fighting the drug, searching for Stavros or Vee.

Arms wrapped around me from behind, hauling me off my feet, then flinging me face down over a shoulder. My body didn't respond when I tried pushing away. The throb from the vampire's punch turned into a band squeezing my head.

Wind whipped hair in my eyes, the vampire rushing away from the fight, my head bouncing with each stride, hot spikes poking my brain with each step. The gold of a California sunrise washed over me, highlighting Josh's tall form running my way, lips moving as he yelled my name, before black drowned out the sun, consciousness, and my guilt.

CHAPTER 2

even-Zero-One

"CLEAR TO ENGAGE." Under the whoosh of waves coming in, and the chatter of the group of human's circled around large yellow vehicles, his handler's whisper carried.

Peering through the sea grass, he ignored the vampire. The ocean breeze brought him information. The fishy taste of creatures that lived in the salt water. The chemical pong of many other vehicles and their fuel. The sweetness of food, remnants smeared on the small humans. His stomach pinched, hunger rising.

He hadn't been fed that night. Or the one before. Only those who obeyed were given rations. Performing well now was his chance to fill the hollowness in his belly.

Still, he watched the humans. The grown ones—women, the name humans and vampires gave their females—and the cubs they served as caretakers for. They had all been inside the building across the road, on the other side of the beach.

The building with the giant ocean creatures on the sides, where there were roads instead of sand, large tanks of water instead of ocean, until moments earlier. In the images his trainers showed him, humans went in and out during the day.

These humans had slept in the building, though. Now they were outside, carrying the kinds of pads he slept on. When he obeyed, and earned one.

"Repeat. Clear to engage the enemy. Now, Seven-Zero-One." The handler's voice slapped at him, the vampire using its aura as a weapon, and he twitched.

He wasn't good at obeying. He'd been on many training exercises. Sometimes he killed the enemies. Those were bigger, other vampires, or enemies with claws.

These enemies were smaller. They carried bedding, and boxes that smelled of the sweet food. He wasn't familiar with this type of enemy-human.

"Seven-Zero-One. Engage."

"They are small and weak. Cubs. The others carry no weapons."

"Irrelevant. They are the enemy. Follow your orders. Eliminate the adults, and retrieve the subjects." The anger twining the vampires voice, that Seven-Zero was familiar with.

He understood growing. He and the batch of littermates he was raised with had once been small. They bit and snapped even then. Sometimes for sport, always for dominance. And for food, a sleeping mat, or one of the good places to rest, one where he could sleep with his back against a wall so others didn't sneak in and attack from behind. They fought more as they grew larger, even though there were fewer of them, the weak culled away.

These cubs didn't act like his. They made loud, high-pitched sounds, and ran around each other, chasing. The faster ones didn't pull the others down when they caught them, though. They didn't smell of anger or violence.

He crept closer. Not to attack. Only to watch them more closely, in their bright uniforms. None the same, and he hadn't puzzled out how they knew which batch they belonged too if they all wore different colors.

As the breeze picked up, he cocked his head and parsed the pheromones coming from the group. For some reason, the not-fighting was allowed—the caretakers didn't shock and discipline the cubs, or encourage them to fight more ferociously.

"They'll grow up, becoming large, armed humans who will attack you, unless we capture and modify them," his handler warned.

"I am studying these enemies." Which was a not-truth. These were a new thing, and new things fascinated him.

"Stop studying, and engage. The sun will be up in twenty-minutes. If I get singed, I will fry your worthless carcass," the vampire barked.

A growl trickled out of Seven-Zero's throat. His handlers disciplined and demanded. This time, maybe he would fry them.

"We have an incoming problem." The tinny voice of the not-handler who stayed inside the vehicle came from the device in the handler's helmet. "Infrared is hot, and the digital signature is consistent with Company soldiers. Unit Two is on the way to intercept them, but they're several minutes behind the humans."

His handler muttered the nonsense words that meant he was angry, and the grass around Seven-Zero rippled. He pivoted, facing the real threat. The vampire was fast, and quiet. Not as fast as Seven's kind, and he met the threat head-on, growl deepening.

Covered head to toe in the special black uniforms needed

to protect their kind's fragile skin from daylight, his handler loomed over Seven-Zero. The blocky training taser hung from a strap around his wrist. "Attack. Now. This is your last chance, you backward excuse for a fighter."

Seven-Zero showed his teeth in threat, the words distorted by his snarl. "I am studying."

His handler's fangs slid out in response, skin on his face thinning, almost translucent and showing the bones underneath. "I'm done with this insubordination." He flipped the smoked visor over his face, palming the taser. Fire sparked from the ends.

Seven-Zero launched from his crouch, fist slamming through his opponent's face shield, shards embedding in his knuckles. He smashed the vampire's face, bones and fangs crunching.

The vampire yelled for his partner, and jammed the taser into Seven-Zero's chest. The fabric of his shirt melted, smoke mixing with the burning meat stink as his skin blistered. Agony seared his nerves, but he was accustomed to pain.

He punched the vampire, its head snapping back, then grabbed its throat. Sand squeaked behind Seven-Zero, the second vampire cornering him, another hated taser ramming against his spine. He fought to hold on, to crush the handler's throat.

Instead, alien electrical impulses spread, his muscles jumping and spasming. His hand twitched, and no matter how hard he tried to tighten his hold, it opened, dropping useless to his side. His entire body shook.

The handler jerked the taser away, whipping it in a circle, then the heavy block connecting with Seven-Zero's skull. More pain erupted against the side of Seven-Zero's head. He dropped, hitting grass and packed sand. The taser bounced to the ground, abandoned. Pulling on the last bit of strength, willing himself to move, kill his tormentor, he managed to roll his head. Looking for his captor.

The handler's gun pointed at Seven-Zero's face.

The other vampire's boots skidded to a stop, inches from Seven-Zero's head. He tried opening his mouth, taking a last bite before they eliminated him as the vampires argued. "We aren't cleared to dispose of experiments."

"This one has always been defective, and I've wasted too damn much time on it. It's untrainable."

"It's also tens of millions of dollars in research funds. R and D can still put it to use, dissecting it to see what went wrong."

Tires screeched, and the shrill noises from the human cubs and caretakers increased, tenor altering. The boots moved. "Fuck. They're here. The lab will add us into their next experiment if we allow a specimen to fall into Company hands."

Footsteps, heavy and fast, pounded over the road. Two sets coming closer. Hands grabbed Seven-Zero's collar, twisting it tight enough his breath wheezed, as another set of hands closed around his ankles. The vampires heaved him up and tossed him. He hit the cold metal of the van, head bouncing, cage lock whirring.

He caught the whistle of guns firing behind them, where the cubs were. Figures rushed his way. Two human soldiers, in mottled gray uniforms, loaded with blades and guns. They split, a smaller one heading for the handler's hiding spot, in the lead.

The last thing he saw was a woman soldier, hair tied up, leaving her heart-shaped face bare, and intense eyes visible, lit from behind by the sun rising over the building. She aimed for the sand bank hiding the van and him.

Doors slammed shut, leaving him in darkness, the motor rumbling and taking him away from the battle. He would have rather died under the open sky, fighting the fierce soldier, instead of under the scalpels of the vampires he was returning to.

* * *

THE BRUSH of frigid air over his blistered skin greeted Seven-Zero. The part of him that understood earth-position threw up an image of digging, and tunnels. Underground, then, the DNA of whatever burrowing cryptid he was composed of believing this was safety.

His nostrils flared, pulling in the bite of chemicals used when his kind were cut up and improved on, and the whir of the machines in the short tunnel that cleaned the vampires when they returned from outside. He was underground, in the vampire's facility that his kind were kept in.

He opened his eyes the smallest bit, keeping the rest of his aching body still, in case he wasn't alone. Hoping for the stone walls and dull metal bars of his batch's sleeping cages. Instead, pure white walls and harsh, buzzing lights greeted him.

The digging part of him was wrong. This was the lab, the bad place.

The vampire scientists here didn't care if he was awake or not to perform their improvements on him. The door whooshed open, vampires walking in. One bringing the rot of old blood with it.

Seven-Zero rolled to a crouch, one hand on the slick white tile bracing him. He slung his head, shaking off the last of the taser effects. From the way the room wavered, they had shot his body full of the bad drug, making sure he didn't wake until he was trapped in this clear cell.

Cowards. He lifted his lip in warning as his handler stopped beside the cell. The vampire's face was healed, nose no longer crushed and the marks of Seven-Zero's fingers around its throat gone.

"I was crystal clear in my assessment report. This specimen is defective, and we are wasting time and resources on it better utilized in training another generation." The vampire spoke, voice whistling, and victory mingled with Seven-Zero's rage. The vampire had only a nub of fang on one side, nothing on the other yet, his regeneration ability inferior to Seven-Zero's.

One of the scientist vampires, who were dominants in the lab, continued walking, sitting a tall cup on her desk, the tang of chemically prepared blood leaking around the lid. She dropped the bag she carried beside the chair, her routine when it was her time in the lab. "The subject rates in the top percentile for agility, speed, and cognitive ability. It almost perfectly matches DNA and blood test parameters to read as human. Only one anomaly, which can be passed off as a minor amino acid elevation. That automatically qualifies it for another attempt at programming."

Seven-Zero was more interested in what was inside her bag than talking vampires.

"Every try has failed, Irene."

The scientist gave off a wave of irritation, the kind when the handler called her by the name instead of *doctor*. "He is also in the top two-percent for aggression. That alone is worth salvaging."

His handler slapped the clear barrier, glaring at Seven-Zero.

Seven-Zero slapped the same spot, from inside. He pointed at his teeth, then the vampire's. "You are defective."

His handler whirled on the scientist. "That. That is the issue. Aggression is great. But it's directed at the. Wrong. Damn. Species."

"Your opinion is noted, although perhaps it's time to

consider that it isn't the subject that's sub-par, but the trainer, *Adam*." The scientist circled the equipment, tapping switches. She nudged the bag under the chair as she went by. "Seven-Zero-One is from the F6 breakthrough batch. That group is even more important due to Welch's disastrous need to show off. Not only did we lose our only adult psy specimen, but now the Company knows we exist."

The bag tipped sideways, top open, drawing Seven-Zero's attention as the vampires continued arguing. Bright pink and green peeked out, along with the silhouette of a human male. Excitement swirled through his system. A new book. His fingers flexed, the feel of the shiny cover and paper fresh, despite not having touched a book in many months.

At the door swooshing open, Seven-Zero pulled his attention from his potential prize. While he had been lost in the hopes of something new, the vampires had stopped arguing. Two large helper vampires walked in. One carried the hated device, a collar, with poles attached on each side.

The barrier vibrated from his growl. He wasn't taken out for training in the lab. Only for pain, being strapped to the cold tables, the bad drugs so he couldn't defend himself. Escaping the helpers wasn't possible, but he would fight until he couldn't anymore.

The vampires all picked up the plugs they put in their ears, and the Irene-scientist pushed the button. Noise, like shrieking and stabbing inside his head, blared. The room wavered, and he wobbled, balance vanishing. Dampness trickled from his ear. He couldn't hear the cage opening, only the change in pressure. He lurched, swinging blindly at the helpers.

Metal hit his throat, then clamped around his neck. He threw himself backward, but couldn't find his center. The pair dragged him out, poles now keeping them out of his reach. They swung him, his back and skull slamming against metal. Next would come the straps, securing him, then the table tilting flat. Humiliation at his weakness, and something else that left him feeling hollow, washed over him.

The needles-in-his-brain noise cut off. The handler and scientist were yelling, but his ears ached, ruptured eardrums not healed enough yet to hear. He concentrated on the scientist's lips, reading the words, the way his batch had learned to speak.

He caught *prisoner* and *val-u-able*. The handler motioned for a helper.

The helper vampires looked to the scientist for orders. She pointed at one and the door. He tossed his pole to his twin and the tension on Seven-Zero's left slacked.

She nodded at the cell. Seven-Zero's ears popped, sound skipping, but hearing returning. "...will have to wait. One of you can handle him...hasn't recovered enough.." She pivoted, going after the handler and helper.

The helper hesitated and Seven-Zero lurched sideways. Legs wobbly he went down, hitting the desk edge, chair skidding away. He threw his arms in front of him as support.

"Idiot lab rat." The helper grunted and shoved, propelling Seven-Zero across the floor on his hands and knees. The helper thrust him into his cell, Seven-Zero hitting the floor face-first.

The helper jerked, collar releasing, then the cell door slammed closed. Seven-Zero lay flat until the helper's footstep's retreated, the whoosh of air marking him exiting to follow his leader.

Seven-Zero rose to his knees, back to the room even as hairs rose on his arms in warning at leaving himself vulnerable to enemies. He hunched over, then scrubbed his face against his shirt, rubbing blood off before it could drip. A quick look over his shoulder proved the lab was empty.

He reached under his waistband, pulling out the book

he'd snatched. He huffed at tricking the helper, as if Seven-Zero would ever fall over like a new cub.

Seven-Zero cradled his prize. The Irene-scientist vampire brought many books, reading them when there were no experiments, and no creatures to hurt. Sometimes she brought the same books, rereading them. This one was new. He wiped his hand against his pants, their fabric cleaner, then traced a finger over the pink lettering on the cover, and the image of a human face hiding behind dark glasses almost like the handler hid behind his helmet cover. The human face was only half visible, an open book held in front covering the lower portion.

A ribbon of satisfaction wove through the dark emptiness inside him. He had read another book from this group. He sounded it out—book two. Books sometimes had numbers, telling their position. The numbers meant which to read first, not which was stronger, the way numbers did in his kind's batches.

He scooted to the solid platform extending from the rear barrier wall, the spot intended for sleeping. He ran his hand along the cold, slick surface underneath, all the way to the back. His fingertip bumped a raised seam, and he worked his nails in enough to pop a corner loose, then removed the square.

Feeling inside the hollow, his fingers brushed against book spines. Two. They were still here where he had hidden them, in the hole he'd scratched out. He rested against the side of the platform and carefully opened the book, to where the story words began.

Books were for studying, the same as the small enemy-cubs. And equally forbidden. His kind were only interested in the things their handlers trained them to see. His batch didn't study. They weren't created to.

His kind didn't have emotions. They were trained to

mimic actions and emotions, long enough to fool humans, and infiltrate and attack. His batch was smarter than other batches. He and the surviving batch were trained to go alone without handlers by their sides, and execute missions. Not to think extra things, or feel emotions. Another way he was defective.

The books were full of emotions, and the people and emotions were more interesting than missions. He didn't understand all he read, though. He hunkered in, enjoying the first pages, because there were always emotions in first pages.

The hero—the male—talked of loyalty. Seven-Zero knew loyalty. That was what was required of his batch, loyalty to the handler and all other Syndicate vampires. If he wasn't loyal, if he snarled at, bit, or punched vampires, he was punished.

Sometimes, heroes fought. So did heroines—the females. He knew fighting, another thing he was trained for.

Not all of the scientist's books had battles. They all had *love*. He needed to understand it, but trainers never showed images or demonstrated how to act out love. There was also kindness and support, more concepts he needed to understand.

There was also always *attraction* with the *love*. Comparing his training to books, he knew attraction. That was when males of his kind were caged with females, to breed. No one in the books commanded the males and females to breed. But often the two were *stranded together* which seemed the same as caging together.

The other emotions, and the actions of the book people… they were confusing. Alien. Like when he tried understanding psy creatures or the venom-lizard creatures, and their scents and behavior.

Finger over the second-first pages, the ones where the

hero males and heroine females crashed into each other, in carriages, or shops with coffee, he stopped. His head buzzing. Not with the sharp discipline pain, but with idea-questions. The book emotions...what if they were real? What if not-humans had them? That would be—*amazing*, the word the scientist used when one of the other female vampires brought her fresh cups of blood, or the red drink that smelled of spoiled berries. The one she whispered when she and the other vampire went into the enclosed experimenting part of the lab, and pheromones that meant mating scented the air.

He slumped against the unforgiving platform. The scientist and helpers would return. Then they would take him to the experimenting table, and do the *reprogramming* to him.

The hollowness increased. He would not be repro-grammed again. He would attack the vampires. He would fight, through the killing noise, through the collar, fight until blood ran from his eyes and ears and he died like other fail-ures from his batch, or until the vampires used their guns and killed him.

Thumps from the lab entryway carried. He wedged the book in with the others, and placed the clawed-out chunk in the hole, pressing until it sealed tight. Prize hidden, he whirled to face the lab as the scientist arrived, snapping orders. "Be careful!"

"We're trying. Ma'am," One of the helpers said, as he and his twin backed it in. Whatever they were holding between them was smaller, not a lizard or ghoul creature, or the stinking four-legged ones.

One helper grunted, then said the angry words. They shoved the captured specimen into a cell, and stabbed the locking button.

The captive spun, back on its feet just as the lock engaged.

Another vampire or one of his kind. Its scent was covered by vampire and blood stink, as it kicked the barrier.

"I'd prefer not to sedate you again," the scientist said. "Members of field units aren't known for their light touch, including with sedatives and captured specimens."

She never spoke to specimens or creatures. Seven-Zero rose for a clearer look, defective curiosity waking

"I'd be happy to relieve her of a pint or two," the first helper said. "Damned thing bit me."

The captured vampire—a female, in a black and gray mottled uniform, nearly identical to theirs, but holsters and weapons stripped off—stepped so she was as close as the barrier allowed. And folded all the fingers on both hands down, except for the middle one. Those she raised in the helpers' faces, the same action he'd seen other vampires use when insulting each other.

She wasn't just defying them. She was *taunting t*hem. He'd never seen anyone challenge the vampires—except him.

"Leave it," the scientist ordered as the offended helpers growled. "I have a meeting with the Director to discuss our unexpected prize. Go scour the transport van for any additional bio remains. Those troops can't tell a viable sample from dead seaweed."

As the trio left, the air pressure in the room shifted, and brought the captive's scent clearly. Vampire musk, the rot of drying blood, vampire and human. Underneath was the faintest trace of vegetation, the kind other species consumed. His nostrils flared. Not only old human blood but...

He inhaled, the refined smell-taste receptors from other donor creatures sorting and cataloging. Sweat. Human. She was a *human.*

She circled the cell, fingers touching the barrier, bending and running them along the corners of the enclosure, around the sleeping platform. She laid on her back, sliding under the platform, repeating her exploration of the underside.

Humans truly were wily. She would have discovered his prize cache. Done with her inspection, she rolled out and to her feet in an enviably smooth motion, despite her torn shirt and scrapes along her wrists.

Climbing onto the platform, she tilted her head back, turning in a tight circle, and scanning the top of the cell. Back where she started, she hopped off and crossed to the side facing him.

He tensed, prepared for her to launch at the barrier in an effort to kill him. She had to have seen there was no escaping from the cell, but humans were vicious and less intelligent than vampires. All of his batch were taught that as cubs.

Instead, she leaned in, watching him, doing something with her hair. Pulling a band out, curls cascading to her shoulders, then pulling them back into a knot and re-securing the band. Like the way the human soldier at the beach had worn her hair, the one in the lead he'd glimpsed.

Scent and memory clicked together. This *was* the lead human soldier.

Instead of yelling threats at him, or making the insulting gestures she gave the helpers, she knocked on the barrier. When he jerked, she waved. Waving him closer.

He hesitated. But she couldn't reach him. And she was different, interesting. He stood, showing her his height and size, impressing he was dominant, not prey.

Once he was paying attention, she tapped her lips, then her ear, and pointed at his. He crossed so that he was closer.

She nodded, and spoke slowly, much slower than vampires, pointing at her lips the entire time. Her voice was rough, and required all his attention, lower than any creature's he'd encountered, even the psy creatures the vampires believed were mute.

But he heard her. "Hey. We are getting out of here. I'll get you out, okay?"

He turned her words different ways inside his head, puzzling them out the same as the words in the books. The words weren't aggressive. Neither was her body language, no posturing or stretching or puffing to appear larger. She stared but not like she was challenging him.

"I only need a little time to plan," she said in that rough-faint, slow voice. She made the words stronger. "I'll kill these monsters, and we will escape."

She put her palm flat against the glass. "I. Promise."

The books always had promises, and the book people kept them, no tricks.

Maybe...maybe this was a true book emotion thing. Like escape and freedom. For the first time, he thought of himself and freedom together.

Their trainers would call this new idea impossible. If it was an exercise, they would tell the batch that many of them would die completing the assignment. There were no other batch members here and no handler backup for this escape-fight, only this human, one without weapons. They were buried far under the ground, with many handlers and scientists between this room and the outside.

But he had nothing to lose.

He put his palm flat against the barrier, mirroring hers. "Yes."

CHAPTER 3

 imi

Vampires really were *the* worst.

Head still aching from the drug after-effects, I circled the holding cell again, slower, pressing close and peering at the mechanized door, like I was the only farsighted agent in Company history. I'd scouted my temporary prison as soon as the vampires tossed me in, half protocol for any agent captured, half proving this wasn't a hallucination or dream, and that I really was inside a faction facility.

This second pass was cover while I studied the room's layout, available equipment, and security setup, totally different from the building housing the vampire-led group our and my sister Liv's teams busted the previous Fall. More realistically, that glitzy cryptid-reveal party was an unsanctioned event by a higher-ranking member, at one of the real businesses the splinter group used to generate income. That the first incident was in Phoenix, and this one was somewhere on the outskirts of L.A., supported my theory.

Squashing the urge to touch the lump inside my boot shaft, I let the unoccupied part of my brain review facts and probabilities. My captors had been thorough, searching and stripping me of weapons. But they hadn't even glanced at the extra zippers on my boots, the thumb drive that my success hinged on tucked where I'd hidden it before our mission went sideways.

Switching to inspecting ceiling and corners for additional cameras, I took a deep breath and finished my circuit, facing deeper into the room. Right across from the only other occupied cell, and the major complication I hadn't factored into any of my scenarios. Nausea stronger than when the sedative hit my bloodstream burned up my esophagus as I ran out of reasons not to look at the other prisoner.

He didn't give off any vampire tells, the micro actions that made civis uncomfortable in a cryptid's presence, that primitive part of our brains recognizing a predator. Even if it was a ghoul hiding under a hoodie and sweats or a vampire in a suit and carrying the newest cell phone, our bodies responded to their otherness. All Company agents spent eighteen-years studying cryptid behavior, though.

After not-watching him via his reflection in my cell glass, this guy still didn't exhibit any red flags. It would've made my mission so much easier if he was simply a vampire that had displeased its Master and gotten tossed inside the lab as punishment.

No such luck. His expression and body language when I arrived...he reminded me of Bruce, my adopted brother, when he believed my sister was dead. That same worn-down hopelessness had curved his shoulders, and dulled his expression.

I *had* to get into the computer system here. The Company's existence, and my family's lives, depended on whatever was stored here. But I also had to get the human across from me free of this nightmare.

He was scuffed up, plain black tee ripped on one side, and sets of charred oval holes on his chest and back exposed the blistered skin underneath. Matching multi-pocketed BDU pants carried mud streaks and the glitter of sand.

Everything about my new roomie screamed he'd been here way longer than my few hours.

His dead expression went in the con column of my calculations as to whether he'd be a help in a violent, precisely planned escape.

In the pro column, the BDUs. They didn't *definitively* prove he was military or LEO, a law enforcement officer, of some type. Paired with his crew cut, black hair little more than stubble, and the old scars visible on his arms and hands, it upped the probability.

Either way, he looked the part, as tall as my brother Josh, carrying as much muscle as our year-mate brother Matteo, but sleeker. Despite simply standing in a cage, he was dangerous. A weapon, hopefully in the same way we were.

Perfectly still, he watched me, the only motion slow blinks and his big chest rising and falling. Like an agent studying their opponent. Or a carnivore watching potential prey.

His hesitation, then agreement when I'd promised him we were leaving this place fresh, I smiled. He'd done great reading my lips, not thrown by my inability to speak. At least the cells weren't soundproof, and I could hear him.

The lab door opened, and I leaned, adding the glimpse of the long, narrow hallway to my building blueprint. The drug they'd hit me with hadn't completely left my system when we'd arrived and my mental map was incomplete. Another mistake on my part, with potentially deadly consequences.

The other prisoner snarled as the vampire in hospital scrubs entered, carrying throwaway plastic trays. The vampire ignored him, tapping a code into the scanner on the cell door, and shoving the tray in the narrow slot that slid sideways. The guy snatched his up, but didn't take his eyes off our guard.

The feeding routine had possibilities. Faking disinterest, I lounged against the cell wall, ideas churning, waiting for my turn. The guard repeated the type and slide process on my cell. I darted in, and hit my knees, grabbing the tray. And left it half in, blocking the mechanism clicking back into place.

"What the hell?" The vampire hesitated.

I pulled the thin film off the top, inspecting the food. Then slapped the neon green gelatin cup back through, to splat on his white pants.

He swore, and I said, "I hate lime," enunciating clearly so he had no trouble reading my lips. I took the rest of the tray and sat on the end of the plastic bunk, crossing my legs and neatly picking up the fork. Politely, I raised a brow, asking if he had a problem.

The vampire stared for a beat. He wasted blood reserves, his rushing to his face, checks and neck neon. "Instead of programming, I hope they harvest you. Slowly." He pointed at the second room, table and operating equipment visible through the same clear walls as our cells.

Pulling on every annoyed Instructor from our Academy days, I gave him a stern look. Exaggerating my lip movements, I said, "No lime. Bring lemon next time."

A grumble of laughter came from the other cell. The vampire's face turned brighter and he hissed, fangs sliding out and face thinning, lips corpse-black.

I opened the paper juice carton, ignoring him, until he stomped to the door, stopping to punch in the code, then resumed stomping out. Not having a door to slam must've sucked. Hopefully, it added to his irritation and anger.

Anger made people and vampires sloppy.

As soon as the door swooshed back, I swiveled around on the seat to check out my roomie, who'd had past lip-reading experience if he picked up on what I said while angled toward the vampire. A definite plus, that I slotted into the resources portion of my potential new plan.

"Hi." I paired it with a wave.

A second of hesitation and he waved back. Which, honestly? *Adorable* coming from a massive probably-soldier.

Testing out the limits of his lip-reading skills, slower but without exaggerating, I held up the tray and spoke. "Is the food drugged?"

He unwrapped his, and frowned, leaning to sniff the food. He shrugged and tore the sandwich in half. "It's fancy food. No bad drugs."

I poked the sandwich, white bread and a slice of what might or might not be ham. Pushing it to the edge, I opted for the bowl of limp iceberg lettuce scattered with a few tomato slivers, and the sugary juice. If this was a step up from what the vampires usually fed prisoners? There couldn't be any humans working here.

When I checked again, Mister Possibly-A-Soldier's tray was empty. He gave my leftovers a hungry look.

So, he'd been trapped here long enough to consider a sandwich that even a gas station wouldn't sell desirable. My already firm promise to free him turned to concrete.

Tapping the drained carton against the tray, I plotted scenarios. Punching the vampire worker's buttons was progressing nicely. Dancing on the fine line between goading the guards into getting sloppy, but not quite to the point where they would shoot me through the feed slot, was unexpected fun.

Buzzed on the drink's high-fructose goodness, the concoction banned in our compound, and the rush of messing with vampires, I bounced up. My fingers itched for a paintbrush, or camera, to channel the energy. Neither of which were available.

Paper, on the other hand, was. Careful not to rip the cardboard, I opened the drink carton along its seams, until it was a flat rectangle, then wiped the inside against my pants. If nothing went FUBAR—say, over-antagonizing a guard, the scientists deciding that whatever they'd been keeping the other human for, now was the perfect time to program or eviscerate him—I'd be back home before the BDUs got super gross. Or, worst case, dead. Either way, no reason to worry about laundry.

Folding the cardboard, I paced corner to corner, humming to myself. One of those too deeply ingrained habits, like actually speaking although no one could hear me. The keypads used to enter and exit the labs and cells were a bonus. I only needed the code, as opposed to keycards and prints or retinas for biological scanners. Being in the first cell and closer to the pad would've been better.

My brain pinged from possibility to possibility for getting the vampires not to stand directly in front of the pad, blocking my view. I needed my sister Liv's height. Then looking over the tops of their heads wouldn't be a problem. Pretty sure the guards would notice my standing on the sleeping platform and peering over their shoulders, though.

Action in the other cell pulled me back into the here and now. The maybe-soldier had finally moved. Nose nearly pressed against the cell wall, looking at me.

Not at me, but at my hands. I made a last fold and tuck, and examined the origami creation. It wasn't exactly cute, the cardboard too stiff, but it was recognizable as a canine.

Finessing the design until it looked like Snuggles, my nieces-by-adoption's Golden Retriever, was a work in progress.

My neighbor was both in the cell closest to the scanner, and unless there was an ex-NBA player turned vampire working as a guard, had the height to see over anyone here. He was also an unknown quantity.

The scientist's code, or one from an equally high-ranking member, was a must. The workers were undoubtedly restricted, not allowed access to certain areas. I needed free access, to make it through the two security points I did remember from my trip in.

Next, weapons. The lab jerks only had small caliber pistols. The real guards carried Glocks, as well as semi-automatics. No knives, which kind of sucked.

Standing on tiptoes, I cataloged the surgical suite. *Bingo.* A disturbing display of scalpels took up one whole counter. They worked in a pinch, at least for close-quarters fighting. Which was unavoidable, especially in the narrow cleaner entry leading out of the lab, and again from the building into the garage. Once in, hot wiring or hacking a vehicle was a gimme.

Other obstacles kept piling up, though. Simply getting out had turned into getting myself *and* the other human out. But leave it to vampires to rip us off on command structure, training, gear, and weaponry, but instead of situating their compounds on isolated backroads, plop them in the middle of population centers.

Stopping teams from pursuing us shot to the top of my growing list. The Company mandate was protecting civilians at all costs. Vampires didn't care who ended up collateral damage during a chase, as long as they recaptured or eliminated me.

Facing reality, my plan had to be perfect and executed ASAP.

Because one, extracting every byte of data was non-negotiable, the only way for us to prevent the vampire uprising from expanding, plus my best possibility for getting closer to research on reversing the virus effects and getting my family off Oversight's chopping block.

And two, I had a fellow human to rescue. Point three, we were in a lab, an area built specifically for medical experiments on subjects.

My roomie and I were those subjects, and the lead scientist looked at me the same way my brother looked at a bag of doughnuts, dying to dig in. I wasn't betting on her having stronger self-control than Josh.

I flopped on the platform, placing the ugly cardboard canine on the floor for my roomie to stare at, and closed my eyes. Mentally sketching out a new painting, trying to replace the ghost image that popped up, of the moment I made a decision without considering probabilities, stepping out of formation, and a ghoul slipping into the opening I'd left, its claws flashing toward my brother's stomach.

Successfully executing my mission might come down to how reliable under pressure the non-Company civi enthralled by a piece of twisted paper was. I had no way to calculate his abilities and factor them into my plan.

On the plus side, Bruce, one sister's fiancé, and Marshall, my other sister's civilian love, always stepped up, protecting those they cared about. Even Kit, our non-human civi, risked his life for us, his new family.

But the only other human in here with me had no such emotional attachment, and the probability of success? Not on my side.

CHAPTER 4

even-Zero-One

THE LAB'S lights were never dimmed, but the part of him created from animals that always knew whether it was day or night told him it was edging closer to time for those creatures who lived in the dark to stretch, and prepare for the hunt. The brief period when few vampires were up and alert was his only time to rest, and it was ending.

Instead of following that basic biological drive to sleep, he had sat and watched the human, who was curled on her side asleep, an arm over her eyes. She was...he didn't have a word for her. *Different* and *new* wasn't enough.

She made magical creatures, the tiny image of the stinking windigo, but without the smell. She produced odd yet pleasing not-word noises. She taunted and laughed at the vampires. She made *him* laugh. An action he wasn't genetically capable of, since he wasn't bred to feel emotions. One had snuck out of him, surprising as a cub ambushing another.

This human wasn't like the ones in the images the vampire caretakers and trainers taught his batch with. She wasn't even like the vampires.

She made him forget the dark, hollow thing in his center. He liked how she made magic. How she looked. How she smelled. She did the smile-action, but it made her eyes different. Happy eyes, not the showing teeth threat his kind used, or the vicious lies kind behind all vampire smiles.

He understood her escaping. He didn't understand why she would take him. His batch was trained only to assist others on missions, and only if instructed.

His back to the lab camera, he ran his thumb over the smooth page of the book he'd brought out once the helper left, and *she* slept. Was saving others a human thing? This book didn't have fights and saving, but the other tucked in his hiding spot, the second he'd taken, had people-animals, werewolves who saved their mate and pack.

She was pure human. He also wasn't sure if he qualified as a were-people. He had parts from many cryptids, but he didn't grow fur, or fangs and claws. Fur was useless, but the claws he would've liked. He didn't know if humans liked were-people, or were-people without claws.

He huffed, a soft blast through his nose. Humans were confusing. She had rejected fancy food. No cryptids *ever* refused food. Was she sick? He hadn't scented the too-sweet rot of decay. Unease slithered in. The vampires killed and disposed of sick things. The unease built, until he whipped his head around, checking whether the human was still breathing.

She sat on the floor, legs tucked under and watching him. Him, with the book in full view. He froze.

She tapped on the cell wall, pointing at her lips again. Was she threatening to tell the helpers? The scientist?

Doing the slow, faint talking, she said, "I wish I had a book. What are you reading?"

He examined her body language, the feel of her words and the emotions under them. All he found was curiosity, like his. This still might be a trick so she could report to the helpers and gain better treatment, though.

She knew nothing of his secret horde. If this book was taken, he had more. He hitched closer, hunching protectively so that all the camera saw was his back, and held the book cover chest high for her to see.

"No freaking way." She bounced in place, and he instinctively jerked back. Faster than before, more excited, she continued. "My sisters and I love that series. I have a signed set."

He knew the words, *series* and *set*, but not how field training maneuvers worked with books.

"Sorry." She sat back, excitement dimming, and went back to slow, mouthing the words, pointing at his hands. "I like the book."

He didn't like her not-excited. Before he could understand why, what he had done improperly, she smiled.

Smiling was good.

So was her looking at him with approval. "Do you like romance? Have you read others?"

"They are all I read." Except the slides the trainers used. He wasn't sure humans were taught the same way, and didn't want her to stop smiling again. "I read book one."

Clearly the correct thing to say. She did the happy-bounce. "The rest of the series is equally good. Have you read her others?"

"No."

"You have to, once we get out of here. Since you liked the

first, you might like a—" She frowned, like she was searching, her fingers moving again. In patterns. Signs. Letters, not exactly like the ones they used to signal during training and missions, or with the ones who didn't speak.

"Spin-off." He tried out the word. A new one.

She blinked at him, and her fingers moved again. Quicker and surer, and without talking. *You understand ASL.*

It took a heartbeat, while he put the signals together. Another new word. "What is A S L?"

The look she gave him wasn't anger over him not knowing the answer, or outrage over daring to ask. Closer to her smiling-one when he showed her the book. He decided he liked this look as well.

She combined the speaking slowly and signing. "I can totally work with this."

Maybe he should tell her that he heard her soft talk, and signs and lip movements weren't required, and that he didn't know all the signs she used. The trainers hadn't taught her combination way of communicating, but vampires said humans weren't to be trusted. Yet she hadn't attempted to insult or attack, except toward the helper-vampires. And *he* would kill all the vampires in this place if he could.

He settled on not risking insulting her human ways, and nodded. "Spin-off?"

"The spin-off is about three sisters," she continued. "They have creative meet-cutes for each instead of the predictable discovering the guy they hooked up with the night before is their new boss, or slamming into each other and dumping coffee on one right before an important event."

She knew about first pages. Excitement rippled under his skin, stronger than when fed, or released on a mission. *Meet-cute.* He had a name for when the hero and heroine slammed together. He tucked the book under his shirt, moved closer, and sat so they faced each other.

"Each couple is different." She scooted so her knees bumped the barrier. "The first is opposites-attract. The next is a second-chance, and the last is enemies-to-lovers, my personal fav."

Enemies, he understood. His curiosity itched at him, like the blankets his batch's caregivers awarded cubs who obeyed. "Were-people and fated mates?"

"Your favs?"

"Do you like them?" Suddenly, that was critical information.

"The fated-mates I'm fifty-fifty on. Objectively, love is a chemical reaction, and fate is more about statistical probabilities." She picked up the magic non-stinking windigo, turning it around in her hands. A faint trickle of guilt wisped off her, and she ducked her head. "With were-creatures, which I argue are hominid cryptids, that's complicated. Once I would've said all cryptids were dangerous. Now, I believe it's case-by-case. A lot are innocent."

He was lost, most of her words strange. Except for one, which he needed to learn more about. "Innocent?"

She looked at him again. "I get it. After this, difficult to believe cryptids are anything but evil, right? But some are only trying to live their lives, never harming humans."

She didn't like some were-people, but did others. He had no desire to harm her. Thus, she didn't hate him. This was good. He made an approving grunt.

Some of her bounciness returned. "Exactly. Oh, I'm Kimi."

He sounded it out, and decided it felt good on his tongue.

"What's your name?" She braced her elbow on her leg, and put her chin in the palm of her hand.

Something like fear hit him, but not the same feeling as being disciplined or reprogrammed. Humans had names. Batches had designations. Seven-Zero-One wasn't a human or were-people name. He twitched and the book spine dug into his stomach. The hero in this book was Owen. O-One. Owen.

He raised his eyes to her oddly patient ones. "I am Owen."

"Nice to meet you, Owen. You aren't familiar with ASL, but you still understood a lot of my signing, primarily those associated with action and orders. Are you SWAT or private security? Special-Ops?"

Special-ops. Human soldiers. Yes. "I am a soldier."

"Perfect." She rested back on her elbows. This smile was predatory. "We are going to have a blast taking these vampires down. Time to refine our exit strategy."

No one had ever called him perfect. He examined the feeling as she stared at the clear cage ceiling, her fingers tapping, though not in any code he'd been taught. He was increasingly sure he hadn't been taught about this type of human, either, and whether this was real or a vicious human trick.

CHAPTER 5

wen

CONDITIONED from the many times he was in this cell, half of his focus automatically went to listening for the vampires to return, his inner clock counting the minutes until his short period of safety from their torture and drugs ended. Bringing the human in had interrupted his reprogramming, but the Irene-scientist wouldn't be stopped for long.

The other half of his focus stayed on *her*.

After many minutes, the human dropped her attention back to him, popped up onto her knees, and spoke-signed even slower than usual. The expression in her eyes matching her body language, serious. Important. "Here's the plan. Well, Plan A. You're closest to the door, and taller. When one of the vampires return, preferably the doctor, position yourself where you'll have the best chance of seeing their access code as they enter it. If you miss one, note its position in the sequence. It'll take longer, but I can extrapolate from there."

She liked that he was tall. He sat straighter. "Yes."

"I'll continue baiting the vampires. Once we have the code, I'll push them over the edge when they feed us." She held up the magic windigo. "I can't get away with the tray thing again, but if they're concentrating on replying to my insults instead of their job, they won't notice when I block that feeding slot mechanism. I can reach far enough through to key in the code, and open the cell, then I'll free you."

He had been correct. She was vampire smart, with many ideas, and fearless. Clearly, she was the leader of the human soldiers, the reason she was in front during the attack on his training exercise.

The part of him bred to obey orders relaxed, even as the chatter of voices from the hallway grew louder. She was the leader, and he would follow her. "This is a good plan. The vampires are awake. The helpers will come soon."

She rose and stretched, like his batch when they were preparing for an exercise.

He hesitated in joining her for a moment, torn over his next dilemma. But she liked meet-cutes. She wouldn't tell the handlers. He slid the book out, and blocking the camera, removed the hiding spot cover, tucking the new book away safely.

When he looked up, she was propped against the barrier.

She raised both thumbs, then spoke-signed. "Virtual high five for keeping a secret library right under their noses. That is *awesome*." She hit the last word harder.

The thumbs must be a non-insulting hand gesture, as was a high five. She was pleased with him. Pleasing handlers meant performing an exercise properly, and not getting disciplined. He liked this new thing, her happy with him even if he didn't grasp her reasoning. Or why her happiness pleased him.

Before he could respond, the faint hum of the hall disinfecting unit carried. "They are here."

He moved to the side facing the entry, closer to the cage door than he preferred. Only foolish creatures stood so close, within jabbing range of the helpers' stun guns. Some liked to torment the cryptids, and his kind, when the scientist wasn't nearby. He healed quickly enough that the helpers didn't risk the scientist discovering their actions and facing her punishment.

The single thumbs-up she, Kimi, gave him, was worth the risk of injury. The door whooshed open, air carrying the stink of vampires. He bristled, lip lifting off his teeth, as a second vampire entered. This helper, larger than the others, was the one who led the helpers in tormenting him.

"How about we fulfill your dietary preferences, princess?" The hated vampire stared at Kimi, malice coating his words, behind his false smile. Instead of the fancy food, he shook a cup of the quivery sugar that she had rejected by tossing on the helper earlier, only this was yellow. A stunner hung from around his wrist, held behind his back out of Kimi's view.

The same unease expanded in Owen's chest as when he'd thought of illness, her, and vampires disposing of her.

She sat on the sleeping platform, one leg curled under, one leg swinging. She gave the vampires the same silent, lengthy exam as when she'd first arrived. Then doing the low-talking and exaggerated lip movements, tipped her head at the first helper. "That bite wound healed yet? I'm super proud of my work, by the way. Would you like a lesson? Your technique isn't great."

Kimi smiled too wide, tapping one of her teeth, the short human fang. She kept her gaze on the leader though, daring him to look away.

"You're a handful. Better be glad I enjoy a challenge, unlike a lot of my co-workers." The lead helper laughed, the sound grating over Owen's eardrums. As false and evil as a vampire's smile. "I suggest you fuel up. You're too valuable to carve into a Frankenstein, so you'll be joining the Syndicate, as one of us. Let's call this a welcome to the club gift."

Kimi stood, and under her relaxed stretch, muscles bunched. The fingers of her right hand hooked over the top pocket in her pants, the waxy white of the tiny magic windigo peeking out at Owen, where she held it cupped and hidden.

Owen pressed against the side of his cage breathing hard against the wall, temporarily fogging the surface and stared at the other cell's keypad. As the bitten helper punched in code and opened the tray slot, Owen traced the numbers into the fogged glass. The lead helper thumbed the switch on the hidden stunner, jerking Owen's attention away. He missed the last number as sparks jumped between the device's evil metal spikes.

He froze, afraid to move and smudge the partial code. Kimi glanced sideways fast, then back to the vampire, as the numbers faded away.

She had her excellent plan. But the vampires were luring her in for their own. She would reach for the food, and they would hit her with the painful shocks. Owen touched the largest melted patch on his shirt, the burn marks underneath deep enough he hadn't regenerated yet.

Kimi was human, and humans didn't regenerate like vampires and his batch. His heart scrambled too fast, the way it did when he was a cub and being disciplined with a doubled training session.

He slammed a fist against the cell barrier, unbreakable material shuddering. The subordinate helper jerked, fingers slipping but the slot whirring open.

The lead helper hadn't even glanced at the commotion,

his attention on Kimi. Another step and she would be in range of the stunner.

Owen drove both fists into the barrier. This time, both helpers looked. He straightened to his full height, leaning forward so he would've towered over the vampire, showing his dominance. "You will feed me first."

The leader snickered, eyes already shifting back to Kimi, who was at the cell door, windigo visible to Owen. The vampire waggled the cup at the same time he brought the stunner up underneath in a flash of speed, too fast for Kimi to see yet. Her hand darted toward the slot, fingertips inches from the burning electric spikes.

He used the forbidden insults. "Now, you piece of shit vampire."

The leader's eyes narrowed.

Owen used the middle finger gestures Kimi employed. "You will do this or I will fry you the way I did the useless, idiot handler."

This time, rage puffed off both vampires and they turned, blocking his view of Kimi. Their faces thinned, the bones Owen longed to crush showing through translucent skin. Fangs dented their blackened lips.

"Oh, I heard what you did." The leader stalked to Owen's cell, swirling silver eyes reflecting. His voice throbbed, not enough to rattle the cell material, but thrumming back from the metal furnishings and tools.

"You may be Doctor Irene's pet project, but accidents happen. Tranq," he ordered the other helper.

Owen heard his death in the cold words.

Both vampires left Owen for the room with the reprogramming table and knives, disappearing between blinks. The leader reappeared first, before Owen could check if Kimi's plan worked, if she figured out the number he had erred and missed, flipping a gleaming saw as long as Owen's forearm. "You have no idea how I've dreamed of this, you defective waste of space."

The lesser helper popped in, and the leader jerked the slot open hard enough the device clunked and circuits smoked, holding his other hand out for the tube with the bad medicine dart inside, without looking.

If this was the end, Owen would die fighting. Kimi...he hoped the human could create another plan, and escape this place once he was dead.

Owen snarled at the leader, who growled back, fangs extended into their full hunting display. The vampire's claws tipped out against the metal of the saw in an eerie squeal that pierced Owen's ears, its other hand rising, the dart aimed at the open slot and Owen's chest.

A shriek rattled the cage barrier and blood splashed over the leader's palm and the floor. Behind him, the lesser vampire dropped to its knees, pawing at a scalpel imbedded in its eye.

Kimi appeared from behind the downed helper, ramming a second scalpel into its other eye. The vampire's shriek rose, and she kicked it in the back. The helper sprawled onto its stomach, and she snatched the small gun at its hip.

The pop of gunfire cut off the helper's scream.

The leader's weight shifted, turning to the fight. Owen rammed his arm through the slot, as far as he could reach, skin peeling against the hard edges, and grabbed the most hated vampire's collar, jerking it against the shatterproof barrier. The vampire's nose broke in a crunch of cartilage, and its chin bounced off of the cell.

Behind them, Kimi vaulted the dead helper and jammed the gun against the leader's spine, emptying the weapon until it locked open, bullets gone. Owen tossed the body sideways, and she tapped in the code for his cell.

Owen's door slid open, and she motioned for him. Then

whisper-signed, "Get the other's gun. Any other weapons we can use, too."

She darted to the machines, the laptop that the scientist and handlers used. Bent over the table, her fingers flew almost too fast for Owen to follow, keys clicking. "Code, code, I need a better exit code," she whisper-talked to herself.

He jerked the tiny gun from the leader's belt, the vampire's silver eyes still blazing, more powerful than the lesser helper, taking longer to die.

They required weapons, and Owen would use one to end the creature at his feet for good. He shoved the gun into his waistband and stepped over the vampire, into the hated room responsible for so much pain.

He scanned for blades, trying not to see the walls of equipment he'd stared at many times while pinned to the table, unable to speak, unable to escape the pain as the scientist sliced into him.

He turned, and the light glinted off the table in the center of the room. Memories swamped him, the burn of the drugs injected into his body, the chatter of the vampires talking about nonsense as his nerves fried.

He jerked the table free from the floor and slung it into the clear-fronted cabinets full of the shining scalpels and wires. Glass shattered, shards and drugs flying. He raked his arm down the longest shelf, the sharp-decay scent blotting out all else as jars cracked, preserved bits of cryptids and failed batches splashing free.

Destroy it all. Then destroy the vampires, make them burn and twitch and—

He caught motion from the corner of his eye, and whirled. The leader, who Owen had forgotten, lost in nightmares. Older than the other helpers, nerves already regenerated enough to move, the leader rose to his feet. He swept up the saw blade originally meant for Owen.

More interested in Kimi and the devices she was still hunched over, the vampire lurched toward the human. Intent on her work, perhaps lost in it and revenge the way Owen had been, her exposed back faced the leader.

No vampire would touch her. Red tinted Owen's vision. He leapt, glass and flesh pulping under his boots. He hit the vampire from behind, Owen's longer arms circling its body. Trapping it against his chest. He grabbed either end of the saw, crushing the vampire's hand wrapped around the handle under his. Pulling it against the leader's neck, he hauled back, muscles straining as the vampire bucked and fought.

The sharp end in his left hand cut Owen's palm, blood dripping, making the metal slippery. The vampire surged, getting an elbow raised under Owen's, pressing outward, saw lifting an inch off the leader's neck. Arms burning, Owen wrapped his damaged hand tighter around the biting edge of the weapon, and threw himself backward, hitting the cell barrier. Blade cutting through the skin of the vampire's throat, lodging in vertebra. Sawing the serrated blade back and forth, Owen strained, beheading the leader the only way to end the creature.

A last heave and bone cracked. The vampire's head lolled to the side, hanging by muscle. Owen jerked the saw free, knocking the leader loose. Then swung, the blade taking the head off the mangled neck. The body dropped, and Owen kicked the head and hated face across the room.

Kimi straightened, attention landing on Owen. Her dark eyes widened, a tangle of hormones puffing off her, too many, too fast for him to sample and decipher.

He tensed, all the training warnings about human disloyalty and trickery returning. He wouldn't be stopped now, wouldn't go back into a vampire's cage, or a human's.

She gave him a thumbs up and a victorious-smile, and

spoke-signed. "Nice. We have one-hundred-twenty seconds before my program locks this place down. I gathered several codes, but, no way of knowing how high their clearance level is, or if they'll automatically change once an alarm is tripped. Garage?"

Pushing the machine aside, she crossed to the wall and keypad. A second later, the door opened. She waved him toward the opening.

When he hesitated, weighing whether to trust her or go alone, she changed direction, and grabbed his sleeve. Motion exaggerated, she spoke. "Are you hurt?" Her other hand patted over his chest, bloody fabric squishing.

Vampires were the liars, not his human. Carefully, he pried Kimi's fingers free. "No. This way."

She followed his sprint, keeping up with his long strides. A siren shrilled, revolving lights strobing along the walls, whoever monitored the cameras finally noticing the dead vampires and destroyed lab.

They cleared the lab's hall, and he angled right. Hitting one of the security points, Kimi slipped past him, punching in the code, her faint "Come on, work," carrying to him.

The panel flickered red, refusing the code. She put numbers in again, and again, whispering forbidden words as the panel flashed red each time.

Under her words, the fainter whump of boots on concrete filtered through. Guards, alerted by the siren. His training screaming a warning to protect himself first, as the doors inched apart, Owen barged in front anyway. He would tear through armor and helmets and shield this human.

A warm hand scrapped against his lower back on the way down, then the metal of the stolen gun barrel left a chilled spot as it was jerked loose from his waistband. The door opened, the pair of guards rushing their way.

Kimi's hand and the gun pushed between his arm and

side, aiming at the soldiers. Two sharp pops, and the guards fell. She wiggled around him and pulled on Owen's sleeve, tugging him forward, and he charged down the corridor with her. Senses strained further than he'd ever tried, pulling in air, ears aching from the siren, he separated scents, and isolated sounds. Searching for vampire heartbeats, the oiliness of guns.

Always aiming up, and for the fuel stink of vehicles, and the whisper of fresh air.

They flew around a blind corner, and the last security point. Its door, thicker than the others, lumbered open, the thump of many heartbeats on the other side. Before he could put himself in front, warn her, Kimi sped up. Then dropped and slid, boots first, through the crack. Hair band catching and ripping out.

She slammed into vampire's knees, the packed guards stumbling and falling. One hit the wall, but its out-flung hand *skreed* down tile, claws popping out and punching through, stopping its fall. Its other hand swept wide, nails catching one of Kimi's pant's pockets. Fabric ripped, and a line of red opened along her thigh. Human blood scented the air.

Tile shattered, the vampire's eyes pure silver, shining through the helmet visor, in full hunting mode, more animal than soldier now. It swung its freed hand, nails shining as bright as it eyes. Dropping its weapon, and crouching.

Kimi rolled to her back, legs bent, as the guard leapt. Her boots catching it in the stomach, she pushed the heavier vampire off. It scrambled to all fours, jerking its helmet loose, exposing its fangs. Going for the downed human again.

Owen's human. Something strange, rage but not, flooded him.

He backhanded the vampire mid-leap, knocking it into

the wall, more tile cracking. Kimi snatched the guard's forgotten gun from the base of the wall, and emptied it into its face.

Owen roared his hate and stomped, crushing downed vampire skulls. Grabbing a last by the helmet and ramming it face-first into the floor. He was dominant and they would never touch what was his again. He would rip them all apart then find more and—

A whistle split the air. He whipped around. Kimi waited at the end of the corridor, fingers against her lips, head cocked. Where she'd signaled him, breaking him from his hunting trance instead of leaving him. "You back?" she whisper-mouthed.

He nodded, and she gestured him to follow, darting ahead.

By the time he caught up and entered the cavernous transport area, a bloody vampire body sprawled out of the tall, narrow room guarding the vehicle parts and exit, scalpels like those she'd used on the helper buried in its chest.

Kimi crossed back and forth, hand traveling over the black and silver bits hanging from hooks. She quit, returning and shoving the dead vampire's sleeve back. Checking the timepiece strapped to its wrist, she said a forbidden word, dropping the arm to bounce against the floor.

She zipped out of the room, and he followed her as she sped up and down rows. She halted and Owen jerked sideways, cryptid reflexes keeping him from knocking her down

She slung her leg over a narrow machine he'd only seen in images. She patted the strange part she perched on, demanding he join her. Waiting for it to fall from his weight, he lowered himself. She flipped something between the horn-like handles, then punched a button. The small vehicle coughed. The noise cut off, machine not moving.

She whispered many more forbidden words, and

punched harder. The vehicle finally rumbled like a grumpy ghoul, and vibrated against Owen's rear.

She felt back, catching his arm and wrapping it around her waist.

Before Owen could interpret her human action, the vehicle jumped. Fast. Heading for the wide black front of the vehicle area that allowed them out on training exercises.

The barrier wasn't open.

The vehicle's speed increased, rows of other vehicles whipping past. His human tilted the fast vehicle, cutting through the narrower exit chute. His balance adjusted in time. Kimi reached out, slapping a raised panel on the yellow and black arch framing the chute.

The barrier rose. Slow. Slower than the vehicle. With the machine's front wheel only inches from the impenetrable expanse of metal, a short slice of outdoors was visible. Barely high enough for a crouched vampire to squeeze through. On instinct he ducked low, chest covering Kimi's crouched back. Still better to die attempting to escape, than in a lab.

They shot under the barrier, metal scraping his back, painful enough that he snarled. Moonlight and air rushed over Owen. Behind them, the door ground to a halt, parts catching and clanking. Then slammed down cryptid-fast. The draft hit the vehicle, Owen's seat wobbling.

Kimi steadied the machine, slowing a beat and grabbing his other arm, anchoring it around her the same as his other. She looked over her shoulder at him, a wide smile in place. The vehicle spun to face the sealed door and building, in a dizzying squeal of burning rubber. They stopped, their perch still rumbling under them.

The human lifted her fingers at the vampires' building. Then swung the speedy vehicle, rocketing down a street, away from the cells and reprogramming. Away from vampires into maybe-freedom with this odd human.

CHAPTER 6

 wen

BUILDINGS, the tall poles that lit the roads at night, and even taller trees with waving tops, rushed past, bringing Owen an onslaught of new scents and tastes. The vehicle wove in and out around larger, slower vehicles. Slowing or stopping at some lights hanging over the road, or from arched posts.

Instinct and training commanded him to impress the route into his memory. To catalogue the feel of the air, the scents, the objects around him. The part of him that was beyond his control did as it was bred to. The rest of him was focused on the small, fierce human he held onto.

He'd never been so close to a human. He'd examined their heart rates and functions from a distance. Learned their hormones and pheromones, those released under stress and through fighting and fear, matching them to behavior.

He couldn't match Kimi's to anything in his memory-base. Now, he worked his way through the lab smells and vampire blood coating her, to hers underneath. Something like the oil in the vehicles, but not, this one green like plants. The hints of other humans on her, two males. One with more fancy-food odors.

The hair blowing into his face held even more scents. He lowered his nose into the curls streaming by his cheeks, inhaling and saving their signature, her imprint. Did the same with the muscles and bones under her smooth skin. The feel of her—it pleased him. Not in a way he'd ever felt though.

Exciting, blood racing. Heart beating harder, despite encountering no threat from humans around them. He considered telling her his balance was excellent, which was true and might please her. But he didn't want to remove his arms from around her and her heat, her pulse tapping against his. Nor did he wish the wind to remove *his* scent from her.

The combination was strange. Illogical. His time with her had been short. She was leader-smart, and he was only a soldier. She made complicated vampire-plans. His training hammered the images of treachery his batch had been forced to study through his brain.

He'd defended her, an action his batch were incapable of unless ordered by vampire superiors. He had *protected* her, not considering his own wellbeing. Even now, he'd tear apart anything that threatened her.

Perhaps this was a breeding response. He was larger and stronger than most in his batch. But he was defective, and hadn't been allowed to breed. Nor did his body react the way he'd experienced on catching whiffs of ovulating females. He'd never cared to speak with them, know about them and what they liked.

Attraction. That was what the books said. What they called the crashing-together emotions when hero and heroines met. He pulled up examples, holding them beside his responses. *They* matched.

Which lead to only one conclusion—this was a meet-cute. A weird one. Kimi had said there were other kinds, and she knew many more books than his three.

This was their special meet-cute. They were to be together. Victory stronger than when he'd torn the lead helper's head free sang through Owen.

Kimi's fingers tapped his wrist and he started. Had she understood his thoughts? Fated-mates did, the were-cryptid creatures, which he might be. But humans...

The vehicle slowed, the mechanical click-click of their turning light ticking in his ears. She guided the machine into a darker building, like the vampires' garage, but taller. Floors and cars stacked up above his head. She drove into the darkest corner, and stopped, the rumbling underneath them vanishing.

She slipped from his hold and stood. Panic replaced the victory. She had spoken of their escaping, but not of what came after. He hadn't either, not capable of imagining freedom. Was he wrong, and she didn't feel the attraction?

Holding up a hand, the wait command, she swung over a barrier, and strode to the middle of the next concrete level. She stood square in a lighted spot, head tilted back, fingers moving in her signs, many he didn't know.

He tracked the point she was staring at. A camera high on the wall. Like those in the lab. She didn't hide her actions from this one, and took her time.

At last, she hopped back over the barrier to their level, landing with knees bent. She gave him her attention, and one of those happy smiles, soft-signing. "You did *great*, Owen. Thanks for the assist in the lab, too. That was amazing."

She was pleased with him again, and praised his fighting ability. When she headed deeper into the complex, rough whisper-humming under her breath, he followed her. He would follow her and her leadership as long as she allowed.

She circled a new vehicle, this one larger, yet open. A roof, but only a frame, not closed in and solid. It was bright, the orange of citrus food. It wasn't the shiniest, dented spots along one section. She patted the biggest dent. Reaching inside she hit some button. At the pop of metal separating, she lifted the lid part, ducking under it.

Owen put his back to a wall, scanning the structure, guarding their position.

Moments later, the lid slammed closed. She wiped her palms against her pants, then spoke-signed. "Before you say anything, we aren't really stealing-stealing, okay? Let's call this borrowing."

"Okay." Stealing was unfamiliar to him. As leader, Kimi knew the correct actions.

When she climbed in the citrus vehicle, he followed. Watching and mimicking her actions as she hooked together the straps hanging by the seats.

He'd never traveled in the front, only in the cage sections of the vampires' vans. These straps were less elaborate than the webbing his batch hooked into, lined side by side on long benches.

Instead of screeching away, she guided them into the traffic again, not speeding or moving between cars. At one of the hanging lights, she leaned, twisting knobs on the panel in front of them. Sounds blared and he twitched back, voices rolling from the machine.

"Sorry," she mouthed, and turned a knob, the volume dropping. Her brow furrowed and she played more. The voices changed, and skipped around, some with other noises behind. She paused on one, then sat back. She pressed a button on her door and the window lowered. One hand on the machine's wheel device, her other lay along the opened window, moving like the ocean waves. Or like she was caressing the air.

He tried the action.

She checked him instead of the road, doing the exaggerated soft-speaking. "You like this song?"

"Yes." Songs. The sounds that humans and mates enjoyed. That they *danced to*. He would learn the dancing. He lifted his face into the breeze, eyelids dropping to block out stimuli.

The vehicle climbed, leaving the crowded buildings and straighter roads. These curved around and around. Dirt, vegetation, animals, rock.

Dirt lifted in a cloud, thick and dry, and he sneezed, clearing his nostrils. Warmth touched his eyelids, and he opened his eyes. The sun rose, bright and all shades of gold instead of faded by the darkened van windows, the few times the vampires raced back to the buildings after late training or missions.

His skin heated. Something in him responded, like his bones melting, but without the pain. A breath escaped him.

A touch brushed across his shoulder. He jerked, but instead of a threat, Kimi's hand rested on him. She squeezed, gentle, then went back to driving, as he searched for what the touch meant. A word to match the bright-warm feel it caused, like a bit of the sunrise had lodged in his chest.

They passed under trees, the sun coming through between branches and leaves, and he sat deeper, head resting against the seat, watching the patterns of sun and shadow.

Beneath the green of plant life and earthiness of baked stones, her scent filtered through from a point ahead of them. Lighter, nearly washed away by time. He straightened, the vehicle slowing, tiny rocks and dirt crunching under the wheels.

Kimi coasted into a bare circle of tiny rocks, in front of a small building, the source of her old, faded scent, plus that of other humans, also worn to almost nothing.

The vehicle turned off, and she tilted her head at him, then his side of the wood building. She tilted hers at the opposite. Holding up three fingers, she folded them down one by one. Counting down to launch a mission.

Instead of utilizing the door, she climbed over and out, crouched low. He rolled out on his side, landing without disturbing the loud rocks. Her shadow moved left, and he went right, circling the building. He threw all his attention into the patrol, searching for signs of hidden enemies.

Unease prickled along his spine as he came to a window. More when he spotted Kimi, her head popping up to peer into the matching windows across from his. They met at the rear, no windows left for her to check, no longer putting herself in the position to be attacked through one of the fragile glass panels.

"There is no one here. I detect no evidence of incendiary devices," he reported.

She nodded and crossed to the front. As her boots thumped up the rough red wood steps, he leapt to the landing, ignoring stairs. She swiped along one of the tree-log pieces making up the building. This piece rotated and slid sideways, exposing a panel like those in the vampires' buildings.

Too like the vampires'. He tensed, sensation of invisible fur lifting under the skin at the back of his neck.

She entered a code, then pressed her finger to the screen. Rotating the tree section back in place after. When she touched the knob on the door, it swung open. He held back, torn between wariness bred and beaten into him, and the new possibilities this human roused.

Her steps crossed back and forth over the floor. Finally, she appeared in the doorway. Soft-signing, she said, "The site is clear. We're good. You're free, no vampires, no cages, Owen. I promise."

When she held her hand out, his found its way into it, the sunrise feeling in his chest expanding. He allowed her to lead him inside.

The building wasn't like any the vampires held. All wood, with the large windows on the sides. He wandered closer, examining the extra sparkle in each.

"Chem-coated mesh."

He dropped into a crouch at the strange, mechanical voice. Balanced to launch at the intruder, gaze searching the room, straining for the thump of vampire heartbeats.

Kimi stilled, her cheek denting in as if she bit the inside, then held up a palm-sized device. One of the communication devices—a phone. "Watch," she mouthed.

She tapped the device and the voice came again, in time with her tapping. "This is a text-to-voice app. I can talk to you now. Even when we aren't facing each other, or one of us is in another room."

He unfurled from the crouch, meeting her. Peering at the device, then at her.

She drew her hand across the front of her throat, fingers following faded scars that ran around the middle. Then played with the device again. "Ghouls. Oh, do you know about ghouls, windigos, and other cryptids besides vampires?"

"Windigos stink. Ghouls also stink, but of carrion. Rotted meat."

She nodded and waggled the device. "A ghoul damaged my voice a long time ago. This helps give it back. Anyway, the mesh is chem-coated, toxic to all cryptids. The house foundation sits on more of the buried mesh, plus it's in the roof insulation. Nothing is getting in without giving us plenty of warning."

He'd heard the handlers complain of the human soldiers' chemical. His batch was created with a resistance to the compound. "Anything that poisons them is good."

"Truth."

When she stretched, the rip in her pants gaped open, exposing a long, narrow slash of red. "Your wound." She was a strong fighter, but he didn't know how long injuries took to heal on humans.

"It's shallow. I'll clean it in a minute. At least vampire claws aren't as nasty as windigos' or ghouls'." She smiled again, and waved at the room. "You can explore while I get us situated. Bathroom is straight back."

She skirted the pieces in the room. Chairs, but with cloth and padding. One long one in the middle, a table covered in a light layer of dust. He circled the space, cautiously entering the hall she'd indicated. Open doors showed rooms on either side, these with sleeping platforms, but as strange as the chairs, thick and covered in blankets. He pushed the last door open. A washing and waste facility.

Kimi was far more interesting. He rejoined her, as she opened wooden cabinets, pressing more panels, wood rolling away and screens appearing, accepting her code, and the entire back of the cabinets disappearing.

She piled objects on the counters under. Knives with the same shimmer as the window mesh. Chem-coated, which she pulled from sheaths, checking edges. She switched, laying out guns, larger than the lab helpers', the style and calibers his batch had been trained on, then adding multiple holsters.

His *attraction* deepened at her fierceness and quiet aggression. All good signs in a mate.

She turned, held up a larger device. Placing it in front of him on the counter, she switched to the phone. "I really hate to ask, but I need to run a DNA test."

He backed away. The warmth in his chest shriveling. More of the hated lab things, more testing. While he didn't know if he qualified as were-human or merely as bits of many cryptids, he did know he wasn't really human, not the way Kimi was.

If she discovered he wasn't human, were or real, would she send him to her labs?

She rubbed at her eyes, before touching the phone. "I know. You shouldn't—you've donated a pound of flesh to those monsters already."

Far more than a pound.

"It only requires a few drops of blood, and rules out that you aren't a vampire, or other humanoid cryptid." The voice didn't hold any inflections, but her body language did. Eyes sad, cheek dented in again. Apology puffed off her. "I'll go first, so you can be comfortable trusting I'm human, too."

They had been in sunlight, without suits and gear—neither were vampire. Both of them looked like normal humans, not the lizard or animal-like cryptids that walked on two legs. Nor the grey-skinned creatures that invaded minds, bred in other labs. This action seemed important to her, demonstrating their loyalty to each other.

She pressed her thumb into a hollow on the device. The copperiness of fresh blood mixed with the stale air. After a beep, she spun the device for him to read. A series of green checks lined up beside clusters of letters, the word *approved human* appearing at the end.

He should kill her now. Escape, instead of trusting the scientist's claims that he would pass all tests and appear human.

The idea of hurting her, extinguishing those compelling brown eyes, not seeing her hands dance as she spoke…

She left the piece of equipment, showing him the pricked spot on her thumb, blood already clotted. Then cupping his hand in both hers, mouthed, "You are safe. One last stupid hoop, okay?"

Injuring her was impossible. If the test failed and she attempted to capture him for her kind's labs and tests, he would smash through the window, past the poison compound, and escape instead.

She kept his hand in hers, gently laying his thumb in the slot, hers rubbing along the back of his hand as a needle jabbed. After a second, he isolated the action from the books. She was *comforting* him.

The green marks appeared between heartbeats, ending with the final *approved* icon lighting up.

She tossed the testing box away as if it had angered her, paying no heed as it skidded, tipping dangerously over the edge of the counter.

She opened another cabinet, and handed him a bottle and wrapped object. Water, and food. She cracked the seal on hers, chugging water, throat with the faded, delicate claw scars working, then tore the edge of the packaging, taking a bite of its contents before dropping both beside the weapons.

He downed the water first, then chewed the bar. Protein, better than any the vampires supplied, this one sweet with less chemical aftertaste. He glanced at her abandoned food, fair game for the strongest cryptid. He also wouldn't ever steal her food, and turned his head away from the temptation.

Another protein bar appeared in front of his nose. She offered it, slow-speaking. "There's more. Here. Shirt, please."

She wanted his shirt in trade. He pulled the dirty, ripped garment over his head, politely handing the bundle to her, then taking the food.

She did the air gasp, face going ashen. She ducked her head, tossing the shirt to the floor, but he still heard her. "Oh, Owen."

Not pained, but something hurt her from her tone. He required more information. "Kimi?"

When she raised her face, her eyes were shimmery-wet, face dry but salt riding the dusty air, replacing the blood trace. "May I?"

He examined the white tube she scooted his way, reading the black printing. Burn cream. He checked his chest. The burns were visible, but far better. He shrugged, but if agreeing made her hurt go away, he was willing. "Yes."

Gently, more carefully than he'd ever been touched or seen others touch, she smoothed the cream over the healing taser remnants, then to those on his back and the long patch of road rash from the garage's slow-rising door. The sensation...was amazing. He wanted more of the touching. To touch her in kind.

His earlier idea turned solid, crystallizing into pure truth. She was smart, a skilled fighter, and leader. She was kind, and shared her food. She was a heroine. Thus he was...the hero. He'd never read about one like him, but this was the only possible explanation.

She had chosen him as her fated mate. He wasn't human, vampire, or cryptid, and he wasn't certain he was allowed this bond.

He would never tell her he was lesser, because he refused to lose her approval and presence. In order to stay by her side, he would kill any who attempted to interfere.

 imi

I TOSSED Owen the last cruddy bar from the box. He deserved more than semi-stale leftovers, from one of our lower-low tier sites. This wasn't even a tertiary base, only a refuel-and-go-in-a-pinch backup.

Owen needed...He needed to have been found and rescued long ago. I'd thought it was awful that he'd been caged long enough that gelatin seemed like a treat, but hadn't even been *close.*

He was covered in more scars and wounds than Vee, who'd had the normal Company agent allotment, then been savaged in the desert by a mixed horde of vampires and windigos. Stavros had saved her, breaking his vow to his god, and barely succeeding in turning her into a vampire her wounds were so severe. But no amount of vampire-virus modified DNA could erase the damage she'd sustained beforehand. Owen's were magnitudes worse.

How he was walking and talking was another sort of miracle. I kept him in my peripheral vision as he wolfed down the last crumb, wandering the room, his fingers tracing along the ratty, camo-themed upholstery, a decorating touch that matched the site's public persona as a hunting and fishing cabin.

He'd seemed oblivious to embarrassment, which, a save I didn't deserve, demanding his shirt without considering what it hid. Anyone raised Company wouldn't care, but Owen was a civilian. By my calculations, they were forty-nine-percent less physically demonstrative, and eighty-two-percent more embarrassed by partial or full nudity.

He was military, true. Well trained and conditioned. He still acted and reacted more like Company than any other military branch.

Now, Owen was more interested in the room than wounds, no hesitation evident. I shuddered at the weepy, blistered patches on his chest and back, and the newer scrapes along his shoulders and back that I suspected were from the garage's lift-door. The analgesic cream couldn't be cutting that pain. His bloodwork hadn't shown any infection, another statistical miracle. Only a mildly elevated Leucine level, the amino acid possibly out of whack due to diet.

Maybe most of the laboratory crew were older vampires, the virus that infected humans and mutated them fully established, and they'd forgotten what humans did and didn't require for optimal health.

The vampire faction behind the population explosion, the mental manipulation that allowed upper species to work together, and the appearance of cryptids from other biomes had *sooo* much to answer for.

I ripped open an antiseptic pad, in lieu of ripping off vampire heads, swabbing the cut on my leg. It was barely more than a superficial scratch, and had stopped bleeding by the time we liberated the motorcycle. Yet Owen was more worried about it and me, than his own injuries. I swiped the gel that all agent med kits carried on the cleaned cut, the blue compound sealing the edges and turning solid, and called it good.

The blip of orange light in the depth of the converted kitchen cabinet put my growing list of imaginative ways to punish vampires on hold. I keyed in the appropriate code, acknowledging our arrival, then snatched the portable blood analysis unit that had basically given Owen flashbacks. Inserting it into the port, I exported my and Owen's test results, then tossed the used slides, cleaning and repacking the unit for the next time we or any other team in this Division needed the site.

My coded message in front of the public parking garage's CCTV cameras had pinged one of our Company agents or Assets positioned in the civi world, who had passed it on to our Region's HQ for verification. Once they green-lighted our authenticity, my team would be on the way.

Phones or any other digital contact a no-go for a ton of reasons, including the standard possibility that any captured agent had been compromised, the lengthier, indirect route had been my best option.

That, and the chilling fact that the vampire-led cryptid uprising was advanced beyond my private almost-worst-case scenario. HQ hadn't even known the facility I'd been detained in existed. We hadn't known, no chatter or rumors from street contacts hitting our team radar, despite the complex sitting in the center of our new Division, miles from our primary home base.

Attaching the thigh and wrist rigs, slotting the regulation Glock and thigh blade, and my fav throwing knives, I let go of the worry I couldn't act on yet, and the associated energy suck. I'd reported my escape and the accompanying rescue of a civi, and Vee would've been notified shortly after. I'd locked the vampire complex down, at least slowing their reprisal or relocation. The program I'd planted in the complex's system was running, scraping files, then rerouting the information to HQ, and off-book, to me. Our current location was secured.

There was nothing else on my agenda until the team arrived. Time to get to know Owen better. That he was serious, physically and mentally capable of executing plans in high-pressure situations, and justifiably angry at his captors was a given.

The part I'd glimpsed when he flashed me the cover of the romance he'd pickpocketed from deep in a vampire research center, his fascination with my amateur canine paper folding, and the easy way he followed my lead? That was the intriguing part.

His capacity to endure pain and hide the effects also made me itchy.

I levered onto the counter. Intensity swirled around him like a second skin, even while he double-checked windows and doors, vaulting onto the rough living area table and running his hands over the ceiling, testing for escape doors and weaknesses.

He studied and touched *everything* he encountered. The book pages he'd mindlessly stroked while reading in the cell, thinking I was asleep. The door, dash, and console of the Jeep. Every furnishing and surface here. Me.

His arms had stayed locked around my waist on the motorcycle, hands politely where I'd positioned them. I hadn't missed how he'd lain over me as we cleared the vampire complex's garage, how tight he'd pressed on the ride, or that he'd sniffed my hair, chin rubbing my head.

I cleared my throat, ensuring he heard me and we wouldn't have another moment where I startled him. His attention snapped to me. Instead of unsettling, his focus energized me, like borrowing one of my sister's caffeine skin hydration masks.

Using the phone, I checked in. "Are you hurt anywhere other than the burns on your chest and back, and the scrapes?"

He stared for a beat, almost as if he was processing, forehead wrinkling before answering. "No. You tended those." Then like he was trying out a new language, added, "Thank you."

I gave the gashes on the hands and knuckles, and the swatch of reddened skin along his right shoulder, a pointed exam, then raised both brows.

Reading my non-verbal cues with an uncanny accuracy that tickled along my nerves, he shook his head. "These are minor, and old. Not true wounds."

Again, he sounded like me, and every agent the Company turned out.

"Now that we can communicate more efficiently, I have a ton of questions." I typed away, then waited for his reaction.

"Okay."

"You don't mind? Please tell me if any are too personal."

"You can ask me anything."

No one, not even my sisters, had ever said that. At least, not after being around me for more than an hour. "Obvs, you're a soldier."

"Yes." That off expression appeared again, like Josh when Bruce caught him sneaking electrolyte drinks into the compound. Super guilty.

"I am—sort of a soldier," he blurted. "Not the same as you. Or other soldiers."

An ugly, cold curl of dread popped to life. He hadn't given a rank or title. Every military Asset and contact I'd met led with their service branch information, minimum. I picked my words carefully. "I'm an agent of Company Alpha Cryptid Containment, Southwest Region Two, Division Four. That breaks down to L.A., Southern California, and a border stretch of Nevada. Our mandate is protecting humanity and its social and political structure from predatory and otherwise dangerous cryptids, including those that can be leveraged to change the balance of power between governments. I've been Company forever—since I was born."

I leaned back on my elbows, giving Owen more space. Removing some of the pressure, from a psychological standpoint.

A bit of the wariness tightening his shoulders left. "I have been with the vampire trainers forever, as well. They are Syndicate. I have no title, and go where they take me."

My stomach flipped, the water churning. He'd mentioned the word before when referring to the vampires. But now, our enemy faction officially had a name, The Syndicate. And Owen's answer hinted at the worst violations imaginable.

"This isn't meant to bring up painful memories, and you always have the right to end any discussion or not answer—"

"I will always answer you." Truth infused his simple reply.

"Thank you. The Syndicate took you as a child, didn't they?"

He looked at a point over my shoulder, but kept his promise. "I don't remember anything other than the vampires, the caretakers, and trainers."

I choked down the rage, requiring confirmation, but hoping to ease in. "You are an excellent fighter in hand-to-hand combat. Fast, strong, incredible instincts."

Owen perked up, like one of Bruce's herb beds at getting water, after we'd been away on an extended mission. He straightened, shoulders back, and a smile blossomed. "You approve of my ability."

"Very much."

He faced me squarely, dark eyes sparking. Thrilled. Like, hey our favorite Academy Sniper Instructor told Josh he had the best semester score, kind of happy.

Basically, he behaved like one of us.

There had been that surveillance van and two vampires that originally brought us out on a mission. I didn't know if the team had gotten to it after I was taken. I had a terrible suspicion they hadn't, because it had already left, with another human prisoner inside.

I spun the phone in a circle, then asked. "Did they take you out in public?"

"For training." His shoulders slumped and he subtly angled his body away, guilt returning. He had less of a poker face than Matteo.

"They were conditioning and training you to fight on their behalf, as one of their soldiers." We'd encountered old fashioned vampire nests who retained a few loyal human servants, thanks to the promise of eventually being infected and turned, or for enormous salaries. This was a whole other level of evil.

Owen stuck with a short, stiff nod.

"Your being in the lab?"

Muscles bunched and slid under his skin, on display without a shirt, as he prowled again, too jittery to remain still. He had less body fat even than Josh. At my question, he morphed from soldier to a weapon, fists clenched, jaw set.

He *looked* dangerous because he *was* dangerous.

The expression in his eyes, how he rose on the balls of his feet, promised that he was willing to commit violence. More akin to cryptids, a ghoul whose only drive was killing and survival.

His deep voiced dropped to a bass rumble, verging on the kind of growl people talked about making, but that only carnivorous animals were able to produce. "I don't follow the rules. I attacked my handler. He was like the leader-helper. He liked hurting me."

"And you hated him. All of them." Of course he refused to follow their rules.

"Yes. Disobeying is forbidden. I disobey, often. Many times. I question the trainers and handlers. I am not aggressive enough. Or in the correct way."

My heart ached. Captured and tortured, and he still held onto his humanity, and defied the vampires. He refused to kill innocent civilians. "And they tossed you in that awful lab."

"It is the place for the defective. I'm taken there to be modified and reprogrammed. It never works." Bitter despair took the place of his rage.

"Oh, Owen." I spoke, slipping into my oldest habit, brain and body too attuned to ever give up the action, even though my voice was inaudible. I went back to the phone app. "I'd hoped my suspicions weren't true."

He flinched, and retreated, back smashing against the door. "I won't return to the vampires and the lab. I won't be modified again."

They hadn't killed his soul, either, the anger a thin veneer over his anguish and hurt. I was so arming the drones and dropping charges on that complex as soon as I got hands on my tablets. Owen had been through too much, simply to survive. He had no one—no team of siblings, not other year-mates, or nurturing Instructors and other agents, for support. And he'd been made to feel wrong and lesser because he didn't fit into a predetermined role.

I ignored the answering surge inside, the one I'd carried since the windigo training exercise, and nearly costing Josh more than scarred vocal cords.

Owen was like us, none of his responses those of civilians. I hopped off the counter, reaching up and gripping his shoulder, speaking slowly to allow him to lip read. "That torture is done. Done."

He studied me. Then the tension left, muscles under my hand relaxing. I joined him, propping against the wood.

He inched, until our hips bumped, then settled. Tears prickled under my eyelids at his show of trust, and I held them open wider to prevent waterworks. No male agent would be offended, so Owen probably wouldn't either. But pity sucked.

The question of why I responded so strongly to him, a brave soldier, but nonetheless a civi, not Company, rose.

Cutting off that line of questioning, I signed and spoke for him. The dang phone might as well be back in my room at the compound, because no, I wasn't budging from beside him to grab it. "Can you explain what the lab researchers were attempting to accomplish? It might give us an edge in stopping them. Otherwise, I'd never bring the topic up."

He frowned down at me. "To correct me so I obey every command in a fight. What else is there?"

Forget the drones. Calling the Assessor most supportive of our mixed vampire and human teams was the way to go. He'd approve a request for a full-on strike team to obliterate the Syndicate site and the researchers who had tried to turn Owen into a robotic killer.

I opened up to the reality of the scars covering every visible part of Owen's body. I reached for his arm, then snatched my fingers back before making contact, settling for signing. "They experimented on you. Chemical and surgical procedures. That is barbaric."

"Bar-bar-ic." He sounded out the letters, then lifted my hand, the one guilty of almost touching him without his permission. He pressed my fingertips over the rows of bumpy needle marks crisscrossing the bends of his elbows, the backs of his hands, even a few along his neck, results of IVs for sedation or biological infusions.

Then opened my hand, placing my palm along a narrow, clean scar running the center of his chest. The line was too precise for claws, the work of a scalpel.

This was why his bloodwork was off. There was no way of knowing the drugs and surgeries they'd tried in order to make him a perfect killer. The anangoas, non-native cryptids that had appeared in our old Division, known to secret a hallucinogenic biochemical venom meant to render prey passive, took on a more disturbing bent.

The Syndicate had imported them, either to milk for venom, or to use in retro engineering a more potent version. One they'd almost certainly subjected Owen to, playing with his body and brain to make him malleable to their manipulation. They'd done their chemical best to strip him of his will and morals.

"There's nothing faulty about you, or anything that needs fixed. You are a survivor." I held out my fist to bump knuckles.

Owen jerked, eyes on my hand.

Because he didn't have a clue about social norms, much less teamwork and congratulations. His day-to-day had been physical abuse, not support and praise. I mouthed, "This is a ritual of congratulations between humans, for jobs well done. Like this." I fisted both of my hands, gently tapping them together.

He followed the motion, focus intense.

"Want to try again?" I mouthed.

"You believe I did well. In killing vampires and following your orders."

"You didn't follow, you worked *with* me. As an equal. And yes, you owned those vampires' asses."

A snort-laugh blasted from him, more goofy than lethal. He made a fist and presented it to me, and we bumped.

The unit in the cabinet flashed, a series of green blips. A starburst pattern followed, the code Liv, Vee, and I had made up as Cadets. Unofficial, but our personal signature. The team was minutes out. Happiness at seeing them again, and them seeing that I was fine, gave way to the familiar bracing for their well-hidden disappointment at the error leading to my capture.

Owen dove for the extra weapons I'd laid out, the largest blade in hand uncannily quick. "A vehicle is approaching. Not a van or an open one as we borrowed."

I hustled between him and the door, hands up to catch his attention. He hit, chest ramming against my palms, staggering me into the door, pain ricocheting up my hip where the doorknob dug in.

Owen froze, nostrils flaring, tensed more like a vibrating piece of stone than a living body. But he looked down at me, fighting some internal battle.

I mouthed, "Easy. I know."

Sliding my palms down his chest, easing the pressure away in degrees, I totally wasn't noticing the angles of his chest, as unforgiving as the rest of him, or passing over the ripple of carved abs. Hands free, I explained. "My family is in that truck. They're here to help, and are our ride back to my home base."

That wrenching push-pull between his wariness and hope played across his face. He straightened. "Family."

"All Company teams consist of sisters and brothers. We're not just kickass soldiers." I grinned, hoping to ease his fight or flight. Which leaned heavily to fight, but, no throwing stones here. So did ours.

"You are an impressive soldier leader," he said, like he was reassuring me.

"Same." Keeping his limited social experience in mind, I elaborated. "We'll debrief by summarizing our escape. You have invaluable information on the Syndicate, which will help in fine-tuning our approach to eliminating them, so there will be a ton of questions. After we have a real meal, and regroup."

As boots crunched on the circle drive's crushed shells and gravel, I kicked my brain back in gear. Owen would debrief, but I was also making sure I was the one who escorted him to HQ, and got him settled in. I was already cobbling together a case for keeping him at our nearby Regional California HQ for debriefing, instead of sending him to the main Southwest HQ.

Then proceed from there, once Owen had a chance to catch his breath, and had an idea of what he wanted and where he wanted to go now that he was in charge of his life.

All I needed were a few concrete facts to convince Vee that I wasn't making a mistake that could injure the team and everyone on it by taking a short leave to accompany him.

Then after bringing them over to the Owen-is-staying-local side, another metric ton of imagination to convince our HQ, then the Assessors who policed our shadow strike team, and ultimately, Oversight, with their *extreme* trust issues.

CHAPTER 8

wen

THE INSTINCT to crash through the weak wooden door and ambush the enemy drummed through Owen. Spill their blood, be done with the threat. The knife handle creaked in his grip.

Kimi's promise held instinct in check. She promised, and he smelled no lies or deceit on her. Only excitement, confusing him again. *Family* seemed a human word for batch, the cubs he was born with. Encountering any of his batch outside of an exercise or mission only resulted in reestablishing dominance and rank within the batch, physically vying for position and any advantages.

His lip curled off his teeth at the hammering of boots, bodies running up the steps. Kimi stood between him and the oncoming soldiers, and whether to obey training and follow her orders as leader, clashed against his new desire to allow nothing to harm her.

The door crashed open, jamb splintering and knob hitting hard enough it lodged in the wall. Kimi breathed one of the forbidden words. The speed of the soldiers' entry created a draft, and funneled the scent of old blood in. The smell of vampires.

Two in the front. They had somehow traveled during the day, intercepted her family-team, murdered them, and were now attacking here. He whipped the blade back, reversing for a stroke that would take the first's head off.

A weight latched onto and hung from his wrist, derailing his aim. He reared to shake off whoever had snuck in behind them. Came nose to forehead with them. The odd plant-not-vehicle-oil, the plastic aftertaste of food bar wrapper, and the older whiff of fancy food coated his sinus.

Kimi. She shifted her weight to one arm, and snapped her fingers in his face, soft-talking. "My family. Remember?"

He got words out around the snarl crawling up his throat. "They are vampires. I won't go back."

With two fingers, she pointed at his eyes, then hers. Demanding attention. "Technically, they are. But not Syndicate. They're like me, and you. Trust me?"

He shouldn't...but she held his gaze, her forehead wrinkled. A human sign of concern. Concern for him. He grunted agreement.

Keeping her arm wrapped around his, she turned to the destroyed entry. The vampires crouched in front, a male whose aura beat against Owen, old, strong, more than any he'd encountered. The small female one beside him felt young, too powerful for the taste of her age, her aura the blazing yellow of the sun instead of the dark mustiness of a vampire. Both with the long machete blades. Another human, a tall male stood in the gaping doorway, gun trained on the room.

Kimi snapped her fingers at them, the sharp pop explosive. She spoke-signed too fast, even with one arm half imprisoned. Owen recognized the command to stand down. Then more words, her gestures strong.

The human holstered his weapon. "Okay, yes. That was kinda over the top on our part, but, c'mon. You've been gone nearly twenty-four-hours. We missed you, Kimster."

What resembled a growl came from Kimi.

The vampires stood, blades back in thigh holsters. The female's face turning dusky rose. "What Josh said. Sorry?"

The ancient vampire inclined his head. Apologetic. "Lo siento, hija. HQ indeed forwarded your pre-report to us, but I did not control my distress, and it fed your brother and sister's."

Owen had been correct. The three, even the old vampire, obeyed Kimi.

"Está bien, papá." Her demanding signing softened, as did her whisper-talking in the second language. She let go of Owen.

The old vampire's head lifted, scenting like a windigo. "You're injured."

"A water bottle," the younger vampire ordered, and the human turned to flee back out the door.

She pulled out a smaller knife, then hesitated, looking to Kimi. "How bad is it? My blood or Stavros'?

"Never mind. Stavros' blood." Not waiting for an answer, she handed the blade to the larger vampire, who stabbed his thumb, blood welling.

Kimi stiffened, and Owen caught the creak of enamel as she gritted her teeth.

The human rushed in, tossing the bleeding vampire a bottle. The vampire dripped blood in, turning the water pink, and advanced on Kimi.

"Don't let them turn you." Owen had never seen it done, but had been taught how vampires were created. And these vampires that were out in the day without suits, they were more powerful. He fell into a fighting crouch, knife ready.

Kimi held one arm out, toward the vampires, and offered Owen her other. She whisper-mouthed, "They aren't trying to infect me. They're offering to heal me."

She turned her head enough to include the vampires and other human. "Which isn't necessary. *At. All.* If it was, I would ask. Which I'm explicitly not."

The small vampire's face changed color again. The older vampire capped the bottle, knife disappearing. He wiped his thumb against his pants, and the faintest hint of embarrassment came off him.

"Sorry times two?" The bright faced vampire said. Then she and the human rushed them, circling Kimi. *Touching* her.

Owen grabbed Kimi by the waist, swinging her away from the horde.

Her elbow landed in his gut, his breath whooshing out. The hand he'd laid on Kimi went numb from the wrist down. Done breaking his hold, she was in his face again, eyes narrowed.

He dropped his head, averting his eyes in respect. He had disobeyed. He'd touched her without orders.

Her face softened, the way it had with the old vampire, and she whisper-signed. "Are you back with me now?"

"They were touching you," burst out.

"They weren't attacking or attempting to hurt me, or you." She cocked her head, then laid her hand on his shoulder for a moment. "Like this touch. This is a happy thing, another way of sharing comfort and showing you missed family."

He searched through the stored memories from his books. If there was an explanation, it would be from books. Touching, but not as fighting or mating… "Hugging?"

She blinked hard, and the pungent emotion she'd given

off when she saw his scars returned. Anger, but not at him. And the other, the upset-sad one. "Exactly."

Turning away from him, she signed to the human and vampires. Then walked among them, arms wrapped around the two vampires. The tall human threw his arms around all three. The salty scent came back, from the human and small vampire.

They did the hugging for minutes. Many minutes.

They finally separated, but the old vampire caught Kimi's chin, and spoke in the second language. Even his scent was happy-relieved. Kimi patted his hand, then hugged him again.

"You're seriously all right?" The human asked.

"Obvs," Kimi signed, an unexplainable hint of guilt riding her scent. "Stop sniffing or I'll smear that menthol rub on everything again."

The order seemed aimed at the female vampire, who winced. "Super harsh. But, fair."

"Bruce?" Kimi signed a name, and Owen switched to more important information than words and names. Evaluating the hormones and scents, the micro-movements of each member, whose eyes shifted where. Attempting to sort their hierarchy. Who might dare punish Kimi for not completing the mission she had been on.

Most importantly, whether he had the right to defend her then, or if his aid would make her appear weak, and invite more punishment.

Despite blocking out all stimuli except his search, Owen picked up no posturing, or central leader. Nor was Kimi reprimanded, or punishment spoken of. The group's happiness only increased as they hug-touched and talked.

Perhaps family-teams were different. If this was a true fact, then maybe the other book things he read were also real.

He examined the human male more closely. The books had ex-mates, often evil, who attempted separating the heroine and hero. Was this human that threat?

"Owen?" He caught Kimi's whisper-question, turning quickly to see what she required. He fixed his attention on her.

The correct action, as she gestured him closer.

"Owen, this is Vee, one of my sisters and Commanding Officer, Stavros, our father and Lieutenant, and Josh, one of my brothers. Guys, this is Owen."

Perhaps Owen misunderstood what family-team meant. There must also be a command level above C.O., one for Kimi's title as alpha leader.

The human male gave Owen a gesture. A wave. Then held his hand out, in the fist position Kimi had demonstrated. The one indicating a job performed well. "Hey, man."

Under Kimi's gaze, Owen tried out the gesture, bumping his knuckles against the other's.

The male smiled, the non-threatening one Kimi used, and dipped his head at Owen's bare chest. "I've got extras in the truck go-bag that'll fit you, if you want. We're close enough to the same size."

"A shirt?" Owen dared ask for clarification.

"A tee, and BDU's. Dunno if there's hot water in the shower here, but you can at least change into something not coated in gore."

Owen glanced down at his pants. "I killed lab and guard vampires. Kimi killed the first, and many others." It was important to honor his mate's leadership.

Josh held his hand up high, palm to Owen. Clearly expecting a physical response. Presumably like the fist touching. Owen held his out, smacking it against the other soldier's. Josh flashed a bigger smile. "Props, brother. Gimme a sec to grab the gear." He jogged down the stairs to the ground.

This strange male with no alliance to Owen, or orders to work with him, liked Owen's fighting, and was offering him clothing. As Kimi had offered food, water, and aid. The book information *was* true.

Also true, Josh wasn't an ex-mate. Those were always evil, where Josh was good, so, an impossibility. It was one of the book rules.

Kimi watched Owen, from beside the powerful vampire. She didn't smile with her lips, but the edges of her eyes did, approving.

A cough echoed from Owen's side of the room.

He looked down—far down—to the small female vampire, who rested against the cluttered counter, her hands stuffed in her back pockets.

"Hi." She kept her gaze off to the side as she spoke, not locking eyes and challenging. "Would you like anything else from our stash? Josh or I can grab it."

This was a vampire, but one of Kimi's family-team. He kept the growl out of his tone. "I will use the clothes."

"Food? There's at least one pack of doughnuts hidden with the burner phones, and Josh would totally share the sport's drink he snuck out in his bag. Oh, the doughnuts are chocolate."

"Kimi has shared food with me. I don't know chocolate." Later he would ask Kimi if it was fancy food.

The vampire's head shot up, mouth open in surprise. "Seriously?"

"My handlers never spoke of it."

"Vampires are such jerks," she muttered, brows scrunched together. She glanced at his chest, giving off the tangled puff of emotion like Kimi's. "There's a mild painkiller in our med kit. I could—"

"Kimi put burn cream on me."

The vampire chewed on her own nail. "The vampires you mentioned are responsible for your scars?"

"Most."

"I am *so* sorry, Owen."

He tasted the truth. "You are a vampire. Your aura is wrong—not vampire. And you walk in the sun." Those facts had to be related.

"Whoa, you can feel us? I hadn't considered whether close, extended contact with vampires would cause a human to develop a sensitivity." As if his question was an invitation, the vampire wiggled closer. "What's wrong with my aura? Or different, I guess?"

"It is strong, while you are young. It feels like sunshine, and doesn't stink of moldy earth. Why?"

"Kind of a long story. I was an agent. A human Company agent—"

"Like Kimi."

The vampire made a noise, like an injured animal, barely audible, and swiped at her eyes. "Yes. We're sisters, and trained together, and then gained our own Division. Until vampires—" she took a breath "—until the Syndicate vampires attacked us. Well, me and Stavros. He saved me, in his own way. He and I have only ever fed on other vampires. That's why we can stand sunlight, at least, as long as we're all juiced up."

She raised her face, expression fierce, silver banding her dark eyes. "I hate them, too. All of them."

"You kill them?"

"Yes. We always policed them, but now it's our primary mission. We can get to those that even regular teams can't. Stavros and I will end them all one day."

Her words sounded like a promise, as when Kimi had promised to also rescue him.

He should be wary, on guard. All he'd learned said humans were the enemy.

No one here, human or vampire, had challenged him, injured him, or attempted to cage him. They had been the opposite of everything the handlers taught.

Kimi said he was safe, that this was her team. He should have remembered she was the heroine, and it was always correct to trust her, his mate. She'd said he wasn't defective, and that books and questions weren't forbidden and wrong.

"I would like to kill more vampires as well," he shared with her, the tiny vampire, Kimi's family. Vee.

She leaned back to examine his face, hers scrunched again. "The mini-report Kimi sent mentioned you'd been held by the Syndicate for some time. You don't want to get away from the whole cryptid monster world, and back to your family and career?"

"I had nothing except the vampire handlers and cages. I am staying with Kimi," he said. He would be with his mate, and by aiding her family-team, there would also be no more Syndicate to recapture him.

The brother, Josh, halted in the doorway, a bag hanging over his shoulder. His gaze bounced from Vee, to Owen's mate, then back to the vampire. "Oookay, then."

Hot or cold water made no difference to Owen. He took the bag and headed for the bathing area, as everyone in the room turned to Kimi, as was right and proper.

CHAPTER 9

imi

AND I HAD THOUGHT my plan would be controversial

Factoring in his bluntness, his reaction should've been in my top five possibilities, though.

"You discussed him returning to the compound with us?" Vee's tone was all Commander. Not an especially thrilled one, at that.

"Not exactly, no."

Stavros looked between me and Vee, and took a step back, lining up with Josh. Who resembled a giant-eyed anime character as his gaze ping-ponged between me and Vee.

I motioned everyone to the corner, in case Owen emerged from the bath. His vision and hearing were exceptional, and he didn't need to stumble into what might be a vigorous discussion.

Also, I definitely wasn't speculating on whether he'd gotten naked in the primitive shower. My libido was healthy, but my response to a virtual stranger was intense even for me.

They crowded in, Stavros on the outside, also monitoring the unguarded door opening while keeping ears open for Owen. We all turned to signing, our ASL and Company hybrid.

"You saw him," I signed.

"The report said he'd been held long term, and suffered damage, but...dang." Vee crossed her arms like she was cold. Too easy for her to fall back into the nightmare of when she was savaged and infected.

"From all I've gathered to date, he was taken as a toddler," I signed. "He was literally raised in the facility, by what sounds like jailers who were tasked with turning him into a daylight soldier for the Syndicate. He wasn't simply in a cage, he'd been there long enough he had hidden caches. He'd somehow gotten paperbacks—he had a copy of the *Bros Read Romance* contemporary series."

Toss-up whether Josh or Vee had the most massive *OMG!* eyes at the news. Vee's stiff, at-attention posture shifted a few degrees, closer to normal.

"I think most of his information on being human came from the few books he'd stolen," I added.

"Those scars are hardcore. He's been worked over." Josh emphasized the last words, signing harder than I did.

"He was a research subject." The churning rage rose again. "They tried a myriad of chemical and surgical procedures on him. My best guess is in order to make him blindly obedient, yet still able to function independently, similar to the agenda Marshall reported vampires discussing when he snuck into the Franken-Non mission to save Liv."

"Fucking monsters." Josh's hands flexed, like he'd prefer they were around the necks of the skanky vampire partiers who'd set our sister's team up months earlier, planting some sort of lab-grown cryptid for her to capture, that then mentally ensnared and manipulated them. To the point she hadn't recognized Marshall, prepared to eliminate him on the head vampire's order. Her team had been meant as the first wave of Syndicate spies inside the Company. We had almost lost her, our brothers, and Marshall.

"Owen is—" Brave. Unpredictable. Fascinatingly direct. "All he knows is this brutal slavery. It's a given that no civi medical professional will have a clue how to handle any health issues or have a behavioral approach—"

"Our Med and Psych divisions would have the closest chance at understanding his situation," Vee said.

"Agreed. I think the best idea for his introduction to non-Syndicate life is for me to accompany him to our HQ. He trusts me."

"Ours? Cali instead of HQ-HQ?' She frowned. "That isn't protocol. Plus, Oversight will want hands on him, which I totally agree with. He's a goldmine of Syndicate information."

"He's been traumatized like nothing I can imagine. They're only going to add more crap for him to wade through," Josh signed, emphatic. He had every right to hold a grudge against Oversight. "After all that, and having your back, he doesn't deserve more. He has rights."

"He seems to have imprinted on me," I admitted.

"Noticed." Vee went for her cuticle again.

"What he knows about the Syndicate is invaluable." I got straight to the point, my, and Owen's, best leverage. "I'm not sure he would trust anyone else enough to go in-depth into all he knows of Syndicate agenda and methods, or feel safe enough to go into detail as to what was done to him."

"Who can blame the guy?" Josh signed. "He's got no reason to trust anyone other than Kimi. He helped save her, she helped save him."

I shoulder-bumped my brother, thanking him for his support. "If we can prove that he has information the Company needs, and that he will willingly discuss it with me, that's our in."

My subconscious did its thing, tossing up the answer. "We can draw up a set of quick and dirty questions for Owen right now, and have his answers ready when we call HQ. That is tangible proof our idea is valid."

"And *boom*, we have a plan," Josh signed.

I checked with Stavros, who inclined his head in agreement.

"It's settled, then." Vee's signing gentled. "But he is going to have to integrate with HQ life and staff quickly. We can't spare you for long."

She was only stating what we were all thinking. We were barely keeping up with missions and call-outs when it was the four of us. My absence left a hole in the team, a weakness a cryptid or vampires could exploit.

"He is returning," Stavros signed.

We separated seconds before the bathroom door's hinges squeaked. Owen stalked in, intense as Stavros and Vee, who's every movement proclaimed they were predators, despite the effort they put in to be normal, no matter how well they thought they succeeded.

In our everyday gray tee and multi-pocket BDU's, he looked like Company. Aside from the fact that he was broader than my brother, shirt stretched tight. And the towel situation here must've been lacking, the cotton fabric sticking to his damp chest.

He stopped beside me. "Do we go now?"

"Soon, I hope." Vee took over before I could, her phone out and recording app open. "Would you mind clarifying a couple of the things you discussed with Kimi?"

He frowned, looking down at me.

"She means would you mind telling us a little more about how you came to be with the Syndicate?"

"I will answer you." Which wasn't exactly a yes. Or enthusiastic.

"Do you recall when you were first taken?" Vee said.

"All I remember are the vampires, the caretakers and trainers." He repeated what he'd told me.

"Nothing else? No fragments of other humans? A house? Pets?" Vee continued.

"What are *pets*?" He asked me, almost like Vee wasn't in the room.

"Animals, like dogs or cats, that people keep."

"These are for food?"

"No. I mean, humans do keep food animals like cows and chickens—fancy food," I took a guess. "Pets are non-food animals kept for companionship and comfort."

The look he gave me was blank and baffled.

"Not important," Vee tried reassuring him. "We can talk about training instead. What was it like and how long did you train?"

"It was training. To become faster and stronger and a better fighter. I have always trained."

Josh took a turn. "We're just wondering what kind of training?"

"With weapons, guns and blades. With my hands."

"What was the objective, like, what were you trained to do?"

Owen stiffened. "To kill, to follow my handler's commands."

"To kill human's," Vee said, her tone softer.

"I did not kill humans. I disobeyed. Kimi knows this."

That weird tone was back, the one he'd used when he said he was defective, the one that surfaced anytime he mentioned not going back to the vampires. He didn't move,

89

but it felt like he withdrew, as if I turned to look, he wouldn't be beside me.

Before I could sign a warning, Vee said, "Do you remember anything about the treatments or experiments done to you as—as punishment?"

Owen did move, stepping back. Rage and wariness sharpened his voice. "I remember everything. There was always pain. Any creature that disobeys made the scientist-vampires angry. When they reprogramed me, they did not give the bad drugs that made me sleep."

Jace swore, barely audible over Vee's gasp, and Stavros' "¡Santa Madre de Dias!" as he crossed himself.

Stomach churning at the new level of abuse he'd endured, I stepped between the team and Owen. Question time was so over. "We can talk about this later, once you're rested, we've eaten, and had time to process. Would you mind bringing more bottles of water to replace those we drank? They are in the last bedroom, underneath the bed."

He turned without speaking, shoulders hunched, his body language screaming his discomfort.

"They fucking cut him up without even local anesthesia?" Josh's eyelid twitched, a tic that only came out when he was the kind of furious where he was ready to take a swing at someone.

"That is—I don't think I have a good enough word," Vee said.

Stavros did. "It is the vilest evil. This is what demons are driven to, reveling in humans' pain."

I rubbed at the ache in my temples, then signed, "Owen was far more open with me. I don't think he's comfortable around people yet. I also don't think his adapting to life at HQ and with their therapist, much less with whichever Assessor Oversight sends to grill him, will be a quick process."

"How the heck do you get comfortable talking about torture?" Vee whispered, and Stavros laid a hand on her shoulder, comforting her.

Owen barely understood comfort, as evidenced by his reaction to anyone touching me. He'd done what he thought was required to protect me. I owed him the same protection. The idea of him alone at HQ, once I had to return to the team, of agents and Assessors basically forcing him to relive the most horrific parts of his life…I pressed a hand against my queasy stomach.

I couldn't allow that to happen.

"Owen needs to come back to the compound with us," I signed.

Three sets of eyes fastened on me. "He needs space and a friend, not the pressure of strangers demanding answers immediately and without understanding what they're really asking of him."

"He only answered us because of your presence and the bond you have forged," Stavros said, picking up more from hormones and micro-reactions than we ever could. "His emotions when these vampires are brought up is complex, but there is great anger. Were another agent or Assessor to unknowingly press him too hard, and send him back into that memory of torture, he may well react violently before he can separate himself from memory and reality."

The way he'd trashed the lab's surgical suite, and how he'd lost himself while killing the guards between us and the exit came back and I shivered. "He is one of the most formidable fighters I've ever seen. If the worst happened, I'm not sure he could be stopped without potentially fatal consequences."

"Which would also mean losing everything he knows about this Syndicate," Vee finished.

"The more information supplied, the happier Oversight

will be. Maybe our being—okay, Kimi being—the only one he'll talk to will make us more valuable." The same cold logic that allowed Josh to bide his time until a creature was in his sights, then end its life, surfaced

Vee's hand drifted to the back of her neck, where the lethal popper chip was located. Because of a lifetime together, I knew she was thinking of the one in Josh and Stavros, not hers. "I'll call B and get his input, then Liv. You have ideas on the most palatable way to broach him to Oversight?"

A crushing load of apprehension vanished at their implied trust in me. Only to be replaced with another, that I was really doing the right thing. Bringing Owen in would technically violate the harsh rules we lived under, grounds to activate the chips. But we were also basically the OG innovators of carting home civis, and adding them to the team.

"We present him as the most invaluable source of day-to-day activities within this vampire faction, who has now dropped into our hands. One that basically will only deal with me. We go through Jamison." The AIC, Assistant Assessor in Charge of policing us, had been swayed if not to our side, at least to embracing what having Vee and Stavros as Company meant in saving other agents' lives.

He also got our sense of humor.

"I mean, five minutes with Owen, and anyone will recognize his pure hatred of vampires. There's zero chance he'd allow himself to be turned." Oversight's biggest bugaboo was that Vee and Stavros would make a go of turning all of us, then all nearby teams, forming an army of Company-trained vampires.

Points for their inventiveness, but, least likely scenario ever.

"After the way he fought, there's no doubt of his feelings toward vampires in general. He was merciless," I signed. "His training and specialized insights can be presented as another plus, and best used in the field and as part of a team. Similar to how we framed your value," I signed to Stavros.

Vee hesitated, then tipped her chin in question at her Lieutenant. Stavros mostly stayed out of interfamily drama, but he was Vee's second, and an endless source of experienced advice.

Perfectly in synch, partially thanks to his experience, partially from the hive-like biological bond Master vampires shared with any receiving their infected DNA, he understood Vee's request for his input. He dipped his head in agreement. "I concur with Kimora's evaluation. He is human, and must be protected. He is also returning."

Of course Owen's instant negative reaction when he believed Vee wanted to infect me had won Stavros over.

"I'm on it," Vee said aloud.

Owen sat the case of bottles on the counter, underneath the cabinet he'd seen me take ours from. He watched Vee bounce down the steps, and hop into the truck for privacy.

"Thank you for being honest with us, despite how awful those memories are for you," I signed. "Are you still willing to talk about everything you saw and heard from your time with the Syndicate? Our Company will have a lot of questions, and will want to speak with you often. If you prefer, I can ask the questions they send, and you can give me your answers privately."

He deserved to know what wounds HQ would be reopening, everything from his childhood until the point we'd escaped the lab.

"My answers will aid in destroying the vampires?" He stopped toe to toe, way into my personal space even by touchy-feely Company standards.

"It will." I caught and squeezed his hand, and his shoulders straightened.

"You ask this, so I will tell your Company all of my memories, and I will fight beside you and kill all vampires. Except these two." He pointed at Stavros.

"This is the boy's holy mission." Stavros' rough voice held approval. "It is God's will he act as a weapon against the demons."

"Demons?" Owen frowned at me. "I do not know those, but I will kill them if Kimi agrees."

I ignored Josh's choking noise, adding it to his payback tab, along with teasing me earlier over the nickname our year-mate Ridge had given me as Cadets. "Stavros uses demon as another word for vampire. Historically, demons of all faiths and mythologies are evil and torment humans."

Owen grunted agreement. "I require other weapons. Please," he tacked on, as if it just occurred to him.

Holsters, too. The hilt of the knife he'd nearly decapitated Stavros with earlier was slipped through an o-ring at his waistband, where he'd carried it with him to the shower.

A life that left you feeling as if even showering required weapons was my new definition of worst-thing-ever. I back-tracked to the selection of gear I'd laid out.

"You've for real earned some payback." Josh rejoined the convo. "I meant to say it before, but thank you. Not for bringing Kimi back, because she's hella good and would've escaped anyway, but thanks for backing her up, and all."

I handed Owen a pair of standard thigh-rigs.

He attached them without looking, more interested in studying my brother, like he was something strange and fascinating, the way he had my origami dog. Owen slotted the knife in place, then added the longer blade on one thigh, the standard Glock on the other. "This is all?"

"We'll contact our superiors and get you cleared, then I'll load you up from our Armory once we're home. Plus, you can add whatever your specialty or favorite is," I promised.

"We're a go." Vee popped her head around the door, then came the rest of the way in. "I lucked up. B hadn't started restaurant prep yet, and Liv was back from her *short morning run*." She rolled her eyes.

"Do not miss those," Josh muttered.

I took the encrypted laptop she brought in, and went through the protocols to reach Jamison. This was one of the few times I missed my voice, because my hands would be too busy signing to keep my fingers crossed for luck.

Our phones pinged in unison. We all sent the personal I.D. confirmation code, that extra layer of protection proving we had messaged, not some cryptid who'd taken us out and stolen the laptop.

Depositing the laptop on the counter, I motioned Owen closer. I'd examine why Jamison *had* to agree to my request later. Simple triage of priorities, not me avoiding considering my unprecedented emotional reaction to a stranger.

The link opened, blue eyes filling the screen, against a blur of moving green and brown. "Present yourselves." The screen stabilized, probably on the hood of the Hummer only Assessors used, Jamison in the next-gen gray body armor his office had access to first. Scrub, a saguaro cactus cluster, and desert spread behind him.

Vee started the ritual, giving him a clear view plus our team code and her personal C.O. code, then rolled her thumb across the red square in the corner of the keypad. Beside me, Owen twitched, likely a reaction to the drop of blood she'd been forced to donate. A few seconds, and Jamison said, "Verified."

Stavros and Josh went through the same process. I stepped up, signing and submitting to the finger prick that was matched against our stored DNA profile, proving who we were, and once again that I was still human.

A tense second of Jamison's eyes scrolling through the

chemical analysis popping up on his end, then he gave a thumbs up. "Verified. I'm damn glad to see you on the outside and in one piece, Kimi."

Our current situation and relationship with the Assessors wasn't the norm. Assessors were support for teams, evaluating when needed, identifying any weaknesses, and aiding agents and teams in shoring up those vulnerable spots. They joined in the celebration when teams returned to peak condition, or when new teams were formed. They were the best of the best, created to help us. Unless your team consisted of an infected agent and an adopted non-Company vampire father.

At heart though, Jamison was an agent, and agents always had each other's backs.

Quickly reassuring Owen that this was the same as the earlier test, I introduced him. Instead of sticking his finger on the square, he offered his hand to me to test, allowing me to perform the DNA draw.

As it ran, Jamison added, "I'm sending an app, something new R and D came up with, that we're field testing. We're still unsure of the function of the chips this vampire faction has implanted in all of the anomalies you've brought in for us, but this will pick up their presence. Scan the entire skull horizontally."

As our phones pinged and I tapped to download, I had a moment of pure professional jealousy over someone else beating me to creating the program. Then got over it, since they'd finally paid attention to my reports on the weird tech, and this was useful. Plus, I still had a shot at discovering the implant's purpose first. Since they'd also only been found in cryptids and the Syndicate's lab creations, no reason to worry about Owen carrying one, despite Jamison's caution.

Owen bent enough for me to perform the scan, and flip

my phone around to show Jamison the *no chip detected* reading.

A moment later, Jamison gave a relieved smile. "Mister Owen. On behalf of Company Alpha Cryptid Containment, North American segment, welcome. Our Medical and Counseling divisions are already preparing for the team's and your arrival. Whatever you require, we'll provide. Is there anything we may not be aware of that you need or want?"

"No." Owen did that unnerving vibrating intensity. I side-stepped so that our hips bumped together, betting on contact soothing him enough he didn't lump our AAIC in with the bad guys.

Jamison took the answer as Owen not having any requests, as opposed to Owen refusing to go in.

"About that." Vee peeked into frame.

"We have a tactically sound request," I signed, pulse picking up.

The AAIC's gaze drilled into us for a handful of heartbeats.

He jerked his polarized sunglasses out of a pocket and jammed them on, a futile try at blocking us out. "Do not. Do not say what's on the tip of your tongue. Or on the tip of your fingers, Kimi. Once you do, I'm required to report it to Oversight within the half-hour."

I added a mental note to draw Jamison into our Company gamer group. If he didn't find an outlet for his stress, he was going to implode. Super unhealthy.

"We're petitioning Oversight, via our official Assessor channel, to allow Owen, the documented human we rescued from a vampire facility, to accompany us to our primary base. We will cooperate immediately with all requested testing, and any interview schedule that Oversight hands down to HQ," I promised. "Once he is stabilized and ready, he will report for in-person appointments when we do our monthly visits."

"You are the hardest agents in recorded Company history to keep alive." He snatched the glasses off. "Do you know why I'm standing on a West Texas backroad? Because I'm a day away from arriving at your sister's gate, to conduct an evaluation of the non-predatory cryptid—"

"Kit." Josh hung over my shoulder. "The kid's name is Kit."

"Silva, damn it." The camera and screen were high-res, giving a crystal clear view of the vein throbbing in our Assistant AIC's temple.

I was unilaterally adding Jamison to our game tonight. He'd thank me later.

"The kid has been a rock star. How many solid leads has he brought in, that led to eliminating nests? And that pocket of genetically fucked up ghouls that were about to be unleashed on Galveston's Juneteenth parade? That doesn't even count all the non-predatory evolved cryptids sharing info with him, to pass on to us." Josh wasn't letting this go. The fact was, Kit's entire flock, family, siblings, friends, had all been massacred by the Syndicate, too. And when we'd first encountered him, we'd ignorantly treated him as an animal and a threat, when in reality, he was an orphaned, traumatized child.

"He has been good enough to receive provisional Asset status," Vee chimed in. "I.E., the reason you're on your way to Scottsdale."

"I'm aware, Ruiz." His tone was desert-dry. "I've no doubt he'll blend well with the team, *once* introduced into the compound and team itself."

We all kept our *We Are Totally Innocent and Of Course Kit Hasn't Already Been Living In The Compound for Months* faces on. Jamison suspected. Heavily. But suspicion wasn't the same as proof.

"The point being, firstly, that Owen is demonstrably human, not even a small, fruit-eating cryptid kid," Vee said.

"Secondly, Owen has been a captive for the majority of his life. He deserves the freedom to make his own choices," I signed.

Stavros paced to the front, grave and dignified. He dipped his head respectfully to the agent. "This man is a skilled fighter. He chooses to put all he has learned into the service of eliminating this vampire scourge. His is an honorable choice meriting respect."

"Mister Owen." Jamison switched tactics, probably hoping Owen was the more reasonable person in the group. "You don't have to make any decisions now. You have a number of options, and applying to join a team is an involved process, and can't be undone once you're accepted. Our Headquarters is a neutral area where you can regroup, heal, then decide—"

"I stay where Kimi stays. And her family-team." He pressed into me. "Only she has earned trust."

"You already know I'm thorough in data and reporting," I added. "I'll develop a sample set of questions focused on Syndicate—oh, that's what the faction is called—on Syndicate training practices during the drive home, and email them before we hit the front gate. Oversight can elaborate from there, and not have to reinvent the wheel."

Vee retook center stage. As C.O., it was her place to advocate for her team, and take any hits. "Another element is in play here, that Oversight and HQ haven't considered."

"Doubtful." Jamison gave her a look over the top of his glasses.

"Yes, Owen is technically a civilian, innocent, and under Company protection, plus valuable to the Company mission. However, the Syndicate sees him as their property. Sorry. You know how they are." She directed that at Owen with an apologetic wince. "Vampires do not easily give up what's theirs. The territorial drive is...intense." Color rose up her neck, embarrassment clear.

Her inability to give up her Command after being infected had almost caused an impossible rift in the team. Indirectly, it was part of the reason our sister, who had been part of our team since we were children, took the unprecedented and freaking painful move to start her own team.

"This isn't about some basic nest of angry vampires. In effect, the Company is now holding the coveted property of a large, multi-national, intricately organized group of vampires with deep pockets and an overarching terrorist agenda. And we are doing so in what we've just discovered is that group's territory." She made an *I-smelled-a-windigo* face at the Syndicate operating miles from us without our knowledge. "We all know it's preferable to draw that potential for attack away from California HQ, the main Southwest HQ and Academy, and our way. You can admit we are uniquely equipped for the challenge. As Oversight's strike team, this is in our wheelhouse."

Jamison's sigh rattled the speakers.

Vee squeaked, because from him, a put-upon sigh equaled yes. The authorization wasn't a gimme, and his Senior partner was leery of us, but his opinion held weight with her and with Oversight.

"I'll put in an appeal. It's a stroke of luck that Oversight is in a good mood. The vampires triggered a self-destruct, but thanks to Kimi's fast reporting, choppered in teams and Cleaners made it in time to salvage a significant portion of the site and research. That was another reason you were cleared so quickly, and the team given an immediate go-ahead to meet you."

Now to hope that my program finished transferring their

files before the place blew. Out of sight, I found and squeezed Owen's hand.

"This is a time-sensitive situation, but that's your team's M.O.," Jamison said. "Do not move from where you are. Do not add any civilians, vampires, or chupacabras to the team in the fifteen-to-twenty minutes this conference call with Aida and Oversight takes. If Oversight refuses the request—don't put me in the position of having to bring you in."

The screen went dark.

Jamison's statement wasn't a threat. Simply our reality. Living on the edge, as agents facing creatures with extreme powers who preyed on humans was the sort of danger we'd grown up with, or according to Bruce, been indoctrinated into. It barely registered.

The situation with Oversight, though. It was specific to us, and with no warning, the click of a few keys could end my sister, brother, and father. Then the organization our heart and soul belonged to, our reason for being, would eliminate the rest of us. We hadn't just had a threat added to our lives, we'd also had the support and surety we'd been raised with jerked away.

None of us were truly okay. We hadn't been for several years, starting with Bruce's cancer diagnosis, then Vee's disappearance, Liv splitting from the team, and ending with Oversight's threat shadowing our every waking moment.

A sigh snuck out, and I rotated my sore shoulders, giving the hurt a temporary way out.

Owen loomed over me, forehead crinkled, one hand on the knife hilt. "What is wrong? Do we fight?"

Allowing my emotions to negatively affect someone under our protection was another new and unwelcome change.

"I'm impatient, and don't enjoy waiting," I signed. All true, only omitting the personal danger.

"I stay with you, and will only speak with you about the Syndicate, handlers, and modification."

I stuck with a nod. If he was sent to HQ instead...Josh caught my eye, and we shared a moment. It would be a disaster for Owen. My going with him to mediate long-term, if they'd even allow it... No matter how good we were, and the edge Stavros and Vee provided, we really were scrambling to keep up with not only the vampire population explosion, but what were either rejected cryptid experiments getting dumped for funsies or escaping, like the ghouls who now joined into packs, cryptids defying their biologically coded behavior.

Who even knew what other anomalies waited for us, thanks to the Syndicate's labs.

The laptop pinged and we all crowded back around, Owen behind me. Not touching, but his heat warmed my back. I crossed both sets of fingers, mind racing through Owen's options and possible reactions if Oversight rejected our proposal.

Jamison popped back into being, at parade rest, his back stiff and hands folded in front of him. He had a cap on and the wraparound sunglasses back in place. Maybe shielding from the sun, maybe hiding his expression from us. "Your request is granted, on a temporary, provisional basis. In addition to your current requirements, you'll make Mister Owen available within five minutes of any HQ or Oversight request, you'll turn in a daily report on any new information Mister Owen shares, and you will evaluate and turn in daily reports on his proficiency and scores on all exercises required of full agents—hand-to-hand and knife drills, speed, agility, shooting range, cryptic identification and habits, and urban and rural tracking. You will also note any areas he lacks training and any area that promises to become his specialization. Aida and I will be conducting a formal visit, after we evaluate Commander Muñez's team, to evaluate and rule on whether to allow the team alteration to remain in effect, or *immediately* pursue other placements."

"Yes, sir," we chorused, me signing. Then, out of camera sight, I caught and squeezed Owen's hand for a second.

Jamison's body language altered and he leaned so his face filled the frame. "The more intel you can provide in the next few days, and the more detailed, the better it will look. Oversight is divided on this, and our visit isn't a formality. Kimi, get on those questions ASAP. Put the greatest emphasis on insights into how the uprising is creating these staggering numbers of new vampires—whether they've engineered a mutation that increases the odds of an infected human turning, or whether there's some other mechanism in play. Also concentrate on detailing any non-native cryptids Mister Owen observed in the facilities, what their powers are, and how they are being utilized. We need to know what other hybrids, like the two psychic creatures you encountered in Phoenix, exist or will roll out in the near future."

"Understood," Vee said. "Thank you for going to bat for us."

"Agents don't thank agents." He repeated the unofficial motto. "Get going."

"Ready?" I turned to Owen. And basically bounced off him, only the thinnest space between us. He reached like he wanted to grab me, then politely dropped his hands to his sides.

Points for trainability.

He watched me as intently as when we'd first encountered each other, but fell in beside me. "Can we borrow another of the small, fast vehicles like the vampires had? The one where I put my arms around you? Not the large, orange one we borrowed after."

Choking noises echoed from behind me. I added giving

my brother a new screensaver and ringtone combo to my list. Something depicting pudgy wombats mating, possibly.

"The fast one is a motorcycle, occasionally referred to as a bike." I patted the Jeep as we walked past. "This is a vehicle meant for traveling off city roads. We'll use the team truck now, though."

Every emotion showed on Owen's face, his disappointment clear.

A motorcycle was a tiny step in showing him a different world. And that life wasn't all about training, fighting, and survival. "Our cleaners will return the Jeep to its owners. I can ask if they'll release the bike to us after they retrieve it, though."

He perked up, trusting me. That he had the ability to trust, and that he'd held onto curiosity and the capacity for enjoyment in that soul-sucking prison was as amazing as him surviving the physical trials.

Stavros slid into the driver's seat, Vee beside him. I didn't give Josh any choice, opening the rear door for Owen, leaving Josh in the middle row where he had less chance of antics, and more chance of Stavros squashing any teasing.

I belted in, Owen copying my technique.

"Can I put my arm around you in this truck? It's important to always ask," he said, deadly serious.

Vee's dreamy sigh carried, for sure visions of our favorite rom-coms playing through her head. Owen's request had little to do with romance, and more to do with traumatic associations. The SUV wasn't exactly one of the dark panel vans the Syndicate used to transport him, but it was still a black, official vehicle. At least there were windows.

"Yes, you may." I pulled my emergency tablet from its slot under the seat, activating the text-to-voice and opening a blank document. Then leaned over him, lowering the window enough for him to feel the breeze, and the sunshine.

Cupping his hand in mine, I settled in, monitoring him, and one-handedly creating a tantalizing set of questions for HQ and Oversight. Questions only Owen could answer.

More relaxed than during our trip here, he had his face mashed against the smoked window glass, watching everything. He couldn't shake the way he examined every aspect of the landscape from a strategic point of view. Another ingrained habit we shared, one we hadn't been aware of, until Bruce pointed it out.

But beside that calculating rundown, was the open enthusiasm of—not a child, but of a tourist in a strange, enthralling new land. Owen didn't attempt to hide or downplay his curiosity, or worry what others thought.

He was lethal and adorable in equal measures. With a huge extra measure of primal attractiveness.

The Company reared all its members to be sex-positive. We didn't do romantic relationships, but sex was always normal, whether it was for fun, stress relief, or a celebration of surviving another mission.

Intellectually, I understood the civilian world didn't function within the same parameters. McKenna, our year-mate Ridge's LEO civi girlfriend, then Bruce, and now Marshall, had all exposed us to the reality of civi biases and rituals around sex.

Owen, though…there was no way to gauge what he had or hadn't learned, aside from brief forays into great romance novels.

He glanced over at me, a ghost smile curving his lips, then went back to absorbing this new world of freedom.

Bile rose in an acid wash at the possibility he had been forced or used sexually while he wasn't in a position to refuse. Or even if it was because he'd been taught that obeying his handlers was the universal way and all he knew.

The fact that I found him attractive was therefore a nonstarter. He'd been violated enough, without my foisting sexual fantasies on him. There was also too much on the line now, keeping his cooperation, adding whatever creatures the Syndicate cooked up to our study-load and integrating new techniques to counter them.

I was an agent teammate, and Owen's guide into being an autonomous person, and his friend. Nothing else.

CHAPTER 10

wen

KIMI TAPPED HIS SHOULDER, a polite request for his attention. He took another deep inhale first. A scent-memory tickled. Not the embedded scent of his batch. Similar, new but not new. He opened his mouth enough that air and scent also filtered across his tongue, seeking more information.

Then it was gone, the vehicle moving too fast. He cut away from the view of stretches of rock, sand, and strange trees, and the other scents of reptilian and warm-blooded animals.

This new place was interesting. Kimi was far more interesting, though.

"We're nearly home," she whisper-signed.

Home seemed the term humans applied to where they slept and ate. Like his batch's cells and runs. The concept didn't warrant the contented puff of emotion Kimi gave off.

He would learn to respond the same way, to please her.

Being with her in this place was already better than his old *home*. After asking him a few questions about any creatures he had seen in the labs and using her device, she had wrapped both of her hands around his, resting them on her leg during this trip. This holding of hands was an acceptable alternative to putting arms around her.

Exaggerating her lip movements again, she said. "Your DNA, the information from the blood you donated, should already be processed and uploaded to our compound security base. If there was a lag in the office posting, there may be an alarm as we enter, but don't worry. It's only programed to respond that way for non-invited people and cryptids." She gave the happy-smile. "Sit very still as we go in."

He wasn't people. He wasn't cryptid. But he had parts of both. He had passed the tests with the small boxes. This was not taking a simple drop of his blood, and he had never been exposed to such a device in training scenarios. Thus, it was impossible to know how the machine would respond on encountering him. Out of her view, his free hand teased the thigh holster open, hand drifting to the gun. He wouldn't harm Kimi's family-team. He would smash the window with the butt of his weapon, and bolt into the mountains.

Tall chain-link gates rolled sideways, the truck passing through. At the edges of his visual range, a faint red ultraviolet beam swept them, though Kimi and her family-team seemed not to notice or care. A hollow hissing accompanied the beam, registering on the upper edges of his auditory range.

The gate rolled closed behind Owen, and that feel of hair just under his skin rising swept him. He tensed, shifting his weight in preparation for his escape.

A simple three note chime echoed in the vehicle.

"See?" She signed. "You are official. All good."

He took his fingers off the weapon, pressing the fastening back.

"Welcome to home sweet home. This is our primary compound." From in front of Owen, Josh stretched, fingers tickling the truck's ceiling.

The truck continued along a road, flanked by a scattering of the low, wiry grasses and plants that would flower briefly during the rains. The ground rose steadily as they advanced, leaving the valley behind. The inherited locating ability he carried told him they had progressed over two miles when another fence and gate appeared. They repeated passing through the gate, and the beam.

The road branched in three directions. The truck followed the left fork.

Kimi pointed, then signed. "The middle leads to our Armory, repair garage, and gym. The last goes to our training areas—outdoor courses, track, shooting and munitions range, and a holding area."

The truck crested the ridge, giving a clear view of the road and valley on three sides, a sheer rock face on the last. A large steel structure sprawled at the end of the drive, rising two stories. Sun glinted off the wall of glass circling the upper level.

Ahead of them, a metal wall rolled up, and they drove into a garage. Not as large as the vampires', but with equipment and tall red chests along the furthest wall. They stopped beside another of the black trucks. There was an empty space, then a red vehicle that looked like a cross between the trucks and the orange vehicle Kimi had borrowed, and two open, four-wheeled bike vehicles. Many other slots were empty.

Light flared, harsh and white, then dropped back to the level humans and vampires used.

"UV lights. Safety precaution in case of ghouls and vampires," Kimi whisper-signed.

"When are you going to by-pass those again?" Josh asked, a whine like a cub's in his tone.

"How about when we aren't on probation with Oversight, and subject to surprise Assessor visits?" Kimi signed. Then leaned forward and flicked Josh's ear.

He swatted, but far too slow, then rubbed where she'd connected.

Owen waited, gauging whether the sibling posturing would escalate to a fight for position, and whether Josh was challenging Kimi's leadership.

The old vampire muttered in the second language, and the vehicle shifted as he exited. The rest abandoned their seats, doors whumping closed. As if the squabble meant nothing. When Kimi reached across Owen, and opened the door, he followed her unspoken command, falling in beside her.

"Decontamination protocol, then the tour," Kimi signed.

He followed her, walking through a door to the left. A hall with the familiar scents of the lab's cleaning hallway greeted him, cold air shooting across him from both sides of the corridor. He moved closer to his mate, her curls brushing against his shoulder.

Kimi continued on, a clear door panel sliding closed behind them. "This is the lower level. Laundry, since it's way easier to strip here and toss gunked-up uniforms into either the wash or incinerator."

He would happily strip in here with Kimi. "I have never done laundry. Clothing was supplied or taken away."

Her face tightened, then she indicated the machines, bright silver against gray tile walls and floor. "I'll show you how. Washer first, then dryer. Drop boots in here, if they're covered in ick. Our other teammate has very strict rules about tracking cryptid remains inside."

She kept going, pushing doors open. She propped the first open with her hip, and signed. "Medical, for injuries. I'm the team medic."

He didn't step inside the sterile room, with the metal tables and equipment. Too much like the scientist's lab, with its experiments and pain. The bite of alcohol and chemicals ruffled the hair along his arms, even though the only hints of blood he detected were human, and no jars of cryptid remains lined the shelves.

"I'm sorry. I wasn't thinking," she whisper-signed, the door swinging closed. Then she was rubbing his arm, banishing the chill bumps.

He enjoyed the warmth of her palm sliding against his skin, and almost didn't ask why in case she stopped. But he didn't understand her reaction, and understanding a mate was important. "It smells of the lab and I hate it. You did nothing wrong. Why do you take blame?"

"I should have considered the bad associations the room would bring."

He turned the idea around, examining it as Kimi continued deeper into the building. "You were being—thoughtful." He tried out one of the words he'd read, but not had a definition for.

"It's what friends and family do. This is the—"

"Food area." The aroma of meats, vegetation, and milk swamped his senses. Too many types of fancy food. Counters and free-standing areas were covered in a glossy gray-mottled stone. The machines here were even shinier than those in the laundering room. Racks hung overhead, polished vessels hanging from them, the silver of metals he knew, and a brownish-gold he hadn't encountered.

Under it all was the sharper scent of paint, and the mellower one of cut wood and sawdust. "This is new."

Kimi snort-laughed. Owen stored the sound. He would find other ways to elicit the happy sound from her.

"This isn't our original home. Our fifth member went on a renovation and redecorating spree when we took over this Division. He has high civilian standards," she continued in her rough-whispery voice paired with signs.

"Civilian?" He knew soldiers, lab helpers, scientists, handlers, vampires, and humans

"He is a chef. A very well-known one. A cryptid targeted him a few years ago, we sheltered him until the creature was eliminated, and he never left."

He understood *cryptid* and *eliminating* one. For the rest, perhaps he was putting her signs together improperly.

She studied him for a moment, head tilted. "Let's try that again. Our definition of a civilian is any human not part of the Company, and not engaged in protecting humanity from cryptids."

"Only humans?"

She ducked her head away. "That is a complicated question. Basically, yes." Her head came up, something like fear in her eyes. "Only our two teams and Oversight know what Vee and Stavros are. You can't mention it to anyone else, ever. If anyone, Company or otherwise, learn they are infected, we will all be executed."

He bit down on the snarl fighting to break free. Snarling wasn't human. And only humans deserved protection. As well as rare vampires who were once Kimi's human Company soldiers. "I won't betray you or your family-team."

"Thank you."

She entrusted him with important information, and didn't assume he would make errors. The warm, swirly emotion inside him must be part of the fated-mate bond.

He stuck as close to her side as possible, while she wove around the kitchen food place.

"Eat-in bar," she signed as they passed another long stone counter, this one with tall backless chairs. "It's primarily for quickie meals. Occasionally for hanging out while Bruce works." She frowned. "Actually, forget that last, and give him privacy. The kitchen is his domain."

Discreetly, he sampled the web of scents, picking out the heaviest, the one belonging to the human who spent the most time in this area. He stored the scent signature of the territorial human. Owen would be prepared if challenged.

Kimi stopped at an arched opening with no door, leaning around, but not entering. "Dining room."

He copied her, curving around her to look, her back pressed to his chest. Almost as close as on the motorcycle, and equally pleasant. A long reddish wood table ran down the center of the room, but its edges curled like waves instead of straight lines. Many chairs lined both sides. "Like the eating-in bar?"

He caught himself before asking why humans had entire rooms for feeding.

She looked up at him, the movement pressing them tighter, a move his cock approved of. "This is where we have most meals. It is also a time to relax, and talk with each other. Learning how free people live will take some time, but I think you'll like the change."

"Yes." He already liked being here with her. The way her hands danced when she communicated, the softness of her whisper-voice and laugh, her fierceness and intelligence.

He also liked the way her body fit against his. The way her hand wrapped around his, as it did now. She squeezed it, but let go, circling to the last room, as he hunted for excuses for her to touch him again.

"Family room. This is where everyone usually hangs out

between missions and call-outs. Games, movies, most of the fun stuff," she signed and walked in.

This room had a stronger web than even the food room. Stone like in the kitchen covered most of a wall, with an inset with an open stone and black metal area that held the smokiness of a fire, though no cooking food smells. Over it was a giant, glass screened black square, similar to the ones trainers used to show his batch images of killer humans, weapons, and plans for training missions. Smaller boxes sat under, connected with cables to the square.

He turned to the rest of the room. The chairs with cushions sat in a circle, small devices and headpieces also sometimes used with the training images tossed on the seats. A long chair that would hold many ran along another wall, separated from a shorter one by a table far too small for food.

Different handheld devices lay on it, along with colorful pillars smelling of bees and blooming plants, and a flat box with a strange green feline on the cover. He read the words underneath. "Why do we explode kittens? Is this for training?"

"It is a game, for fun. One with a silly title," Kimi sign-whispered. "You can explore, and ask as many questions as you like."

With her permission, he ran his hand along the long chair, stroking the fabric. A blanket hung over the back, and he rubbed the corner between his fingers. It felt the way clouds looked, fluffy and softer than any blanket he had ever known.

The puffy objects he had seen on the cabin sleeping platforms were everywhere, scattered on the chairs, and between them on the floor. All bright, in reds, pinks, oranges, not the white or scratchy gray he knew. He squatted, picking one up that appeared to have fur on it, though it smelled of no animal or cryptid.

He checked with Kimi. "This is for sleeping?"

"You can nap on it, but it isn't a bed. This is another place where we relax and spend time. We do online gaming with other teams, play card games, watch our favorite movies, or listen to music. Ready to see more?" She held out her hand.

He would ask about *games* and *music* later. Eagerly, he took it and let her lead him up a set of stairs that seemed to float in the air, held by metal wires. They stepped into a circle. A round room. The windows reached from the ceiling to the floor on one side and Owen braced for a moment, until his body and brain processed that he stood on solid ground, and he wasn't falling from the sky.

He turned away from the open air, deeper into the circle room. There were more chairs and pillows, sitting on a piece of fabric that covered most of the floor. And—he stumbled, more unsteady than with the illusion of no ground under his feet. Books. There were rows and rows of *books*. The shelves were as tall as he was, all filled.

Many colors and sizes. Some with stiff covers instead of the bendable paper. Others with glossy golden lettering.

"You can touch them." Kimi came up beside him. Her fingers skimmed along shelves as though searching, and stopped. "Here," she signed. Then pulled a book out, holding the cover up for inspection.

A familiar human face, hidden behind sunglasses and an opened book—"My book!"

The book he had taken from the scientist, and only read the first pages, before having to abandon it in their escape. He reached for it, then dropped his hands. These were Kimi's, not his. He wouldn't steal from his mate.

She lifted his hand, flattened it, and placed the book on his palm. Then whisper-signed, "You can read it."

He stared at the book, then his mate. Who still had her hand curved under his, her thumb rubbing along his wrist. She gave him a happy-smile, whisper-talking, "You can read any of them."

She was sharing with him. She enjoyed touching him, and she was sharing her prized possessions with him. He had the best mate.

The squeak of a boot on tile carried from downstairs. Her books were here in the open, unguarded. "How do you protect them? What if others borrow them?"

She turned away so he couldn't see her lips, and not pairing it with signs, soft-whispered, "I am torching every Syndicate lab in existence."

He politely pretended not to hear, until she faced him again.

"These are for anyone here to read, then put back once they're done. You can re-read them as many times as you like, too. When you finish, here's the third book." She tipped a book out, giving him a view of a pink title, a cap, and a cat. "I need some air."

She stalked down the floating stairs.

If his mate was angry, he would be angry with her. He tucked the book under his shirt, and caught up with her as she jerked open a door in the back of the laundering room.

At the last moment, he dodged around her when she stopped.

"Our outdoor space." She leaned against a stone column. One of four holding up the upper portion of the building that jutted out. There was more of the stone here, a floor despite her saying this was outdoors. More of the padded chairs were scattered under the projection's cover, and a table more like the eating room's. Another of the shiny cooking machines, and a circle of rocks with charcoal remains.

He sampled the air, catching salt and water, almost like the ocean. Fascinated by the impossibility, he wandered past Kimi. A small body of water lay at the end of the outdoor space, enclosed by bright stones and tiles. Steps led down into it.

He knelt, swirling his hand through the water. Warm, clean blue water but no ocean creatures swam in its depths. He rose and dried his hand on his pants.

"This is a saltwater swimming pool," she signed. "It has no purpose other than enjoyment on hot days. Another upgrade that civilians like. So do we."

"I swim." He had learned first in the center, then in the ocean. Learning to ignore the cold or rough waves. Trainers timing them on how long they could stay under. Some of his batch hadn't survived. "I will swim with you."

His offer brought her tiny smile back, gaze tracking over him and cheeks turning an appealing dusky color. She joined him.

The breeze shifted, putting them downwind. The rotted scent of dead ghoul coated the inside of his nose, along with the metallic pong of rancid vampire blood. Old, not enemies lurking to attack them. Underneath both, the gamey scent-taste of fear and hate.

"You have brought cryptids here." He shifted, gaze going past the pool and east. To where the third road led.

"Yes, to the holding area I mentioned." She edged in front of him, as if she was blocking his view. "It isn't a lab. Occasionally we are required to obtain information from a vampire, before we take it to our HQ. We also take in cryptids that the Syndicate has experimented on and that have escaped or been dumped, in order for our group to study, in hopes of understanding what the Syndicate is attempting to do."

The vampires never allowed a creature to escape and

survive. Until Kimi, and him. They didn't dump failures. Those they took apart to see where the mistake was, then burned anything they couldn't reuse. If there were lab cryptids loose, the vampires meant for it to happen.

The Syndicate punished any vampires or handlers who brought human attention, or who left equipment or remains behind after training or missions. Letting reprogrammed creatures go free, and among Kimi's civilians and Company, broke the rules, and—

Hands bracketed either side of his face. He jerked his attention from the distant cage area and the puzzle of vampire reasoning. Kimi stood on her toes, hands shielding his face, brow crinkled.

Slowly, she whisper-mouthed, "The holding area isn't for humans, ever. Its only use is for predatory cryptids and vampires, and then just long enough to gather information that helps save people."

He puzzled out her actions. She was blocking his view of their cage area. Not because he wasn't allowed to look or ask questions. The only other possibility was—because she was worried for him, and bad memories. His mate cared. That swirly warmth returned, stronger now.

Guilt lurked under the happiness. He wasn't only human, or were-human, *and* he was lying. Lying to a mate was forbidden, like touching without asking first. But he wouldn't go back to a cage, Syndicate or Company. And he wouldn't leave Kimi.

The book he'd tucked in his waistband poked his stomach. There were books here, that he was allowed to borrow. Relief bloomed. He would read many more books, and watch her family-team, to learn what to do, a way not to lie yet to remain here.

He turned his face, nuzzling his cheek against Kimi's palm. Letting her scent mark him. Later, he would do the same for her, so that all would know they were a pair. "Thank you."

She shivered, eyes widening. Her pupils shrinking. All good signs. She cupped her hand, thumb stroking over his cheekbone, and he leaned into the caress.

A chime like the one when they arrived sang out. Kimi dropped her hands and stepped back. "That's the final member of our team."

Concentrating, he caught the slam of a vehicle door. Several heartbeats later a raised voice from inside the house echoed, coming closer. The laundering room door opened, the voice clear and demanding, like a trainer's. Scent memory clicked. The territorial one Kimi told him about.

Kimi frowned, then signed, "Let me speak to Bruce, while you wait—"

Owen would show this human that Kimi was Owen's mate, and that Owen was also loud and claimed territory. He strode past Kimi's outstretched hand, to meet this potential threat.

CHAPTER 11

wen

"Vᴇᴇ, damn it. Get down here. Where is Kimi?" the new voice barked.

Vee was vampire, but also his mate's family-team, and hunted Syndicate vampires. Owen would protect her from this new, loud one as well.

The human stepped onto the outside-floor and stopped. Glaring at the overhanging part of the building. Then dropped his gaze, eyes narrowing. He crossed his arms, examining Owen.

This one wasn't like Josh, far shorter, in the brighter clothes shown in training images. The mix of food scents came from his pores, of sweet things, green plants, meat— almost camouflaging his natural smell.

Pale. The human was paler than all of them, including Owen, though Owen could find no signs of illness. Patterns and color covered the exposed parts of his arms, in swirls and lines. Round bits of glass covered his eyes, not tinted black like the daytime eye covering vampires and some humans used in the sun.

He pulled them off, rubbing them against his shirt, still studying Owen. Then replaced them, scrubbing at the hair covering the lower section of his face. "Fucking hell."

Dominance rolled off him, his pheromones, the way he stood, claiming the ground, locking eyes with Owen.

Ex-mates weren't the only threats. There were also often evil people in the books, out to ruin the heroine and hero's happiness. This human looked as if he enjoyed ruining things.

Owen felt Kimi beside him, and checked in with her.

"I'll introduce you," she whisper-signed, looping her arm through his. Firmly, pulling him against her.

Excellent. He should have remembered how fierce his mate was. They would meet this threat together.

When Owen looked again, Vee was there. She launched at the human, wrapping her arms around his neck. Before Owen could join her in the attack, the man's arms circled her, his relief and their combined happiness thick enough Owen sneezed, clearing his nose.

The two touched lips. *Kissing.* This was kissing, and suddenly, Owen very much wanted to try it with his mate. He didn't look away when Josh and the ancient vampire entered from beyond the pool, busy memorizing how kissing was done.

The pair separated, Vee whispering in his ear.

Owen braced as the man approached. He held his arms open, and Kimi abandoned Owen. Hugging the newcomer. The way she had Josh and her family-team. The man let go, but only to hold Kimi out at arm's length, examining her.

Owen easily caught the man's exhale, the same relief as when he had hugged Vee. Voice grumbly-gruff, he asked,

"Did you have a good time exploding vampires and giving me a fucking stroke?"

Kimi happy-bounced in place. "Technically, I didn't explode it. But still, loads of fun. Bruce, this is Owen," she signed.

He, Bruce, put Kimi to the side. The rest of the family-team closed in, Josh and the old vampire flanking Bruce and Owen.

"Owen, this is Bruce," Kimi whisper-signed.

Bruce held out his hand—not high for the high-fives or fist bumping. Owen mimicked the action, holding still as the man gripped Owen's hand then released it.

That got a quick nod. "Thank you for your part in destroying that damned facility and everything in it. You had your freedom and basic human rights stolen. Looking at you, it's clear you were tortured and subjected to horrors no one should have to endure."

Bruce took the two steps that put them toe to toe, intensity radiating off him. Josh said one of the forbidden words. "I am sympathetic to your suffering, and the fact that you seem to be a competent soldier. However, that only buys you leeway, or my support, to the point where your presence here or actions put the team in any form of danger. Every person living under this roof has been molded into a noble, self-sacrificing Company hero. Except me. I'll turn you over to the Company or eliminate you myself if it comes down to your life versus that of any of my family. Are we clear?"

Vee attached herself to Bruce, while the male members made a wall between Owen and the others. Kimi locked her hand around Owen's wrist, her face too ashy.

He examined the information he'd gathered. The human's behavior, the way he and Vee had greeted each other. Their words and the emotion under them. They were also a fated-mate pair.

As Vee's mate, Bruce had given Owen the rules, the consequences, and a warning. He was protecting her, and their home territory, the correct course of action for a mate. "I understand."

Kimi, her brother, and sister shared some communication, without signs or speech, only body language.

"We aren't going to turn on you, man," Josh said, scowling at Vee's mate.

"The rules are fair, and I accept them," Owen said, and dared lay his hand over Kimi's.

She blinked up at him, and the stress hormones she'd been shedding abruptly switched to relief. And then to another pheromone scent, very like when Vee had spotted her grumbly mate.

He promised her, "I will never bring harm to you or your family-team."

"The boy speaks the truth," Stavros added, as Vee gave one of the happy squeaks. Josh as well, though his was deeper.

All Owen cared about was the way Kimi's hand slid down his wrist, trading the grip on it for linking her fingers through his.

"For fuck's sake. You two clean up," Bruce ordered Owen and Kimi, then pointed at his mate and Josh. "You two set the table. You've got twenty minutes until dinner."

As the rest left, Vee's mate stomping impressively despite his size, Owen examined his borrowed clothing.

Kimi did the rough snort-laugh, freeing her hands to sign. "You're fine. Bruce likes to impress his dining rules from the get-go. I'm taking a quick shower. If you want to hang out here, I'll come get you for dinner."

"Can I look at the books instead?"

"Of course. Come on."

This time, the floating view had no effect on him. He

hesitated as Kimi continued past the books, to the other side of the room, and an opening he hadn't noticed the first time. He braced for the discipline at having been foolish and unaware of surroundings. Except there were no trainers or handlers here, only Kimi.

"Our rooms and the showers are through here," she whisper-signed.

"I will wait."

She gave him the thumbs-up sign, and he watched until she disappeared, squashing the wisp of concern at her leaving his sight. Instead, he began at the first bookshelves, getting lost in the colors, the slickness of covers under his touch.

At a rough cough, he bolted up from where he'd bent to inspect a book with a fabric cover, velvety and purple.

Kimi was framed in the hall opening. In very short pants and a shirt with no sleeves, her legs and arms were fascinatingly bare, only a thin line of bluish chemical where her wound had been. Her skin glowed, and the plant-oil scent from before was joined by another, more like green fruit. Her hair was no longer tied up. Now, it hung in spirals, the shiny brownish-gold of the utensils in the cooking room.

He searched through the stored words from his books. "Beautiful." The word slipped out before he could decide if it was allowed or not. He caught no offense from her, and she joined him by the books. "You are beautiful."

The color on her checks changed, brighter, like the pink cat creature on her shirt, wearing the large training earpieces over its pointed ears. "So are you," she whisper-signed.

The new tone in her soft words...a heat built inside him. He would definitely like to try the kissing soon.

"Do you need a refresher course on how to tell time?" Vee's mate boomed from downstairs.

They both twitched. Kimi drew away, and rolled her eyes.

She signed, "I appreciate your calm with Bruce earlier. He's gotten overprotective."

"Overprotective?" Unclear on the difference between protective and overprotective, Owen frowned.

Kimi fiddled with the band around her wrist, like the one that had been in her hair at the lab, then whisper-signed. "I suppose it isn't overprotective. He has cause. Vee was—" her fingers stilled for a moment, a sheen in her eyes. She blinked hard and continued. "Vee was taken from us, for a while. It was horrible. Now, Bruce is always afraid it will happen again in some way, or to one of us."

Vee had told him she had been human and Company, then wasn't. "The Syndicate."

Kimi nodded, that sadness still in her eyes. Owen would remove the sadness and make sure it never happened again. "We will kill them. Bruce is correct in his actions, and in protecting his mate. And family-team," he added.

The look Kimi gave him this time, he didn't understand. He fell in behind her down the steps. Fancy food smells assaulted his senses as they stepped into the food area. Too rich and complex, alien to him.

Kimi's stomach growled. "I am starving," she whisper-signed.

She had refused food in the lab, then they had escaped before the next feeding, and she had given him extra bars from her food at the cabin. An odd guilt settled over him. He had taken his mate's food, leaving her in need.

They entered the feeding room, full with the entire family-team, including the vampires. Unease joined the guilt. There were no solitary runs and eating alone here.

He moved beside her, drawing onto the balls of his feet. He would need to protect his share of the food and Kimi's, and she was already hungry due to aiding him.

Bruce stood at the end of the long table, holding a tray of

the food. Owen calculated—better to posture and try to intimidate him, or better to launch over the table and snatch the food immediately?

Kimi tapped Owen's shoulder, and signed. "Sit here."

A whine built deep in his throat as she pointed at two chairs, by their end of the table. Too far from Vee's mate and the food. The position wasn't strategic.

Stiff, he did as his mate asked, but perched on the very edge of the seat, feet under him in a half-crouch, prepared to spring up and snatch their share as soon as the tray came close.

Bruce sat a plate at his spot, and handed Vee a plate next. Understandable.

But then he did the same with Josh, and Stavros. He finally gave one to Kimi. Instead of claiming it, she passed it to Owen. His mate was giving him her share again.

Before he could grab the remaining plate and present it to her, Bruce did.

Owen scooted his chair against Kimi's, and curved his arm around his portion, wishing he could reach far enough across to do the same with hers. Especially as she didn't immediately start eating.

Owen glared around the table, silently warning to the others, doing his best to prevent theft.

"Bow your damn heads," Bruce ordered.

This was a ploy, then. While Owen wasn't looking, the others would take the food. Bruce first, not the largest or strongest in the room, but the alpha the rest deferred to anyway.

Owen refused, keeping arm and attention on their share even while Kimi fell for the trick, as Bruce said words that made no sense, undoubtedly part of the distraction.

Except no one tried for anyone else's plate. Instead, they took the cloth squares on the table, putting the bit of fabric across their legs, and taking the silver implements beside each plate. Owen palmed the knife, though it was dull.

When Bruce stabbed his food, Owen fell on his, glaring around again as he wolfed it down, the way his batch had been forced to as cubs, only the strongest eating. This fancy food was as rich as its smell, and worth fighting for even had Kimi not been starving.

His plate empty, he angled to help defend Kimi's, a growl trickling out before he could stop the natural reaction.

"Dude..." Josh paused, food speared on the other utensil, not putting it in his mouth.

A hand rested on his forearm. He already knew the weight and heat of his mate's touch. He dared take his eyes off the others, checking to see what she required.

She did the exaggerated lip whisper-talking, keeping her hand on him. "Owen, what's wrong?"

"You must eat, quickly. You are starving."

"There's no rush. We also talk, and take our time over meals. Remember?"

He darted a glance at Josh, who still hadn't eaten the bite. And who still had most of his food left on the plate. Owen frowned, checking the rest. The vampires were the same, although he had rarely seen vampires bother with real food. But Bruce's plate was also full, like Kimi's, and the man stared at Owen, face even paler. Horrified, like he was confronting an unfed ghoul, not another human.

Another strange emotion prickled through Owen. Like performing incorrectly, but not. Not fearing punishment. This...he didn't behave as the others did, and he didn't care for the feeling of being different.

Worse, being different than Kimi. Not acting as her mate should.

He wasn't behaving as Kimi and her family-team did, and thus, he wasn't acting properly. Not in a human manner.

It was the old vampire who spoke, in his slower cadence. "The foul demons who held you didn't feed you, as part of their vile torment. It is understandable that you are far hungrier than we are. There's no shame in that. You need not fear such treatment again. You have my word."

Shame. That was the term for Owen. He shamed himself, and by association, Kimi.

He eased further into his chair, back rigid. Kimi patted his hand, and scooted so her knee rested against his.

When the others started talking, he stayed silent, watching. Studying the way they held themselves, how they ate, what they said. He must learn, and be as human seeming as they were. Quickly, before they noticed more ways he was different, not human enough.

He still tensed as Bruce stood and left, though no one else moved. The human came back with another tray, and small plates.

This time, Owen sat, hands flat on his knees. Waiting until the others took a utensil. He copied their moves, scooping up a tiny amount in the curved utensil. He tried it, and the sugary-sweet smell of the cubs' food, from the beach training, exploded over his tongue.

He tried the food again. The others not-watched him, speaking to each other, but their attention on him.

When he looked, Kimi was watching him. She laid her utensil down to sign. "Do you like it?"

"Yes. I have never had this. It is excellent. Better than the sweet food you threw at the lab helpers, which was my favorite," he confided.

"Congratulations. You've now had chocolate." She held her fist out and he bumped it, gaining a smile from her..

His mate and Vee had been correct, again. "Vampires are jerks." He agreed with her opinion when she'd discovered they had never offered his batch chocolate.

He quickly leaned around Kimi. He had almost forgotten Vee. "Except you. You are not a jerk," he reassured the tiny vampire. He included Stavros as well. "Or you."

At a choking noise, he whirled to see if Josh required aid. The man seemed fine though.

Owen checked with Kimi. Had he acted incorrectly again? The shame returned.

Kimi pinned her brother-family with a narrow-eyed glare.

The human eased his entire chair backward. "Yeah, man. Definitely not jerks. Hey, I'm gonna go grab you some gear while you finish dessert."

He made a wide loop around Kimi, shoulder blades nearly scraping the wall as he exited.

She tapped Owen's plate, and he took that as a request, and finished his chocolate. The proper response, as she rose the moment he dropped his licked-clean utensil on the plate. "This has been a long day. Owen needs time to—process. *Everyone* should." Her hand movements were stiff and exaggerated, as she shared a look with Vee.

"Exactly. You guys are totally exhausted," Vee said. "Go chill and we'll see you in the morning. If you see Josh—"

"I'll inform him he is doing clean-up and dishes," Kimi whisper-signed, with the same smugness she'd used on the lab-handler.

As they climbed the stairs, he reached for a way to apologize. To promise his mate he would perform better. "I am sorry."

"You have nothing to be sorry about. This is all new to you, and you are handling the change wonderfully." She bumped her shoulder into his gently. "Go, you."

Combined with her smile, he took that as a good thing. Especially when she offered him her hand.

They passed through the book room, and into the hall she

had disappeared down before. The hall wrapped around the other side of the building, and had to be part of what hung over the outdoor area.

"Showers, hot tub, and sauna." Kimi pointed to the left. "Also new. Our rooms." She turned him to the right.

"Stavros is the last one. We are kind of a lot for him. He hadn't been around humans, until Vee and joining us, so he has the old C.O. suite where he can put some distance between our talking and dropping emotions all over him."

Owen felt a moment of understanding with the old vampire.

"What was the first two rooms are now the C.O. quarters for Vee and Bruce." She walked past them. "Josh's room."

The scent of rubber came through the open door, and Owen glimpsed shirts hung on the wall in cases, as well as many shoes arranged on shelves, as though they were valuable books.

"My studio." She waved at the next room, its door closed.

Josh met them, arms full, and one of the large canvas bags over his shoulder. "Perfect timing."

Kimi pushed open a door, and Josh ducked in. Looking over his shoulder and moving faster as Kimi entered behind him.

"Who does this room belong to?" Owen detected only faded ghosts of scents, nothing strong and recent.

"This is yours, man." Josh stacked two boxes on a long wooden piece of furniture with many handles. "Toothbrush, soap, all the basics. I threw in some of my favorite shampoo, and moisturizers. Dry air is terrible for your skin."

Owen was too busy taking in Josh's simple statement. That this was Owen's area. The room was far larger than his old run. The sleeping platform was like the cabin's, but larger, covered with blankets and the fluffy objects. A chair with padding sat beside the outer wall, fabric hanging over a section of wall in a manner he'd never seen.

Kimi pulled the fabric away. An expanse of sandy soil and the short plants greeted them, the area by the pool. A window. "This room has a *window*." None of his kind, or any other cryptid, had ever been allowed a window, as it was both a source of distraction and a potential means of escape from the hated handlers and scientists.

"Hey, I get it," Josh said. "Windows seem like the mother of all security risks. Don't worry, though. Everything here is next-gen security, and chem laced. The site is basically surrounded by it. Nothing cryptid or vamp is getting inside the compound, much less the house."

Kimi went to the wooden furnishing, pulling on a handle. A compartment slid open. She unzipped the bag, and laid out clothing. "You can decide where you want clothes to go. There's also a closet."

She touched a wall panel, sliding it sideways. A series of triangular objects hung from bars, the devices handlers placed their gear on.

"We'll requisition basics, and go shopping for everything else you want. Hey, do you ball?" Josh asked.

Owen checked with Kimi.

Who planted both hands on her brother's chest, and shoved. Hard.

He stumbled back. "Dang, Kimi. Payback already?"

"Your payback hasn't even begun." She smiled, with teeth, and closed the door in Josh's face.

"Is this okay?" She turned to Owen. "We can find out what else you like, and you can make this your personal space to relax."

He struggled with ideas and words, none good enough to express what freedom, Kimi, and her acceptance meant.

Proving again that they were meant to be, she signed,

"Silly questions, right? It is totally normal to be overwhelmed, confused, or both. Once you discover things you like and don't like, we can make changes."

He already knew one thing he'd never change. "I like you. Everything you."

The color appeared on her cheeks again, along with a mixed trickle of pleasure and what smelled like the same reaction he'd had when putting arms around her during their motorcycle escape. "I think you're pretty great, too."

He edged closer, so that they bumped at hip and shoulders again—or her shoulder at his chest. When they touched, that rush of wanting to do the kissing hit.

Kimi sucked in a breath, lids dipping over her eyes. Then moved away, signing, "It really has been an insane twenty-four-ish hours. Get some rest. We'll explore more tomorrow." She opened the door.

He lurched toward the door and her retreating back. "Where are you going?"

"To my room."

Had this been in the books? It seemed that in the pages, there was always only one bed, and of course, the heroine and hero had to share it. "Is your room here? Is it close?"

She motioned for him. After two more doors, she stopped, and used a key, unlocking the room. She pushed the door open, and tapped the wall, lights coming on. "This is mine. I'm close, see?"

"Can I sleep outside your door?" If there was to be no only-one-bed-sharing, he didn't require a bed.

Her eyes did that shiny-sad thing. Because he hadn't performed correctly, again, and now she would see—

She caught his hands, and worked the balled fists open. Slowly, whisper-mouthing, she said, "How about I leave my door open? Then if you need anything, or have a nightmare, you can come in and wake me. Will that work?"

He still preferred staying outside her door. But it was also important to listen to mates. "I will leave my door open. I have excellent hearing, if you need me during the sleeping time."

His reward was her pressing close for an instant, arms wrapped around him. *A hug.* His first, *and* from his mate.

When she turned loose, still smelling pleased, he made himself walk away. He stood in his doorway though, long after Kimi went in hers and her room went dark.

 imi

I STARED AT THE CEILING, the pool's reflection shining through the window, tiny ripples dancing along the wood and plaster. I wanted to blame my insomnia on the itchy-twitchy sensation between my shoulder blades from leaving my door not only unlocked, but standing open. The door accounted for only forty-percent of the problem.

Owen was the greater percentage, and the fact that I willingly offered to leave my sanctuary open for him. He was huge and unimaginably dangerous. And when he realized he was meant to sleep alone in his room, had the same expression as one of my adopted nieces during a thunder storm. The request to sleep on the stupid floor outside my door—a ghoul couldn't have gutted me any more painfully.

I totally felt as if I had abandoned him, despite him only being three doors away. The urge to pull him into my room had been way too real. And unnervingly intense. Forcing myself to let him go after the hug...

He felt like any of my Company hookups, insanely muscled, full of the same contained energy every agent seemed to exude, and thanks to the borrowed BDU's, even smelled familiar, of our detergent and the dryer sheets with the cute bear on them.

But I'd never responded so fast and so hard, certainly not from a few touches.

Which was one-hundred-percent plus of a reason to stop, and review the data, before proceeding.

Grabbing a tablet, earbuds, and phone from the night-stand, I scooted against the headboard, and crossed my legs under me. It was close enough to dawn that Liv should be getting ready for one of her marathon morning runs. I texted her and Vee with one hand, setting up the tablet with the other.

The link opened on Liv's face, colorful Mexican tile and aged canyon oak behind her. A beat later, another pane opened, Vee framed by the rosy-soft lighting of the vanity Bruce had installed for her in their bath, high-end granite now covered in makeup palettes, straightening iron, and hair products. I popped earbuds in so we didn't disturb anyone else. Owen did have remarkably keen hearing.

"Need to talk?" Liv stood, prepared to abandon her spot in the kitchen for the privacy of her office. Vee's old office, and the hurt from leaving behind our first home, of splitting the three of us up, still throbbed. There had already been too many unanticipated changes, yet another reason for me to put any experiments, sexual or otherwise, in a hard lockdown. Rushing led to mistakes, and I couldn't afford another major error.

"You're good where you are," I signed, reassuring Liv.

Vee wiggled further into focus. "Nightmares?"

A valid question, after capture during a mission. We'd all spent hundreds of hours huddled together comforting whoever had had a horrible experience in training or in the field, including Josh and the guys. I'd taken the chance on Vee being up because she also routinely woke from nightmares of Oversight detonating the poppers in Josh and Stavros.

Yet every time one of them asked, it felt like the aftermath of the day I'd missed my mark on our cadet canned hunt, nearly getting teammates killed. I kept my hand off the scarred reminder decorating my throat.

"All good," I promised.

"Owen then," Vee said, with a dreamy sigh.

"Owen." I wasn't sure what the point of my spur of the moment group chat was, since I didn't have any specifics in mind to act on. But if there was one to be teased out of my subconscious, it would be with my sisters.

"Oh my god, his scars. You said he'd been tortured, but I can't even imagine." Vee shuddered.

"How is he psychologically?" Liv got to the heart of practical concerns, her specialty.

"At dinner last night..." Vee hesitated, easing into the question.

"Right?" She wasn't the only one pondering his behavior. We had no frame of reference for what he might have lived with daily, not when his life included things like being cut into without anesthesia or pain meds.

"I mean, even Josh was in awe of how fast he ate," Vee said. "The rest of us hadn't taken the first bite."

"It seemed like he thought we were going to take his food, or that he was going to have to fight for it." The way he'd hunched over his plate was pretty much inked into my memory. As was the noise he'd made, almost a growl.

Looking back, it seemed like he'd also tried to protect my plate.

"And the stress pheromones coming off him were intense," Vee admitted. "Also, I was not sniffing-sniffing, they were just that strong. Thus, no menthol rub retaliation."

"Fair point," Liv said.

"The way he protected his food—"

"And yours."

Of course she had noticed. It was what C.O.'s did.

But also, my sister and her relationship fixation. Yet also valid this time. "Granted. His reactions are heavily slanted towards survival in day-to-day scenarios. I tried a fist bump, and he shied away, assuming I was attempting to hit him."

"When we arrived and hugged Kimi, he also freaked."

"He thought you were all attacking me. Like, when I explained it was a happy greeting he actually asked if it was hugging. He hadn't ever *seen* anyone hug before." Which hurt and infuriated me at the same time.

"That is the saddest thing ever." Liv's cheek dented in, where she chewed on it, her go-to worry tic. "When you said he'd been a captive, I envisioned a short-term prisoner. Not this complete lack of exposure and trauma. Is this something better addressed at HQ or even one of the specialty clinics for agents?"

"*Definitely not.*" At her eyes widening, I pulled back on the drama, relaxing my hands and signing. "I mean, I don't think he'll allow it. He has basically imprinted on me."

"And you don't want him to go. Which is understandable," Vee hurried to add, as Liv's attention went from me, to our sister, and back to me.

An auburn head popped into the frame on Liv's end, saving me from her questions, the ones I felt on the tip of her tongue. "Kimi, tell Bruce I do so need those new headphones." Kit, the adolescent cryptid who was totally living at the compound already, jammed his face against the screen.

We'd discovered that with his advanced auditory system, similar to fruit bats, he could usually hear me when I inevitably forgot and spoke along with my signing.

His timely save also kept me from admitting that no, I didn't want Owen to go. Not after the period I'd originally envisioned, where he hit Cali HQ, reintegrated into human society and then went on with his life, as an Asset or into civi life locally. Most certainly not after being here, so close, just down the hall from me.

Fine. I didn't jump headfirst like Vee, or over-evaluate instead of admitting emotions like Liv. I was sexually attracted to Owen. I was also attracted to him on an emotional level, beyond him being a fellow agent. He had already earned a spot on the team, but I'd never be able to think of him as a brother like Josh and Bruce.

At the annoyed squeak from the other end of our call, I shifted my attention back to tangible concerns. Kit had come out of his shell in the past few months, and finally trusted someone other than Marshall, his guardian and Company liaison.

According to Bruce, we spoiled Kit. He had no family remaining though, a heartbreak we all understood. Plus, we had treated him like a prisoner when we first met him. Admittedly, there was an element of guilt involved, which might or might not manifest as us buying him anything new and fun that caught our eye.

He also required structure, though.

"Technically, you don't need them, since you have a pair less than six months old, and earbuds," I spoke as I signed. "Realistically though, there's no such thing as too many headphones."

Triumph lit his triangular face, starved hollows under his

cheekbones finally filled out, and his previously tufty hair trimmed. He'd joined our gamer group, taking to CoW, Cogs of War, our preferred game, and was one of the team's secret weapons.

"However, you have a report due on the civilian American Revolution, and its impact on Company structure in the New World." I raised my brows, the way our Fourth Year history Instructor had when busting us for late homework.

Aside from being a child who deserved an education, part of Oversight's hush-hush agreement in granting him immunity was his role as *the* test case for integrating non-predatory humanoid cryptids as Company Assets and allies. That meant observing him with humans and agents. The best way for now was listing him as a human child Liv's team had taken in. He was enrolled online in the same Academy classes as any cadet his age.

I gave it ninety-nine-percent odds that Liv's ultimate goal was his full acceptance as a cadet, and training to become an agent. Kit didn't do violence, although Matteo and Jace, Josh's twin, were teaching him how to defend himself. He was already an amazing street resource, and would fit in perfectly with the Intelligence division, or as an agent planted in a civilian version.

He did that epic eyeroll only tweens and teens were capable of. "But we're taking on the Galveston HQ team this weekend and—"

"Three days is perfect. You finish and hand in the assignment, and the headphones will be delivered to Liv's postal box by Friday."

"*Fine.*" He'd also mastered the martyred *OMG, adults* tone.

"What do you say, Kit?" Marshall's deep burr asked from somewhere in their kitchen.

"I want the green pair?"

I rolled my lips in to keep from laughing, even as Liv

massaged the spot between her eyes that meant she was courting a headache.

"What do you say when someone gives you a gift?" Marshall tried again, in his ultra-patient way.

"Oh, yeah. Thank you. Bye." Kit's head disappeared. Then popped back into focus for a second. "Don't tell Bruce."

The little dynamo vanished and I gave in, laughing at his unrepentant cheekiness. "He's doing great, Marsh."

"Only you would say that," Liv muttered.

A coffee mug, complete with foamed milk, made an appearance, Liv accepting it with a warm smile. She scooted to make room, and Marshall leaned into view, his big arm with the dusting of ginger hairs lighter than Kit's settling along the back of her chair.

"He made a B-plus on his math exam. Thanks for the tutoring help," he said.

No mystery why Liv was suddenly cheery. Marshall had that effect on people. Broad and tall enough to make Liv seem petite, he should have been intimidating. Instead, in a superhero tee that matched his blue eyes, Marshall exuded kindness and calm.

He'd also come a long way from the withdrawn, wary victim of what we now knew was a Syndicate human trafficking ring. With the team, he'd found a home and family that supported him and his general awesomeness, not treating his neurodivergence as a problem.

Liv did that unconscious thing, shifting the fraction that put her back in contact with Marshall's arm. He did the same, his hand drifting from the chair to her shoulder.

We were all raised to be direct and honest about feelings, and physically expressing affection, concern, or support. Every Company agent was far more touchy-feely than civilians, according to Bruce. Liv and Marshall's intimacy was next-level, same as Vee and Bruce's.

And my thoughts went straight to Owen.

I'd devise a way to impress Oversight and keep him here, the same way Liv had with Marshall.

For the rest—I wasn't even certain I'd ever consider more than sex with anyone, anyway. Liv and Vee's intensity and focus on their partners hadn't detracted from their roles as agents. They didn't have the kind of near-death mistake on the record that I did, though. All odds pointed toward the intensity and fascination Owen brought out in me only intensifying if we slept together, or took it further. I couldn't risk that distraction. I'd been young and full of myself when I'd mis-stepped on our cadet hunt, but all my energy and focus had still been directed into that exercise.

Any of mine being diverted to a romance now, when we were full agents on missions with no support... It couldn't happen. I couldn't be that self-centered, and take that chance of putting my team and family at risk. Even if I was the one that went down under a cryptid's claws or vampire's fangs, it left a hole in the team, weakening it, putting everyone else at risk.

I also had enough people hovering, with their suffocating concern, without adding another. Especially one as potentially overprotective as a single-minded soldier raised only to kill, and treated like an animal.

"Thanks for the morning chat. I'm off to order the perfect headset, in green," I signed, fast, before they saw the stupid dampness burning my eyes. "Miss you guys."

"Miss you, too," Liv said.

I purposely overlooked Vee's faint frown over the abrupt-ish goodbye. False dawn was turning the sky from black to navy. There was an excellent chance Owen was trained to be an early riser, like every other soldier. He also had minimal social exposure, as evidenced by basically all of yesterday. Bruce was also an early riser, usually up preparing a decent breakfast for us before heading off for pop-ups or other business. Which, not a promising combo, when Owen still seemed to see Bruce as a challenger.

I traded sleep shorts for tactical pants and tee, speed brushing my teeth. Quietly, in case he was resting, I peeked into his room. The curtain was pulled back, exactly the way I'd left it.

Owen sat on the floor, engrossed in a book. What looked like half the library covered his bed.

Maybe I should clarify the generally understood definition of *borrowing*, as opposed to my version. I hesitated at pulling him away from the story he was engrossed in, then tapped lightly on the doorframe.

He was crouched on the balls of his feet between blinks. Prepared to launch at a threat.

Keeping it low-key, I signed, "Good morning."

Automatically, he slid the book in his hands behind him, glancing at the bed. The guilt on his face was easy to read.

I was buying new bookshelves, installing them in his room, and filling them with books. From now on, I'd also make sure he had a block of time to read every day. Maybe I'd add a matching one for myself. In case he had questions mid-story.

"When I can't sleep, I like to read, too. So does my sister Liv."

Some of the hair-trigger tension left him. "I have almost finished one book."

"Nice. Breakfast won't be ready for another hour. Want to go outside?"

"We are training?" He rose, putting the book on the bed with the others.

There was zero point in suggesting he take it easy for a while, take time to acclimate, before jumping back into physically and mentally demanding training drills. Plus, giving him the familiarity of training might help him feel more at-home and confident. "Later. I want to show you something, if you don't mind?"

He was beside me before I finished the last sign. Angling in almost like Marshall had with Liv. Then he frowned. "Will there be food if we don't train?"

"Access to food isn't based on performance. Everyone here eats, no matter what." Signs relaxed, I hid the horror and anger that he'd lived in a world where he had to ask that question, where meals were withheld as some sort of punishment. Operation Ease Owen into Real Life was starting *now*.

"This way." Once outside, I wound around the outdoor kitchen and pool, continuing until the house was out of sight.

Owen didn't question where we were going or why, seeming content to walk beside me, close enough that our arms brushed as we moved. Despite all his energy, he was also sort of restful.

My favorite part of the new compound rose before us, on a hill. The inspiration had hit the day we arrived, the lone oak having somehow survived when everything else taller than a weed had been removed due to security concerns, the usual Company practice. I'd sketched the design in half an hour. Building the circular platform treehouse had taken forever, missions pulling us away constantly.

I climbed the sturdy wooden ladder framing a section of trunk, and swung onto the platform that circled the entire tree. I hoped Owen would enjoy the getaway as much as I did. The pool and grill had taken the place of our old compound's rooftop retreat as the central gathering place for outdoor family fun. The treehouse was sort of my baby.

Owen joined me, agile and silent. He surveyed the compound and cliffs beyond, expression calculating. "A higher vantage point to watch for intruders, and ambush our enemies. You are an excellent fighter-leader." His tone was admiring again.

"That is a valid point," I spoke without exaggerating, and signed. He was memorizing ASL incredibly quickly, even faster than our papá had. I pointed at the hills, the sun cresting the top, in a saturated yellow and blue blaze. "I love sunrises and sunsets, and this gives me an unobstructed view to watch the sky slowly change and the intensity of the colors. This is also a good place to sit and absorb some of the land's calm."

The sheer age of the tree and mountains around us offered serenity that helped me deal with all the recent changes. Almost losing Bruce, losing Vee but her returning so changed, Liv leaving, then adding onto our family in the form of first Stavros, then Marshall, then a cryptid child who challenged everything I'd ever learned and believed about non-humans. Maybe it would also offer Owen a measure of healing and peace.

Pulling a cushion from the stack by the tree trunk, I leaned back on my elbows, closed my eyes and lifted my face to the sky. The morning rays kissed my skin, and painted abstracts on my closed lids.

I felt Owen beside me. And when the ever-present intensity he almost vibrated with eased. He was a different kind of warmth along my side than the morning rays, and possibly equally dangerous if misused.

Not opening my eyes, I spoke-signed. "How did you choose which book to read last night?"

He tensed, then that calm returned. "It was the first book in the spin-off you told me of. It has a family group of women. I need to know more about what family is. The sisters and brothers."

That he was putting such effort into something important to me found and melted my hidden gooey center, that lived for the scene where the hero made the huge gesture to win over the heroine in all our favorite movies. "Did the story help?"

"I understand more. Vee is your sister, so you are of course bonded, like the sisters in the books."

An horrific thought hit, one I should've considered as soon as Owen said he'd been trained by the Syndicate. The group that had basically copied and twisted every aspect of the Company. He said he had been a prisoner since he was a baby, and I hadn't even considered the other awful implications.

I twisted to face him, eyes snapping open. Heart racing, I signed, "Do you have any family? Were they in the lab, or in other facilities?"

"There are none like me. None alive." Voice harsh, lines carved his face and his whole body stiffened, withdrawing without physically moving. "Defectiveness is not allowed. Failures are disposed of early so resources are not wasted. I am not obedient and properly aggressive. The handler said this was the last time they would attempt to modify me, before I was also disposed of."

Vampires were composed of the absolute worst parts of human behaviors and urges, the infection retooling DNA, suppressing any emotions or objectives that didn't aid survival, and amping up parts of the brain and endocrine system that controlled aggression, selfishness, and dominance. What Owen described was more barbaric than any vampire acts we'd ever encountered.

Owen's absolute surety that he was completely alone was equally awful. In a way, I understood.

"May I?" I gestured at his hand.

Eagerly, he offered it to me.

I pressed it against my throat. He cupped my neck, gentle as if I was as valuable as one of his books. There was no such thing as an agent without scars, and no one paid attention to each other's. Most scars weren't a reminder of an agent's failure, though.

When I signed, he watched me, not removing his hand. "This injury happened when I was young. It was our first training hunt using a ghoul that the Instructors had caught, and released for us."

I had never *discussed*-discussed the accident with anyone other than our therapist, blowing it off and treating any concern from my family as unnecessary, because I didn't want, or couldn't deal with, their pity.

Above the rest of the world, in the calm solitude among tree branches and the flutter of birds waking, telling Owen about the most shameful moment of my life was…not easy, but oddly natural.

He watched me as if I was the only thing in the world, all his attention centered on me. The heat from his rough palm was more like a caress, letting the words and signs flow just between the two of us. "I made a mistake, one we had all been warned about in our coursework and veered out of the search formation our Instructors drilled into us, leaving an opening. I was positive I could drop back behind and circle wide, use the element of surprise, and take the hostile out. The ghoul used in the exercise exploited my error, erupting from a culvert, slashing at Josh's stomach." I'd barely intercepted its return slash that would've gutted him in time, blow grazing my throat instead.

"I wasn't paying enough attention, or I was arrogant, thinking we—I—was the best and infallible. Instead, because I messed up, a teammate was injured. He could have died because of me, before we ever went on our first mission."

Josh acted as if he'd forgotten. Everyone did, concentrating on my injury. But it was an indelible part of us now. "They all love me and would never do what the Syndicate did to you and the others that were like you. Instead, they sort of hover. They're subconsciously waiting for me to make another mistake. Not on purpose-on purpose, but it's wired into them on a level they don't realize, that part of our brain that's about survival."

"No." Owen scrambled onto his knees, and then was holding my shoulders, his face inches from mine. "You are not defective. You are ideal. It is not possible to modify-improve on you."

His passion washed over me. Like a fluffy blanket, warm from the dryer. Except in the form of a six-foot-plus soldier, who was wildly determined that I was perfect.

A chill invaded that no blanket, real or metaphorical, could ease. I wasn't perfect. I'd been caught as unaware by the vampire that had snatched me during our mission as I was all those years ago by the ghoul. Instead of going into a Syndicate facility sharp and alert as I'd planned, I'd been drugged and missed details that would've helped in the escape plan. We'd barely made it out, the wounds on Owen's back as he'd protected me when I blew under an only partially-raised garage barrier the result.

I so wasn't infallible. It was dangerous for Owen to believe I was.

If I messed up again, what were the odds he'd still be so supportive, so sure I was great? Owen eventually looking at me the way my family did, braced for my next colossal error...seeing that doubt on his face was too much of a risk for me to face.

He was also at least as dramatic as Bruce, king of the drama llama moments and theatrical gestures. I cobbled together a laugh, a better option than crying, since tears might freak Owen out, stress he didn't deserve. "Thank you. No one is truly perfect. It's part of what makes us human and who we are."

He watched me, like he was trying to peer inside of me and read me the way he did the books.

"Seriously, Owen. Perfection also isn't a requirement in order to be accepted and valued here." Since he seemed highly pro-physical affection with me, I wiggled up, and hugged him. My chin hitting at neck level, I felt him inhale. Then his arms wrapped around me, tucking me against him, his face turned and buried in my hair.

I really, really hoped I hadn't lied about attaining perfection, because cradled against Owen, his breath warming my scalp, felt unsettlingly close to the P word.

wen

OWEN FOUGHT to remember every detail of their time in the tall tree platform. He would save the memories, then determine how he had made Kimi laugh, and do the putting of arms around him. The arms around her on the motorcycle had been excellent. This way, with her face against his chest and her arms also around him, was far better.

Her ideas about his worth were strange. Yet she was the leader, and smart, owning so many books. He weighed her ideas about mistakes and perfection. Perhaps this was his way to no longer lie to her, and still remain. If not being all-human was possibly like the mistakes and non-perfection, and thus permissible.

Kimi shifted against him. Unsure if the movement was a request for space, he drew away. Forcing his arms to drop to his sides. Talking with mates was important. "I like the hugging. Very much."

"We are also pro-hugging here." She stood and offered her hand. "Bruce will have breakfast ready in a couple of minutes. He takes being on time way seriously."

He had no need of help rising, and thought of telling her. But any chance to hold her hand was to be taken. He accepted long enough to climb to his feet, and give her hand the kind of soft squeeze she gave him. "I will never be late for food."

She gave another of the snort-laughs as she dropped his hand to climb down, and he added that to his list of actions to examine, along with the others.

The smell of charring meat and fancy food had escaped the house, swirling around the outdoor room. Owen rushed for the door. Then recalled dinner and the way Kimi and the team-family had looked at him. And how there was no fighting for a share. He held the door open for Kimi, the way it was done in books. She gave him one of her tiny, special smiles.

As they walked through the cooking room, food sitting on counters for anyone to steal, he pressed down on the instinct to snatch food and go. He stuck by his mate's side. She gathered a stack of plates, though they were empty, and handed them to Owen, keeping the utensils and bits of fabric. "I usually set the table. One plate at each chair," she mouthed, tilting her head at the table.

He did as asked, and she followed, laying utensils and fabric precisely at each, occasionally moving the plate one way or another. He memorized the ritual and the correct way of leaving utensils, clearly an important human action.

Kimi darted out as he finished, back before he could follow. She placed one cup of liquid where she had sat the night before, the other by what must then be his designated seat. He sniffed the steam rising from the cup.

"That is coffee," Kimi whisper-signed.

"Those monsters never gave you coffee?" Vee, Kimi's sister-vampire appeared, voice rising to a horrified squeak.

When Kimi lifted her mug, he did the same. Bitter, scorching dirt-water burned across his tongue, and he wrinkled his nose.

"I feel you," Josh said, taking his designated spot. He held a different type of cup, and the faint hint of chlorine carried. Water like what had been provided Owen's batch. "Coffee is a religion with these two." He aimed his cup at Vee and then Kimi.

"It's an acquired taste. I'll get you water or juice." Kimi pushed her chair back.

He knew the fancy food juice, from time in the lab. He liked the juice. Coffee was important to his mate, so it had to be important to him. He took another swallow. "I drink coffee."

"You can add other things to coffee, to change the taste. Milk, sugar, chocolate." Vee recited a list. "I do cream and sugar."

"I will do chocolate," he promptly replied.

"Already indoctrinated, I see." Vee's mate snorted. He carried a tray with containers of food this time, the old vampire appearing behind him.

The vampire handed Vee a container, and Owen locked his hands over his knees, repeating Kimi's promise that food was shared. Vee deposited food on her plate, then passed the bowl to Kimi.

With an utensil left in the container, his mate added food to her plate, and to his.

"I made extra." Bruce spoke to Kimi, who nodded, and gave him one of her happy-smiles. She added another measure of food for Owen.

More containers were passed around, Owen's portion always larger. Vee's mate did the bowing of heads, as saliva pooled in Owen's mouth and he puzzled over why he was allowed extra food.

Done, he watched Kimi, memorizing her actions with the bit of cloth, and the utensils, so he wouldn't shame his mate again. Mimicking her, he cut a chunk of meat with the dull knife.

His plate was still empty before anyone else's. Though Kimi's brother's was also nearly gone.

Kimi gave Owen a thumbs-up, and happiness spiraled through him at her approval.

"There's always more food available here. Have some damn snacks between meals," Bruce grumble-offered.

Owen would ask Kimi later what snacks were. He had other questions for now. As her team-family spoke to each other, he turned to his mate. "Do we train to kill vampires soon?"

"As soon as breakfast is over." Reading his confusion as a mate should, she whisper-signed, "This is breakfast, the first meal in the morning. Then lunch mid-day, and dinner at night, assuming there are no call-outs or missions."

Before he absorbed the wonder of food available at all times, the old vampire rose. "We have little enough time before the Assessor visits us, and the possibility of being called away from even that is high. Best to ascertain the boy's strengths and weaknesses now."

"Agreed." Vee popped up, then looked to her mate.

"I'll clean up today." Bruce narrowed his eyes at Josh. "Don't take this as a free pass. I'm still not your domestic help."

During the back-and-forth conversation, it took Owen a moment to realize that the vampire meant him. *Boy* was the term for human cubs. If this part of Kimi's family-team viewed him as nothing but a cub, impressing them was more vital than ever. He already needed to show Kimi his ability as a fighter. If he was useful to her family-team, she might forgive that he was non-human and had lied to her.

He took in the rest of the compound as they left. The training course was much like those the vampires used, with tall walls, areas that required low-crawling, and ropes and boards suspended high in the air, where a misstep meant crashing to the ground. The courses for his batch were all indoors. This, under the sky, was far better.

"A quick run first, to warm up," Kimi whisper-signed, as the others bent and stretched parts of their bodies.

He joined the group as they finally headed onto the circular track, its surface already heating. He shoved to the front in the first lap, but no one tried to race past him, even the vampires. After more laps, the rest slowed, and left the track.

"Man, you could keep up with one of Liv's marathon runs." Josh held up his hand, for the high-fiving.

Owen had stayed in the lead, but none of the others had challenged him, so he didn't grasp why the other soldier was impressed. "I can do better."

"Save it for the course. This is Kimi's favorite part," her brother said. "Watch."

Excellent information. His mate was fast, and graceful, balancing on the ropes as if they were flat ground. At the end, she topped the steep wall, dropping lightly to her feet on the other side. He searched through the book terms, attempting to match one to the look Kimi shot him as she finished. *Teasing.* She found this exercise enjoyable, and wished him to share it with her.

Not waiting, he leapt, grabbing the rope at the beginning, climbing to the swinging planks. For his mate, he pushed harder than even when rations were the reward for excelling. For the first time, enjoying the exertion, the opportunity to show off.

He was greeted by noise when he finished. Josh and Vee slapping their palms together. His mate had her fingers between her lips, giving a loud whistle. She held up a device for the others for a moment, then tucked it away and whisper-signed, "He beat the Company record by a full one-point-three-seconds."

Owen froze, searching for a sign whether he had performed correctly, or displeased the team-family.

"An excellent beginning." The old vampire hadn't joined in the noise, but approval laced his rough voice. "Come."

Owen had pleased the father-vampire, then, as well as Kimi's family-team. He would continue pushing, and make his mate...proud.

An empty version of human buildings and streets took up a large area of the training ground, covering many acres. The vampire stopped in an open, flat area though.

"Basic hand to hand first, since we're seeing more and more up-close action. After, we'll try out knife work and the range. We'll save the closed urban course for this afternoon." Vee's gaze swept the soldiers lined up in front of her. "For today, let's keep it human to human. Owen, you'll spar with Josh. First contact only, no super rough stuff. That means touch instead of full body blows, and tapping out to show you're done, okay?" She looked at Owen.

He nodded. This part, he also knew. His batch were often pitted against each other. It was one way leadership was determined. But if the handlers had a mission exercise planned, any of his kind who truly injured another, so that the loser could not take part in the exercise, were punished.

Kimi was a leader. Thus, he must be smart, perform well enough to be her mate, keep to the family-team rules.

He dropped into a crouch, facing Josh. The other was taller, but not as heavy as Owen. They circled, Owen cataloguing his opponent's speed as they feinted at each other, the nearly invisible twitches and weight shifts. Measuring his reach as they dodged. Josh landed a hit to Owen's knee and hip, Owen's face heating at missing the other soldier's surprise sideways lunge.

Owen recalculated the other's skill and agility. His enemy aimed, seemingly a kick meant for Owen's face, but pivoting and hitting the side of his knee, Owen stumbling.

He couldn't be found weak in front of his mate again.

As the other fighter lunged, Owen stood square, grunting and staggering as the blow connected. But solid enough not to fall. While the other was recovering, Owen charged. Lifting his lighter enemy high. Slamming him to the ground. Stomping down. His opponent rolled, but too slow. Owen missed the killing blow to his enemy's chest, foot glancing off the other's side. Ribs crunched under Owen's boot.

The fighter rolled, coming to his feet. An arm wrapped around his ribs. Yet still challenging Owen. The sun vanished, replaced by red hazing his vision. He would not be cheated of his food, his blanket. He would not be punished, sent for improvement, to the hated helpers with their stunners and the scientist and her knives.

Owen spun, kick meant to hit the wounded side, finish disarming his opponent, and then snap his neck.

In a blur, the soldier was gone, sandy dirt lifting. A vampire crouched in the other's place, silver tinting her eyes as soil pattered down. "Enough. Stand down."

Owen's fists knotted, prepared to jab. Punch through the despised vampire's face, give it as much pain as vampires gave him. Rip its head free.

The greenness of not-oil and the bitter-dirt drink clogged his nostrils, and his mate was there, between Owen and the vampire. He couldn't stop his lips lifting off his teeth, the growl trickling out, the vampire too close. He angled, to go around, to finally remove this vampire, all vampires—

Owen's mate intercepted his path. She dropped and lashed out, boot taking him in the side of his sore knee and dropping him, impact jarring his teeth. She landed straddling him, her knee on his chest, hand gripping his jaw. *"Stop."*

Her scent and touch flooded him, banishing the haze. The burning need to kill. Returning him to this new place, sand under him instead of a a cell's concrete, and yellow sun overhead instead of harsh white lab lights. He went limp, turning his head and offering her his bared neck. The old vampire stood between Owen and the defeated soldier.

Josh. Vee.

His opponents were his mate's family-team. Part of him had forgotten, instead seeing handlers, lab-helpers, and scientists.

Moving only his eyes, he checked with Kimi. Her grip didn't waver, lips pressed hard together. He had slipped, forgetting the tiny vampire who had taken Josh's place was her sister.

Hand on Owen, she watched her sister and brother, her fear flowing over him as the breeze shifted. Coppery vampire blood scented the air. The sister-vampire was there, finger slit, dripping blood into one of the water bottles that had been left by the track.

"I did not mean to try to kill your sister." He waited for Kimi to release him. Hoping she would offer him her hand to take.

"And my brother?" Kimi mouthed the question.

The other soldier crouched, face ashy-gray, breath hitching.

Owen didn't understand why Vee had intervened, taking Josh's place. He did understand that he'd treated a family-team member like one of his batch, when he had agreed not to. "I didn't—I did not intend him pain."

Josh accepted the bottle one-handed, gasping as broken

ribs grated. Kimi stood but didn't try to touch or aid Owen, hurrying to her brother as her heart rate spiked. She knelt by him, taking the bottle and shaking it until the contents were pink. She tilted it so he didn't have to move, and he slowly drained it. Josh grunted, the crunch of bones realigning carrying. Along with the other's acrid pain-sweat, as he said forbidden words.

Vee stood over Owen, eyes human brown again. She offered her hand, hauling him up. "Take a beat, Owen. Go for a swim, or a walk."

He understood the subtext. They didn't wish to be around him. Including Kimi. He had performed incorrectly. The family-team was angry with him. Worse, his mate was displeased. Instead of proving his skill and demonstrating his right to stay with her, he had done the opposite.

He slipped away as the tiny vampire turned her back on him, joining the others around her brother.

CHAPTER 14

imi

I PALPATED JOSH'S CHEST, double-checking his sternum, then moved sideways, hand traveling along his ribs. Plural, four on the side Owen had kicked, broken in multiple places. The calluses of healing bones, advanced as if it had been weeks instead of minutes, bumped under my fingers.

Some of the pure terror when my brother went down hard and I'd thought a rib punctured his lung lifted. I still pressed the stethoscope Stavros had grabbed from the medical bay to Josh's chest and mouthed, "Slowly take a deeper breath."

Josh took a hesitant sip of air. When I nodded, he tried a couple of deeper breaths, and when his chest expanded without a painful hit, stretched and rubbed his side.

I draped the stethoscope around my neck, and signed, "You're good. But no more PT today."

He stood, capping the empty bottle. "Damn. Owen packs a punch."

And because my brother had a huge heart and didn't hold grudges, added, "I can't wait to see him on a mission, knocking some Syndicate heads together."

Vee did that thing, biting the inside of her cheek. "I think he needs to learn how to pull back first. Like when I had to learn that I was stronger after I was infected, and how best to utilize the new ability in a different way than I'd been taught as an agent. Except Owen has to learn control as far as when not to go all out, which I think is his only setting."

I winced, but she wasn't wrong. And although Josh's healing was on fast-forward thanks to the diluted virus DNA from Vee's blood, he wasn't one-hundred-percent. From past calculations when we were injured and I'd documented Vee's blood and healing time, it would be a good twelve to sixteen-hours before Josh was completely healed. Stavros' blood was reserved for true crises, his fear of ever accidentally infecting one of us always looming. Until then, if a call-out or mission came in, we'd have a vulnerability in our team formation.

"I don't think he was trying to take me out permanently." Josh came to Owen's defense.

Neither did I. Owen's reactions in the lab, and with the last of the facility guards surfaced. He'd kind of gotten lost in…memories, maybe. Mindless revenge, definitely. I turned to check on Owen, hoping he hadn't overheard us.

"The boy left during the commotion." Stavros joined our conversation, face carefully blank. "I suspect he may also be unable to process mistakes. He felt great shame, and fear, as he left."

My relief turned to too familiar guilt. Despite Owen's conversations revealing their brutality, instead of considering that the Syndicate had altered our Company training to something more violent and unforgiving, I'd gone blithely along assuming he'd been taught the same way we had, and understood the same rules. He barely understood what teamwork was, since he'd sounded like all his training and missions were solitary, with only a vampire handler. Which matched what I'd seen during the aquarium mission.

I also hadn't reassured him, once we realized Josh was okay. I handed Stavros the medical equipment with a questioning tilt of my head.

He took the bundle. "I will return these to medical. Owen went north."

As our papá and brother left, Vee lowered her voice and stepped closer. "This can't happen again."

"Agreed." We couldn't afford being a member down. Not to mention, family didn't harm family. Our effectiveness was based largely on our absolute trust in each other.

Vee turned to follow the rest, but looked back over her shoulder. "Stavros and I can't really help with this one. I think we still trigger some really awful memories for Owen. Which I totally understand, but, facts."

I understood what she didn't say. This entire situation was on me. I'd pushed to bring Owen in. Now, it was up to me to make sure that he could find his place on the team, a new purpose, without endangering himself or the team.

I headed north in search of Owen, hoping he was still speaking to me after my seemingly turning my back on him. Also hoping I came up with a plan to help, that he'd accept, by the time I found him.

CHAPTER 15

 wen

OWEN SAT, the rough bark at the base of Kimi's tree digging into his back. He didn't deserve the platform with the puffy objects and the view his mate liked.

He picked at the tangle of emotions lodged in his center, hoping to end the confusion. So many new feelings wrapped and twisted, defying matching them with a term.

All except one. He had shamed himself in front of Kimi and her family-team. That feeling came closest to his emotion directed at Josh. *Ashamed.* Owen was ashamed.

He *liked* Josh. Not in the way he did Kimi, but the way he did her sister, who shared his hatred of vampires and joy in eliminating them, and told him about chocolate coffee. He had never liked anyone, not in his batch, not among the vampires. Josh had offered clothing and high-fiving. Yet Owen had injured Josh.

Nearly as alien was the desire for Kimi's family-team to

be pleased with him. Owen wished for them to like him. And for the first time, that hope had nothing to do with a fear of punishment.

He let his head thunk against the trunk. He deserved the pain of a jarred brain. Staring through the fluttering leaves to the patches of blue sky, he let the dirty, bruise-purple shame and regret swallow him.

The breeze shifted, leaves flipping in the opposite direction. Wind bringing him Kimi's familiar scent. He dropped his head, tension rushing back.

She stood a yard away, watching him. He had no way of knowing how long she had been there, too lost in his own head. Yet another error, leaving his mate standing as if ignoring her.

"Am I being disciplined for behaving incorrectly?" He couldn't voice his real fear, the one that had replaced punishment and reprogramming. That he would be forced to leave this place, and his mate.

He ducked his head as his mate approached. She sat, legs criss-crossed under. He folded his so that his knees touched hers, perhaps the last contact he would ever be allowed.

"Of course not. This isn't your fault." She wiggled closer, whisper-signing. "That isn't how we do things. You made a mistake, but so did I. Despite seeing your scars, and the stories you shared, I didn't consider that your training wasn't exactly like ours. You were *amazing* on the track and the course, and I made assumptions. I should have asked if you had questions, and really explained the concept of first-contact. I am so sorry."

She had liked his performance.

The brief burst of happiness drained away, more important facts resurfacing. "I did know the term. I did not mean to harm Josh, or your sister. I have great shame for injuring him."

He didn't want to lie, even if she punished him. "Failing in a fight meant lower ranking, less food, many more fights as others challenged the loser. Josh is an excellent agent-fighter and I forgot who I faced. I will ask many more questions next time."

She patted his knee, and instead of stopping, he finished telling the truth. "But also when I saw your sister and the old one, all I knew was anger."

Kimi hesitated, then signed, "I think that's natural."

"I will do better."

Her smile now was soft, as if he had passed some test. He tasted her relief as she whisper-signed, "When we make mistakes, we apologize and learn from them."

"I will do the apologizing to your brother and sister." The ugly cloud of shame burned off at her wide smile, the way the sun burned off morning fog.

"Good. Now come here." She bounced from seated to on her feet, impossibly graceful. "We're going to spar."

He shoved back, tree bark grinding into his spine. Horror replaced his relief.

She was the leader. She was *his mate*. How was he to face her? The possibility of harming Kimi made his stomach churn the way it had when he had once eaten ghoul carrion.

Heroes didn't attack heroines. Or other women. Even women who hit *hard*. That was a rule in every book.

Reading him again, she squatted, resting her hand on his knee. "I have an idea about how to teach you restraint. How to think instead of react, and practice without injuring teammates. Willing to give it a try?"

His mate was using the comforting gestures, forgiving him. Something new washed over him, starting from where her hand met his body. *Joy.* He would do anything she asked.

Instead of returning to the area devoted to training, she moved a few feet away, choosing the most level area near her tree. Motioning him over, she pointed to a spot, then put herself facing him.

"This is called tai chi. It's a form of meditation and fighting," she whisper-signed.

"I do not know meditation." He pointed out his need for more information fast, her lesson on avoiding mistakes fresh.

"In this instance, meditation is a term that means being aware of your body, calm and fully in control, as opposed to mindless instinct. First, feel your breath." She demonstrated, pulling in a deep breath through her nose, letting it out.

His body knew to breathe.

Kimi joined him, her hand low on his chest, palm flat. He would breathe as many ways as she liked, if it meant her touching him. She pressed, and mouthed, "Breathe from here."

He did as she asked, regretting it when she nodded and returned to her spot.

"These are defensive moves, but slowed down. One move flows into another." She bent her knees, back straight. Her hands sketched large circles at chest level. Then she bent to the side, before doing the same, one leg raised.

He concentrated, shoving away the sharp, immediate instinct to catalogue weaknesses, and watch for an opening while his opponent was distracted. His batch had been taught to strike first, always. He held himself away, stiff.

Biting down on the snarl snaking out of his throat, twisting his face.

She left her spot at different points, pressing his palm flat, gently correcting his form. A hand on his hip, the other on his shoulder, shifting him and altering his balance. Each bit of contact, her green-not-oil scent on his skin, the familiar flutter of her heart, took away part of the trainers' voices. Erased a slice of the need to hit and not stop until his opponent was destroyed.

Neither spoke, or signed. His body loosened, matched to hers, their motions in synch. This close, no one else to disturb the silence, he concentrated on his mate. Gazes fixed, but without threat. Instead, a connection built, stronger as they moved together. The calm she spoke of pushed out his worry, replacing it with an ease he'd never known existed.

Returning to their original position, she nodded. "Perfect. Now, watch."

She burst into motion, hands as a moving shield, her body bending away from an imaginary opponent. Balancing on one leg again, but striking out almost vampire fast. The same forms they had done, but sped up, now for fighting.

Pride in his mate's many skills brought out a smile.

She grinned back, eyes happy-squinting.

"Transfer that restraint when you attack or defend while sparring," she signed. "Especially since we aren't wearing pads or gloves."

He interpreted no pads as being without added protection.

Without warning, she repeated Josh's attack, feinting with one hand, the other aimed at Owen's eyes.

He twisted, like switching from the frontal pose to the side. Dodging her. Anticipating her employing her same attack directed at his knees, whirling out of her reach.

Instead, she launched, using his hip as a base, shoulder as balance. Twisting fast, her legs clamping around his neck, flipping them.

His back hit the dirt. Anger flared, hot and fast. He drew in a deep breath, of his mate and her tree and the salty not-ocean, and the anger cooled.

He bucked, but with half force, shaking her loose. Rolling, and elbow aiming for her stomach, pulling the blow at the last second.

She gave that look again, the one when she'd finished the obstacle course. Laughter in her eyes.

His mate was challenging him, yet with play involved. Daring him. He did the toothy smile. And grabbed, pinning her back against his chest, forearm across her throat, the lightest pressure instead of choking her out. His other arm around her waist, hand splayed over her navel.

Excitement drummed through his body in place of the drive to crush an enemy, the heat of her body molding against him, canceling any desire of tossing an opponent away.

Between blinks, she bent, top of her head brushing the dirt, leg shoved behind his. Flipping him forward, and over her back. Twisting free, but her fingers trailing over his chest as she did.

That same connection as when performing the tai chi snapped into being. He followed her lead again, eyes locked, rolling and pivoting against each other, legs and arms catching, taps on chins and thighs instead of blows. Palms and cheeks rubbing in more of a caress then debilitating holds. Lingering in evading the other's charge.

Heat and desire burned under his skin. Hotter than if he had fought batch mates and creatures for hours. Still wanting Kimi pressed against him.

Her face was flushed the dusky pink, shirt clinging to her, chest heaving. Leaving him wishing for more, for the shirt to vanish.

She came at him, another feint. But he caught her. Jerking her in tight, chest to chest. Her leg slipped between his, knee raised to crush his cock and balls, and he braced for the explosion of discomfort. Instead, she grazed him, and stopped. Thigh pressing into him.

He pulled her tighter, joining them from chest to hips. Her breaths vibrating through him, down to his hard cock.

Urging him to grind against her, her desire rising from her pores.

Her eyes were huge, lips parted. And he wanted to do the kissing, those lips pressed to his. Tasting his mate.

Kimi froze, only her chest moving. He caught himself, and changed leaning over her for a kiss into loosening his hold. This, this was too much like the fight with Josh. Owen not thinking, his body taking over. Resulting in his mate's anger.

His lesson was about restraining himself, and thinking before acting. He hadn't asked what she wanted. And from the books, he'd seen humans, even were-humans, didn't grab and force the way his kind mated. Even now, Kimi's leg dropped and pressure on his arms increased. Silently telling him to let go.

He dropped his arms, stepping back. Kimi mirrored him.

"I—I have drone footage to review," she whisper-signed, her whisper strained.

"And I have...running. I will run the perimeter. To patrol for—things."

They whirled, Kimi going for the house area, while he bolted for the other end of the compound.

Working to outrun his near-shame. His stride pounded in time to the warnings crowding his head. He had behaved incorrectly, first in thinking her family-team's touching was harming her, then with the food, today in attacking her brother and sister.

His eyes on the terrain, he automatically mapped his new home. Frowning at a section where the towering fence was looser between the posts. Noting the outcropping on the edge of the wall of stone bounding this remote end of their territory. The projection was barely enough for the edge of a boot. But he, his batch, had learned to balance on less, a gift

167

from some unknown cryptid's DNA. To stab fingers into rock, punching tiny handholds if necessary.

He slowed automatically, that almost-familiar tang of a cryptid from his ride here again rising, this time from far below the outcropping. When he inhaled, the scent was gone though. He circled back, with the same result.

He aimed for the perimeter again, body reacting, following orders programmed into him from other creatures, and from trainers and handlers. Reacting the same way as with Josh.

The way he had almost reacted to his mate, their bodies entwined. But his mate wasn't cryptid. Kimi was human, and he had erred again and again, not acting appropriately human. He couldn't make that mistake with his mate and sex.

With mating there would be no apologies and second chances. Fighting the urge to turn and race to her again, he ran harder, searching for the correct human way to be her perfect hero instead of a monster she would hate.

 imi

DRONES HAD TO WAIT. On the way to my room for non-sweaty clothes, I ducked inside the group bath, stuck my arm in and switched the shower head to heat up, another Bruce upgrade, from the rain setting to full blast. Not desperate enough for truly cold water, I set it to lukewarm.

What started as a totally legit project teaching Owen restraint, and to think critically, took a hormone-infused turn. A situation that rested on my shoulders. I'd all but challenged Owen on the obstacle course, showing off. And wow, had he responded.

Our escape had been bumpy enough that I hadn't truly seen him fight. Even watching him prowl the cabin and compound hadn't prepared me for Peak Owen. He took the course like it was his natural habitat. His sheer power, the way he twisted and tackled, was more like a dance. Pure art.

I paused at the idea of painting him. Capturing his intensity, and the way muscle rolled under his skin. The primal streak, but his hope, and love of books, and the touch of humor hidden underneath.

How he'd watched me, first on the course, then during the tai chi lesson. He followed my slightest cue. Almost like he read my mind. He'd stared, digging deep inside me, and the connection had felt like the sunrise earlier. Deceptively quiet and simple, until between blinks, it burst into full blaze.

Our sparring turned the blaze into an inferno, as we matched each other move for move. Anything outside the two of us had ceased to exist for those minutes, Owen's grip, strong but holding back. His scarred hands sliding over my sweaty skin, always stopping that inch short of going too far. Teasing, and playing.

Hot water rushed over my outstretched hand and I yelped, jerking it from under the shower spray, half of my tee already soaked. Not paying attention, I'd let the water heat to almost scalding.

The universe wasn't being *at all* subtle today.

Owen wasn't a pretty sunrise. He was a hardened soldier, who'd known only brutality and pain, and had seriously injured Josh. Possibly would have killed him, then gone after Vee. Owen was wrestling with tempering and overcoming his conditioning. I owed it to him to help, not make the situation more difficult because we were busy concentrating on sexy times instead of working through his issues.

And again, who knew how he responded to sex and relationships? We didn't get possessive or hold grudges against sexual partners. Sex was fun, no strings, between friends, because our true ties were with our team.

That wasn't the case with civis. And it was impossible to gauge where Owen fell on that scale—logical and accepting like Company, or prone to ugly blow-ups and hurt feelings like civilians? Most of his responses were closer to primal, which did not bode well.

If Owen couldn't grasp teamwork, his emotions would take over. If friends with benefits failed and he refused to work with me or the team as retaliation, it meant him getting shipped to a HQ facility, which was worse. And our losing Oversight's trust and a measure of our value to them, *plus*, now there was a non-agent who knew what Vee and Stavros were, and as well as who we really reported to.

Keeping my family safe was paramount. Providing Owen a stable, accepting environment and real connections was a close second. Acting on my attraction dropped to the very bottom of the priority list.

"Yo." Josh's voice boomed, amplified by the tile, and stuck his head around the corner, eyes covered.

I whirled, my hair swishing under the edge of the shower. Droplets flew in his face.

He swiped at the mini-shower, rubbing his face on his tee, and opening his eyes since I clearly wasn't in the shower yet. "Why bother cleaning up when we've got more training this afternoon?"

I graced him with one of my inscrutable looks. They had freaked him out nicely since I'd perfected the expression as a pre-teen.

"Hey, just asking." He held both hands up. "Besides, Vee's planning a walkabout. She swore there was a flicker on one of the security videos. Stavros didn't see it, but…"

But, our disbelief when our sister had originally brought up the cryptid weirdness was partially the reason she was a vampire now. None of us ignored her hunches anymore.

"The armory was already overdue for an inventory when we were pulled away for the call out, and Stavros is working on a private report Oversight requested ASAP." Josh winced.

Teaching a four-hundred-plus-year-old hermit ascetic

vampire about modern laptops and daily reports was a work in progress. He didn't totally trust technology. Plus, he hadn't lost that formal, ultra-detailed and flowery written form he'd been taught as a child. And when Oversight wanted something ASAP, we provided it.

"I'll take Vee, you take the armory," I signed, then shut the water off, wringing out my shirt hem. Work was a better method of re-centering than a cool shower anyway. "Your ribs?"

"A couple bruises, but otherwise nearly good as new. I don't think I'll ever get used to how bones realign after a dose of Vee or Stavros though." He stretched arms up and back for me, proof he was healed enough for missions. He dropped the easy going front. "Hey, about Owen."

"He feels *awful* about injuring you."

Josh paused at my leaping to Owen's defense. Leaping wasn't inscrutable, or my thing.

"I should've factored in him not being Company. Those fucking scars." Josh shook his head. "That shit is messed up. I can see how it'd fuck with his head. We'll take it slower going forward."

I tackle-hugged my brother, surprising a grunt out of him.

He hugged back, ignoring the water dripping onto his boots. "This gets me off the payback list?"

I let go, and shrugged.

"It does. Right?"

I walked backward, smiling. There were still mating wombats in his future.

Josh's plaintive, "Kimi. C'mon," followed me out.

A walkabout was shorthand for a sweep outside the compound fences. There were too many hills, mountains, and outcroppings here, which made us all twitchy. Outer rim patrols were now part of our protocol. Occasionally, the outer fence as well.

After grabbing dry clothes, I took the stairs three at a time, hit the armory to weapon up, then cut back through the breezeway, not prepared to meet Owen face to face yet. Vee was already in the house garage, armed and perched on one of the four-wheelers able to handle our rugged terrain.

They were also awesome to race across the flatter parts of the valley for fun.

Owen would enjoy one, in place of the motorcycle we might or might not get back from the Cleaners.

Aaand, now he was invading my every thought.

Vee cocked her head, like she was one of those movie-type psychic vampires. Or, she was cheating and sniffing. I straddled the second machine of our pair, and punched the ignition, the burst of fuel drowning out anything organic.

She smacked the button between the four-wheeler's handle-bars, and the garage door rose. I hung a foot back as we passed through the first gate, and on to the second. We turned as the outer gate rolled closed behind us, and waved at the camera.

When I pointed toward the valley, Vee didn't move.

I stopped and waited, not super surprised we were having an Owen Behaving Badly chat, and possibly a Kimi Behaving Badly one as well. This far out, even Stavros couldn't hear us. Our backs were to the cameras, blocking the view of anything we signed.

"The Syndicate. Facilities in our back yard. Your capture, and then, oh look at that, tons of invaluable new facts about their tech." Vee preferred the indirect route.

Startled, my grip on the handlebars slipped and the motor hiccuped. I had expected a super subtle are-you-really-okay-because-you-slipped-up-again convo. Not my sister guessing my eventual infiltration objective.

"I didn't purposely let myself be captured." That plan had been put on hold the moment we saw children and chaperones spread out in the parking area, and vulnerable.

"I'm positive you could crack a security and lockdown code in any situation you found yourself in. But going in cold, it would require way more time than you had while inside that facility. You used that skeleton key on their system. That's also where all the encrypted information flowing into HQ's Intel division came from."

It was also flowing into mine.

Vee frowned, like she heard me.

I signed, "You knew I was working on a theoretical universal key, then copies we could each carry for potential opportunities, not just for the vampire faction use. I'd just finished a prototype for field testing, and tossed it with my other gear for the next mission, whenever one hit." Which was true. Just not the whole truth.

When her shoulders relaxed, immediately accepting the fact that of course I'd made a misstep and found myself in trouble, I kept my expression neutral.

Hers brightened, changing topics whiplash fast, as only Vee could. "How did working with Owen go?" Like a good C.O., she knew her team, and could predict our actions, as long as it didn't involve the prejudice that I didn't always make good choices.

I picked my phrasing carefully. I'd felt the violence deep inside him as he worked to think instead of giving in to rage. "He admitted he didn't fully understand our version of training, and we'll both ask for clarification going forward. Since he learns best by example, I led him through a tai chi session. His second attempt at sparring went perfectly."

Even as the sensation of Owen's palms sliding across my stomach sent goosebumps over my skin, I stayed analytical. The years of covering my emotions so that both my guilt, and my resentment, weren't allowed to impact my relationship with my family or our performance in the field, had become automatic.

"Excellent. This morning on our chat?"

"It wasn't doubts about Owen's ability, or the decision to ask that he remain here." I hit the signs way too vigorously, not able to stop my rogue emotions emerging this time.

Vee's brow shot up at my defensiveness. Time to reexamine my shielding ability.

"It also wasn't only an everyday *hey, how are you guys* checking-in chat," she said.

Liv loved her new team, Marshall and Kit finally turning them from the orphaned remnants of three different teams, to a real family. But *we* were her family first. Both teams dealt with siblings out on missions without our backup by reassuring video convos after. If I hadn't initiated one this morning, Liv would've by lunch at the latest.

Vee had that look, where she picked through her words ultra-carefully. "I think Owen has gone further than imprinting on you as another soldier who aided in freeing him."

Not really an avenue of discussion I wanted to go down. I nudged the conversation toward a different destination. "He's never had any sort of equal relationship or observed one—siblings, friends, true teammates, supportive teachers. Clearly, the Syndicate encouraged a viciously competitive environment. Owen has no frame of reference. We are *literally* the first humans he's had contact with."

"Owen likes me, I think. I mean, just going by the whole *killing every vampire but you two* clause he adds. And aside from redlining during the session today, he likes Josh." Absently, she tugged the cuffs of the long-sleeved tee to cover her hands, then slid the wraparound sunglasses from the top of her head to her eyes.

My guilt multiplied. She wasn't in a tee and plain BDU's because she'd used up energy healing Josh, and now was forced to conserve what she had left. Her sun-proofing would be the first thing to go. All my fault for not thinking how different Owen's situation had been from what we grew up with, and paying attention as soon as we hit the obstacle course. Kind of like how I also hadn't been paying enough attention, when nabbed by the stupid Syndicate vampire.

There wouldn't be a chance for her to fuel back up until we got another mission or call-out involving vampires. The bit of preserved vampire blood we kept stocked was direst emergency use only, and nowhere near as potent as fresh. The DNA alterations from the virus degraded rapidly. I was still working on calculating their half-life, and better preservation mediums, since it wasn't exactly something the Labs were pursuing.

"But he acts way different with you." Vee pulled me out of the recriminations into the here and now. "It's a little weird how protective he is, but he completely defers to you at the same time."

True, but I liked the combination. A lot.

"He had three books stashed. Two were the *Bro* series. When we talked about favorite tropes, though, he asked if I liked Were-creatures." Exposing his throat this morning, not meeting my eyes when I was upset with him, all understandable if the majority of his education came from paranormal romances, where creature's actions were loosely based on real animal behavior.

We sat there for a handful of heartbeats, ideas bubbling behind my sister's deceptive calm.

"You don't think—I mean, you are both human, not cryptids." She finally waved her covered arm and hand at herself. "You don't even have any after-market add-ons like freaky virus mutations."

I tilted my head, asking for more info to fill in the gaps between what she'd said, and what she meant. Like, from Vee-speak to normal agent speak.

"Were-creatures and shifters? What do they all have in common in the stories? Hello, that whole fated-mates trope?"

We stared at each other, the possibilities tumbling through my brain and lining up observed behaviors, all of his actions since we had entered the cabin. Because the first assumption that popped into my head had to be the overly artistic, right side part of me, not the analytical left side. Owen was pure human. So was I.

Vee chewed on her thumbnail. "Maybe he totally thinks—"

I jumped in before she said it. "Fate isn't a real thing. There's no scientific basis for the concept, only touchy-feely civi wishful thinking. Don't even say—"

Of course she blurted out what we were both thinking. Or trying not to think on my part? "You two are fated to be together. Owen believes you guys are fated-mates."

My startled expression reflected back from her mirrored shades. "That is—" my stomach did a flip. But underneath the denial and automatic calculations on how mathematically impossible the theory was, and my arguments on why I couldn't be more than a teammate and friend, excitement hummed through me.

But again, not real. Like our CoW matches, it was all imaginary fun. Basically for entertainment purposes only.

"I know you aren't about enjoying romance as anything other than a literary fantasy." She crossed her arms, only eyebrows visible over the top of her glasses. Highly judgmental eyebrows. "But seriously. After the tag-team action we pulled on Liv when she was waffling and doing the *eek, I don't know if I should* thing about Marshall and owning her feelings, don't even say you've never thought about it."

Rolling my eyes at Vee's selective memory, I signed, "Do you also remember the part where I told her I understood the hesitation of giving away a huge part of yourself, including your privacy, and then having that person leave? It would be shattering. *We* don't have to face that risk, because *we* have our teams."

"Fated. Mates. That isn't someone who will get bored and bail, right?"

Owen had been treated as more of an animal than a person, and dang, did that explain some of his reactions. Taking it one step further—he could be looking for the permanence we took for granted. And the mate-bond thing was how he manifested that universal desire.

"Assuming you find him sexually attractive?" Vee hesitated.

That part was easy. "If he had been another agent, our sparring would've ended with us naked. But he isn't an agent, and hasn't been raised to think of sex and emotions the way we do. Or in any healthy way, probably." Heat still crawled up my chest and neck. I wouldn't be surprised if my dreams tonight featured Owen and sweaty, nude tai chi action.

"There is that. However, sex can be healing."

"He has so much to learn about real life. On top of that, there's our team situation. What if he and I don't work out, once he learns more about what he prefers?" I acknowledged the scariest, most destructive possibility. "What if it *does*, but Oversight refuses our request for him to stay?"

"Kimi—"

Nope. This was so not turning into a *Kimi be reasonable* conversation. "What if we try and I don't enjoy the whole all-in romantic, one person forever, thing?" Or I did and screwed it up? We hadn't had Academy courses on romance and monogamous relationships. I had no means to calculate whether it was in my skill set, or whether there was room for another mistake and a potential heart-rending disaster.

Vee nibbled at a cuticle, actually listening to and considering my facts. "Bruce had been around during some heavy stuff when we fell for each other, and Marshall was at Liv's for months before they initiated anything romantic. So she and I had time and circumstances to realistically evaluate whether we felt more than sexual attraction. Where Owen has only been here a day. Two, I guess, if you count the vampire lab. Sorry—I wasn't really thinking."

Her posture shifted. Her curious sister half now satisfied, she flipped back to practical C.O.. "Those are all significant question marks, too. *He* doesn't know that *we* know his take on the two of you and fate. Play clueless, like you don't notice. Be his friend, his liaison with our world, and his teammate."

Practical, and all fitting into the pro column. That I kinda wanted to obliterate the super reasonable plan the way I did rival gamer teams was potentially a problem. My problem.

The matter settled as far as she was concerned, Vee squinted at the sky, and the sun beating down on us. "The blip on the surveillance feed might've been a bird, and there was no way to orient which direction it came from or went."

Reaching into the mesh compartment behind my seat, I pulled out a ball cap that snipers preferred, and tossed it to her. "I donated this to the keep-our-sister-from-bursting-into-flames cause on Josh's behalf." I double-checked the com unit snug in my ear, slapped my sunglasses on in solidarity, and revved the four-wheeler, a decent means of burning off energy for the moment, and shot right, on our first loop.

"That isn't the definition of donation," she yelled, dirt flying up from her tires, and hanging in the breezeless air.

This low on blood, her senses weren't sharp enough to

warrant taking point and searching for scent trails or odd sounds. Vee stayed even with me until we hit the split. She motioned down, going for the longer, lower trail.

I shifted, climbing the upper trail. My teeth rattled hard enough that I slowed, more carefully picking my way over and through the gullies and fallen rocks. The trail turned into more of a goat track, a sheer drop-off on my left. The four wheeler's sides scraped against the rough rock face on my right, sacrificing paint as I hugged the wall.

Ahead, the climbing path widened, where at some point in the far past, a generation of agents had carved and blasted through solid rock, creating a shorter patrol route that was more of a tunnel. Shadows from the sheer sandstone fell over me and the temperature dropped as I sped up, walls on both sides rising far over my head.

Minor tremors were common, and the friable stone was prone to minor rockslides. Or to outright collapse, with a major enough quake. I'd scanned my drone's footage days before, doing a routine all-clear check. Topography could change fast, though.

Pebbles rattled down the wall on my right, a puff of dirt following and drifting in front of the four-wheeler.

More scree rolled down, like a rocky rain. Pinging off the sandstone on its way. Squinting, I cranked my neck at a painful angle, searching for the weak spot above, and whether this was a race forward or gun it in reverse situation.

One of the enormous boulders near the edge, feet ahead, rattled. There was too much of a grade to reverse the four-wheeler and run backwards. If the enormous chunk of stone fell, it would roll straight at me. Death by boulder wasn't high on my list.

The boulder creaked, and larger chips hit, stinging my face and hands. Shoulders hunching as my body caught up with my brain and recognized the danger we were in, I twisted the handle, lurching forward. Keeping the falling rock in view from the corner of my eye.

With a shriek of millennia-old formations ripping free, the rock pitched, falling. The tunnel walls shook, the guttural rumbling of part of a peak crashing drowning out everything but the hammering of blood in my ears.

The tunnel ended feet ahead, hazy blue sky and clear trail visible. My pulse raced, as fast as the four-wheeler.

The boulder hit, the shockwave catching the tail of the vehicle. Slewing sideways, my elbow cracked into the wall, pain radiating to my fingertips, leaving them stiff and partially numb. I jerked the handlebars, straightening.

Another shadow balanced on the edge of the wall. Swearing, I pushed for more speed, before whatever chain reaction the first rockslide triggered covered the road and me.

The second rock's shadow altered. Stretching and elongating. The stench of rancid trash coated my nose, as the shadow shifted, standing on its hind legs, sun falling in a bar over red eyes.

The windigo dropped its head, glare fixed on me. A growl thrummed, fallen stones vibrating, counterpoint to the boulder grinding to a halt, stuck between the tunnel walls.

Where there was one windigo, there were more. Letting go of the handlebar for a beat, I tapped out the code for windigo horde, warning Vee.

The cryptid jumped, black claws out. Hundreds of pounds plunging straight down, aiming to land on my shoulders. I shoved the ATV to its limits, back wheels clearing the tunnel edge.

Metal shrieked, claws slashing the rear panel and catching. The creature heaved, and the ATV spun in a half circle. I locked it down, the char of burned rubber mixing with rotted garbage, machine rocking to a stop.

The windigo snarled, shaking its forelegs, claws stuck in the metal frame. Enormous muscles stood out under the cryptid's gleaming black coat, and the ATV shuddered and jumped.

This was a horde alpha. But it was enormous, more bull than canine. Magnitudes larger than even the first oversized horde leader we encountered at the start of the cryptid upheaval.

Right arm still partially numb, I caved, leaving my knives in place, jerking the regulation nine mil out. Sighting, and firing. A bullet ripped into its shoulder, reddish-green cryptid blood spouting. The windigo wrenched one paw free, slashing at me. I bent backward, crown almost touching the seat and claws whistled past my throat. The backswing snatched the gun from my grip.

With a squeak like ginormous nails across a chalkboard, the stuck claws came half-way out of the metal. Two more seconds, and the giant would be free. It snapped, hot breath washing my face, inches from my drawn in chin. A tooth scored down my glasses, cracking the lens.

I slapped the gear button with one throbbing hand, the other resting on the throttle, as the creature's claws flew loose from the ATV. The windigo lunged, straight across the handlebars.

Letting go of the brake, I jammed the throttle and threw myself sideways. Hitting shale and rock. Front tires spinning a finger's length from my nose, spitting debris in my face.

The ATV sped backward at full speed, windigo tangled between the bars. Machine and cryptid flying off the narrow ledge, into the blue.

Metal and rubber smashed, bouncing off the sandstone on its way down. A paw grabbed the edge of the trail, scrabbling for a hold. Its other slapped down closer, broken claws catching the rubber of my boot sole.

I rolled, finally flicking my babies free, slamming the pair of chem-coated blades into the windigo's paws. Snatching my second favorites from their slots in my boot shaft, driving the bright knives in as deep as they'd go, slicing tendons.

The horde leader howled, calling for help, pitch rising. My ears ached. Its paws screeched along the rocky cliff edge, leaving bloody streaks, slipping. Jerking my leg, the claw lodged in it, the 'digo's weight taking me along. I jammed my free leg against rock. Twisting in half, my hand found and wrapped around the hilt of the closest imbedded blade. Jerking it from a useless paw.

I slammed my version of a claw into a narrow crevice where tunnel rock met the trail, wedging it and kicking hard at the stuck cryptid. Putting everything into hanging on, arms burning. The porous rock split deeper, knife sliding back an inch. My chest and bare arms scraped across the rocky ground.

Pulling, bending both legs as far as I could, I kicked out a last time. Rubber popped, part of my boot tearing. The windigo fell, bouncing along off the rock wall the way the ATV had. The crunch of metal came an instant before a last howl, cut short.

I slithered around, doing a half push-up and peering over the ledge.

Familiar claws wrapped around my ankle, hauling me back. I twisted and rolled to my butt, doing an awkward sit-up and carefully stashing my beat-up blade back in my boot sheath. Then signed at my sister. "Hello? I was looking at splatted windigo."

Even through the polarized glasses, a hint of silver flashed. Vee let go, and rose from a crouch. "Oops? But also, accidentally crashing down on top of splatted windigo would be highly embarrassing."

I shook my arms out, the pins and needles feeling easing and full sensation returning. Signing more clearly, I asked, "You get the rest of its horde?"

Taking her hand, I hopped up, then kept going, eying the stuck boulder that a freaking windigo had pushed up and off a cliff, like some stinky canid Sisyphus, attempting to flatten me.

"There wasn't a horde. At least not anywhere close to me."

I checked over my shoulder at her. That wasn't possible. Windigos did nothing alone. Maybe, *maybe*, a young overly-pesky male got kicked out of the horde and went it alone, but even then, their first instinct was to find another group immediately. And the 'digo that I'd just splatted sure as heck wasn't a juvie male.

"For real." She flashed her phone. "Okay, calling Stavros before he freaks and bulldozes through the fence checking for why I just shot adrenalin-fight vibes through his aura."

I fished my phone out, too, but not to reassure a vampire sire that I'd overreacted. Flipping to the text to voice app, I said, "Tell him to pull my extra set of blades from the armory. And the extra-extra one underneath those. Oh, and requisition a new four-wheeler."

Flipping to the custom app, I checked both drones.

Owen. He'd gone for his run as I left. Despite the fact he was a formidable soldier, he hadn't been prepared for a true patrol, only armed with the basic boot knife we all carried.

Hastily widening the search, I flicked through the recorded footage, doing double search duty, for cryptids and him. Footage showed him returning to the house and entering, and the tightness in my throat eased.

I signed, "There seriously isn't a horde. Hasn't been one here, period."

After sending a text, I climbed over the boulder, and headed for the impact site. I had questions about suddenly solitary cryptids with MENSA level-intelligence. At least, MENSA level for a windigo.

A couple minutes later, Vee caught up, and I checked with her. "Papá?"

"Requisitioning as we speak."

"After the lecture?" Teaching a new vampire, even one as miraculous as Vee, how to walk the knife edge and not burn through stolen vampire blood, was as much a work in progress as his typing efforts. Racing up the trail on foot had depleted more of her thin remaining power.

"After the lecture. Only a tiny one, though. He'll dispose of the 'digo after sunset."

I jogged the rest of the way, hurrying as much to get her out of the sun as to get to my slightly squishy prize. Pushing, I shoved her safely into the thin shade of an overhang, then circled the carcass and destroyed ATV.

Using my phone, I measured and documented the cryptid. Which was as freakishly large dead as it had been looming over me when it was alive. I ignored Vee fidgeting in the background, shirt over her nose. I was basted in 'digo, so poking the carcass wasn't going to make me reek any worse.

At the rumble of the truck, and the protest of shocks bumping over the dirt, I pulled the tiny pot of menthol rub from one of my BDU pockets and held it out to Josh without looking. His muttering about windigo ook, and then the clank of him tossing ATV parts onto the flat trailer hitched to the truck, was my white noise.

"Machete," I signed at Vee.

"Oh, no freaking way. You really gotta do that?" Josh gagged when she lent me her weapon and I angled the borrowed blade, as long as my arm, over the windigo's neck.

My answer was to throw my weight against the insanely

sharp machete's handle, until edge hit bone. I pushed harder and bone crackled, the dented head separating.

"It's research. I think," Vee said.

"Why does science have to smell so bad?" Josh muttered.

Nudging the head to the side, I switched for my leftover knife. I felt along the creature's twisted shoulder and foreleg, for the too geometrically perfect lump I'd noticed when it was mauling my four-wheeler. Making a neat slit, I dug under the skin, fingertip brushing non-organic material. Using fingers and the tip of the knife, I worked the object out and held it up to the fading light.

"Another chip?" Vee leaned as close as not moving her feet allowed.

"Different," I mouthed, this one thicker but smaller than any we'd collected so far. Digging into another of the BDU's multi-pockets, I pulled out a gauze pad, wrapping the chip in it and folding the cover over both. Switching, I rolled the windigo head so that it sat upright on the stump of its spine.

Gleaming silver knives appeared over my shoulder. I leaned my head back, giving Stavros a smile, and mouthed, "Gracias papá."

"You are well?"

I stashed my blunted knife, accepting the set he'd brought, then signed, "Of course." Choosing the smallest, I cut across the cryptid's bulging forehead, peeling the skin away.

"On that note, I'm out." Josh retreated to the SUV, its load of parts, and the ATV frame he and Stavros had loaded.

"Ride back with him," I signed. "Both of you." I was re-armed, and had set the app to notify me if anything larger than a chupacabra moved. Not that we had any nearby. I kind of missed the little burrowing pests.

"I will remove the remains," Stavros said.

"I'll grab Vee's four-wheeler and drag the leftovers out for the birds," I signed, despite the warm rush his offer gave me. Until Vee, he had only hunted vampires, considering true cryptids simply dangerous vermin. Windigos especially offended him, yet he willingly took on the most unpleasant part of dealing with them, for us.

"Niña—"

I paused. "Are you drinking from this carcass? Either of you?"

At Vee's gagging noise, and his curled lip, I pointed the knife at them and mouthed, "Exactly. So you clearly weren't proposing doing anything as irresponsible as wasting power, with no meal in sight for an indeterminate amount of time, on a chore I can do with a well-fueled vehicle."

They both slunk off, the tips of Stavros' ears rosy at getting called out, him muttering in Nahuatl.

I couldn't wait to surprise him with my new ability to read and write in one of his native languages, thanks to the online course I'd nearly completed. He might be able to help me with the pronunciation, to the point where I spoke it well enough for lip reading.

Chains clinked and landed in a neat coil, Josh tossing extras from the SUV for me, as I went back to work.

With no one to judge my gravelly tone, I hummed as I carefully separated the creature's frontal cortex. The familiar white of an expected implant, the one Oversight had developed the scanning app for, came clear amid the grayish-pink flesh. We'd discovered the first in a pair of anangoas, assuming a civi collector had brought them in as exotic pets, chipped them like dogs, and then been eaten by his poorly thought-out choices. After multiple ghouls and a starving, mindless vampire had presented with them, the theory went by the wayside.

Now we knew they were inserted by Syndicate researchers. The tech wasn't about keeping track of their creatures, more about influencing their behavior, the reason the vampires targeted not just predatory cryptid species for their use, but sentient ones.

Now there was another type of chip in play. This was officially one of those *I've got a bad feeling about this* movie moments.

Poking around in the gray matter, I compared morphology with textbook windigo anatomy, and that of the few anomalies we'd sent to the Labs. Certain sections of lobes were larger. Far larger than the increased body mass could account for.

The physical size was another red flag, though.

The vampires were playing with mutations and DNA sequencing, at the very least.

I flipped my knife over and over as I thought, the sun reflecting in a sparkling, merry dance, the opposite of my thoughts.

The windigo had executed a plan to attack me. Not hunting, not with its horde. Alone, and tailoring to the circumstances. The species' flexible rear leg joints were a precursor to becoming bipedal, assuming no extinction event occurred first. This, though—the Syndicate had pushed windigo evolution forward tens of thousands of years minimum, probably in less than a few decades. The Company didn't have anything this sophisticated, not even Oversight's cutting edge, hush-hush labs. Who really needed to improve their cyber security.

Vee and Liv threw warnings around about hacking into Oversight files. If the Company didn't want me peeking, they shouldn't have such an easy-peasy backdoor.

I added the second chip into the gauze packet, gathered my chains, and headed for Vee's abandoned four-wheeler and disposal duty.

CHAPTER 17

wen

OWEN REARRANGED the opened books in order of most often used mating cues, careful not to damage their covers and pages. The most common on the bed, lesser used on the floor. He hesitated a moment over two with especially bright covers, one with a tall metal tower, the other with a beach and many blooming plants.

Both locations seemed especially important for courting mates with *proposals*, and *honeymoons*, which seemed some sort of ritual after mates acknowledged their bond. Kimi liked tall places such as her tree platform, and the beach plants were the color of the sunrise she also liked.

However, neither story featured Were creatures, and he hadn't determined each location's distance nor what vehicles he would need to borrow in order to reach them. He stacked the *proposal* books onto the pile sitting on the wooden box with its many drawers meant for holding supplies.

The bathing supplies Josh had shared lined one side of the box. A distinctly attractive scent was the most common mating cue, one he understood and approved of. His new favorite scent was now Kimi's green plant and not-oil blend, beating out the sugary lab food, his previous favorite.

His stomach rumbled. Even without the miraculous window, his body told him it was sundown and the time most vampires were active. Kimi and her sister-vampire had left the interior compound, soon followed by the old vampire and Josh.

With the risk of offending Kimi and her team-family suspended, Owen had returned indoors to research how to be a proper mate. As well as how to do the apologizing to Josh. The action occurred in some of the books, although he was unsure whether the presenting of bright plants, chocolate food, and music worked with non-mates.

Owen hadn't used the bathing facility on his return, too busy with his reading. Now was an optimal point. He opened the tops of the bathing bottles. He sneezed over the first, an especially musky one. The next few proved fresher, like the citrus food and forest. Pleasing scents. Kimi's team-brother was indeed excellent, providing Owen with items to attract Kimi. Hopefully, these would be enough, even if he didn't produce the *man smell* usually mixed into the scent combination according to the books.

When he came out of the large showering room, the funk of windigo met him. As did the voices of Kimi's family-team.

"Yo, man." Josh rushed into the hall.

Before Owen could attempt the apologizing, Kimi's team-brother ducked into his room, coming back out with clothing.

"There was a windigo incursion?" Sampling the air, Owen only picked up second-hand traces, and none of the excitement-adrenaline from a hunt.

"One extra-freaky alpha." He tipped his chin at the bottles in Owen's possession as he passed. His voice echoed from inside the bathing area. "You had some perfect timing. Stavros will hit the showers as soon as his report is in. Vee too, but she has a private one."

Josh stuck his head out, shirt already gone, showing old claw marks and a raised mound of scar tissue in the middle of his chest. "Kimi is fine. She's mutilating the carcass in the name of science, but she'll be back soon."

Of course his mate was well. "Kimi could easily defeat a stinking windigo. As well as extra-freaky ones."

"Fact. But she's scary enough, without padding her ego." Josh withdrew, to the pounding of water.

Owen returned to his room and books to discover *ego*, proud of his frightening mate. Part of his attention always directed outward and waiting for Kimi, the fast, steady rhythm of her heart carried upstairs as the air pressure in the house altered.

He was posed in the entry between the library room and hall when she bounced up the stairs, near the vent propelling cold air so his new scent would greet her.

She paused for a heartbeat, head tilted and examining him. His heart sped up in anticipation. Droplets hung from her curls, and her skin shone. Her training clothing was gone, but not replaced with the short ones of the night before. Only a puffy length of fabric used for drying wrapped her from mid chest to her thighs.

She smiled, the pleasing scents working, and he edged closer to aid her weaker human senses.

Using her elbow to keep the fabric in place, she signed, "I know. Windigo. I did my mandatory pre-shower and tossing clothes in the incinerator in the gym. Second scrubbing coming up."

She walked away, without sniffing the corner of his jaw

and neck, the spot also clearly indicated as the favored area for mates in the books.

Somehow, he hadn't mastered the pleasant-smelling action. He spent time reviewing the next cues on his list, memorizing so that he performed them properly.

Done, he listened for Kimi's heart or her rough-soft whispering. He followed both down, and past the gathering room. A short hallway Kimi hadn't shown him led from it, to a door with the lighted security panels instead of a knob.

The door was open, Kimi sitting on one of the two desk tables instead of in the stiff rolling chairs, or more comfortable-seeming puffy chairs in the corner.

She glanced up from the silver computer device in her lab. Leaving off pressing keys, she signed, "This is the office. It's restricted access unless one of us is also in here." She motioned him in.

"I have no need to be in here without you." He lifted one of the puffy chairs, depositing it at the desk beside her. Finding an empty space amid the circle of devices in front of her, he rested his elbows, displaying his forearms, another powerful cue.

Since he had no sleeves to roll up first in order to attract attention, he was unsure if his action would be strong enough. Best to use a combination. He wiggled closer until his knees jammed into the desk leg, staring into her eyes.

He was unclear what a soul was or felt like, but the books were clear that souls meeting was required, and that could best be accomplished via eye contact. His mate had brown eyes, like the coffee drink, but much more interesting, with a calming darker circle around them instead of the hated vampire silver.

His mate leaned toward him.

Then tapped between his eyes, and mouthed, "Are you in

there? Wait, how long was your run today? Are you feeling dizzy? Did you stop sweating?"

Footsteps pattered from the gathering room, and Vee was there, sandwiching Owen between the tiny vampire, and his mate.

"Heat stroke?" Vee asked.

She squished in and before he understood, pressing the back of her hand against his forehead, firm but...gentle. Perhaps this was another comfort-touch. Not the same as Kimi's touch, but oddly pleasant. He would add this to his list of new human actions to use with the family-team.

He stayed still, as she leaned around him to speak to Kimi. "He does feel kinda hot."

Kimi pushed her devices aside, and left off her perch. She placed her hand in front of his eyes, part of her fingers folded down. "How many fingers am I holding up?"

"I'll grab a couple of Josh's sports drinks," Vee whirled for the door. "We can restock during the mail run tomorrow."

Heat scorched up Owen's throat and face. He had erred again. Ruining the cues, enough his mate and her team-sister believed him ill and weak. He rose, grabbing the chair and moving it, demonstrating his strength. "I am not heat stroked. You should—do your work."

He backed away.

"Oh, maybe it's low blood sugar?" Vee said. "I think we all missed official lunch, and dinner is late, since B is late."

"There's always cereal," Kimi signed. "Healthy one's in the cupboard by the coffee. The really good ones are in that weird narrow cupboard all the way on top. There's protein powder in front as camouflage, but just reach all the way to the back."

Owen escaped, not even asking what cereal was, or looked like.

Food. Special food was one of the very best cues. This cue made sense to Owen. Special mate food was powerful. Clearly, Vee had agreed to accept her mate due to his food skills.

He turned his retreat into a new plan, rushing to the food preparation room. With no one observing, he inhaled, lips parted, gathering and sorting taste-smells. He stumbled, the hard stone counter edge jabbing his hip. Overwhelmed by the flood of information. Even among the scientist vampires, or during training surrounded by human sites, he'd never been surrounded by so much.

There was food *everywhere* here.

Hidden in tiers of wooden cabinets lining the area. Tucked into earthenware pots and containers underneath. He tracked the different sources, quartering the open area. Then followed more into a room full of open shelves, bottles, boxes, and jars arranged to fill the space. These…he recognized some as bits of other food the vampires and humans used.

All were dried, like old grass.

Circling back to the main room, he opened the machine taking up most of a wall, as tall as Owen and wider than his outstretched arms.

He tugged on one of the lower handles. Cold air flowed over him, all frozen things, and he closed the compartment. He inspected the middle sections. The fresh green of plants occupied a quarter. Fruits another. Many bottles as well, some the milk and juice he knew.

The last section—Owen shoved into the machine. Meat. Fresh, in paper and in sealed wrappers. Aside from sweet food and chocolate, meat was the most desirable food. He chose the largest chunk and dropped it onto a board that held the faintest trace of previous meat.

He stared at his prize. His batch ate raw meat when necessary. Humans didn't. Therefore, there was a means in this room to turn it from raw to not raw. Humans also had weaker teeth, and required smaller chunks.

He did understand turning large pieces into small. Prowling, he bypassed the dull, useless knives from the meals, as well as the scooping and stabbing utensils. A separate drawer held a long bundle of dried skin. He untied the thong, and unrolled the bundle.

Knives. Small ones, long ones, one almost like an axe, all with wickedly sharp edges, though coated with none of the compound designed to poison vampires. He admired the cunning of hiding important weapons in such a manner.

He slapped the two largest on the counter beside the meat.

"Why the fuck are you in my kitchen?" Vee's mate's bark echoed around the tile and metal room, and Owen jumped.

Kimi had decreed this food room Bruce's territory. However, she had also decreed no one, family-team or Owen, went hungry. And he required human food to court his mate.

Perhaps Vee's mate would aid Owen, as Josh had. Owen picked up the largest knife. "Kimi and Vee are hungry. I will make them the food. For Josh as well." Meat seemed a more acceptable apology to Kimi's team-brother than bright plants.

The human's face turned an alarming red. An impressive snarl began low in Bruce's chest, where Kimi had taught Owen to breathe from, and erupted. "You do not touch anything in this kitchen without my direct orders and supervision."

He dropped another leather bundle on the counter, and stalked forward. "There are dozens of snacks, clearly fucking labelled, plus whatever shit Josh smuggled in and hid, which I will find."

Vee's mate pointed at a board with writing, on the food preservation unit. "You don't fuck with my meal planning, and waste ingredients."

Finally coming toe-to-toe with Owen, Bruce barked, "And you sure as hell never, ever touch my damn knives."

Owen turned away, shoulders drooping. He understood the other's anger. Knives were vital weapons, and he wouldn't steal food or weapons from Kimi's family-team. He must discover another way to win her attention, and do the apologizing.

Bruce followed Owen, nearly walking over Owen's heels, aggression enveloping him like a dust cloud. "Haul your overgrown ass out of my kitchen, don't ever screw around in here again, or I'll put you on the damn menu. Out!"

The snarl burst out of Owen, and he whipped to face Vee's mate. Pulling himself tall and towering over the other. "You will not."

"Nice fucking try. You think you can intimidate me?" Bruce jabbed Owen in the stomach. "I am engaged to a vampire with minimal exposure to the real world and no filter."

Jab. "More importantly, I'm engaged to a *non-Jewish* vampire with minimal exposure, no filter, and my *entire* family is involved in planning a ceremony to rival the last royal wedding. You don't even rate on my shit-to-worry-about radar."

Jab. "Out, out, *out.*" The human's voice had risen with each word, ending on a bellow that made Owen's ears ring.

"Guys." Vee's calm voice floated over the charged atmosphere.

He found himself once more between his mate and Kimi's sister. Josh and the ancient vampire crowded behind them.

Owen bent his head to Kimi, shame and confusion swamping him. "I will not take his knives. *But I'm not food.*"

She herded him to the outer edge of the room, and whisper-signed. "Bruce doesn't intend to use you as food. He wasn't being literal, but using a dramatic type of speech, hyperbole, to emphasize his point."

Frustration eclipsed his shame. "Why is this speech so confusing? Food is food. *People* are *not* food."

"C'mon with me." Josh sidled between Kimi and Owen. "Let's take a beat."

His body needing to move, to burn off the emotions, and do so before he displeased Kimi, Owen followed. Josh circled the outdoor and water area, stopping at a square space with a tall pole, a net hanging from it. He scooped a ball from the bench that divided the square from the other space.

"Bruce gets intense, but don't take it personally. Just sorta nod and ignore him, and he'll get over it. He was a civi once. Now, he's Company all the way, where it matters, and I'd trust him with my life any day. I have, more times than I can keep track of," Josh said, bouncing the ball from hand to hand.

Kimi's team-brother was once again offering Owen aid, despite Owen's actions on the practice field. "I did not fully understand the rules for fight-sparring, and how to train with those who don't intend me harm, and that I don't intend to harm. I wished to do the apologizing to you with making food."

"Gotcha." He balanced on his toes, and threw the ball so that it went into the net.

"I don't know this training exercise, either," Owen admitted. "Nor the proper way to apologize, and not offend you. Or the rules with—with people. This, I'm not good at. Peopling and speaking." He slumped to the bench, studying the dark surface under his feet.

"We're cool. Seriously. We're all only human, and humans make mistakes. Apologize, learn from it, and then do better next time." Josh echoed Kimi's earlier speech.

When Owen looked up, Josh had his fist out for thumping.

Owen bumped knuckles, even as more guilt swallowed him. He wasn't human. Josh provided him aid, while Owen was lying to him.

Kimi's team brother looked at Owen, rubbing a hand over his hair, almost as short as Owen's. Probably reading Owen's guilt.

He let the ball drop, putting a foot on it to stop it rolling. "Look, I can't even begin to wrap my head around the shit you've been through, and what those skanky vampires did. I can't imagine being alone like that all these years."

"There were others." This, Owen could be truthful about.

"Ah, hell. I hadn't even though about teammates or friends you lost. I'm sorry, man." Josh sat beside him. "Listen, my brother would be a good person for you to talk to. He and his teammate Matteo. Jace and Matteo both lost their original teams, too. They understand survivor's guilt, and trying to make a place for yourself from scratch. Doctor Jill and the other therapists are always available when you're ready, but sometimes talking to people who've walked the path you're on is what you need. Let me see if they're free."

Josh pulled out one of the phone devices, thumbs moving almost as fast as Kimi's.

Owen sifted through Josh's words. The part about making a new place for himself, that was key.

When Josh flipped the phone sideways, and propped it on the back of the bench, Owen squeezed in beside him.

An image appeared, two human males indoors on one of the long, fluffy chairs. Boxes and cables like the one in the gathering room here surrounded them.

"Hey." The one who spoke—Owen glanced to confirm Josh was still beside him, not somehow vanished and reappeared in the strange room.

Josh laughed, the sound warm and lacking the bite of those instances handlers and lab helpers laughed at Owen. "I forgot to warn you. Jace and I are twins."

"Visual proof here, I'm the smoother, hotter brother," the other, Jace, the not-Josh said. When Owen concentrated, the difference in timbre and tone between the pair came clear.

"Whereas, I'm the GOAT as far as the peak of agent attractiveness." The speaker beside Jace was large, wider and thicker than Owen. The sleeves had been removed from his shirt, heavily muscled arms visible. "I'm Matteo."

"I'm gonna need some empirical evidence to support your greatest of all time claim," Josh said.

Owen detected no challenge in either human's voice or posture, toward each other or Owen. He tried out *polite*, which seemed to have little to do with observable fact, a ritual between humans to prevent offense or fights. "I find you all equally great."

"Guys, this is Owen."

"Back at you."

Owen checked with Jace.

"They mean they think you're also great." Josh turned to the screen. "Owen hasn't been exposed much to human day-to-day shit, slang and pop-culture."

Owen suspected Josh was now being polite. "I lived in runs, or the lab cell, never around humans. Vampires are jerks."

"We heard from Kimi that you had some moves when it came to killing vamps. Thanks for having her back, escaping and torching that damn site," Jace said.

"I will always have her back and follow her, and kill every vampire we find, except for hers. I am better at fighting than being human." He never would've been so foolish as to admit to a weakness with his batch, or the vampires. Josh and the rest of Kimi's family-team didn't take advantage of each other, or torment those they lived with for dominance.

An ache opened in Owen. Not the dark one from when he had nothing but labs and fighting until he was disposed of as defective. A new kind where he saw something good, that he wanted.

"Vampires are sadistic fucking monsters," the huge soldier added, and leaned so his face filled the device. "I'm sorry as hell that they held and tortured you. We can't erase that shit, but we'll help you however you need now. You deserve some support."

"I—don't wish to be alone." For the first time, Owen *wanted* others around him. Like Josh. Like these two, Josh's batch-family. Not only because of needing to fit in so as to be with his mate, but for himself. "I wish to fight for a family-team, instead of only fighting beside others like me to harm the civilian humans and their young."

A hand grasped his shoulder. Josh squeezed, gently instead of in anger. Yet another comfort gesture. "You're home."

Far away, Jace cleared his throat, as if enemy bits were stuck in it. His eyes were shiny, as was the other's, Matteo. "You're where you belong. We fight for family. We'll help with whatever you need."

"I need to learn how to be a true human. To be civilized."

* * *

MANY MINUTES LATER, the sun long gone and small night creatures scurrying around the deserted training area, Matteo sat back. "That's what civilized and human means for us. It ain't the same as the civi world, but being real, civis

AGENT OF CHANGE

confuse us on the regular. They don't always act the way you'd expect. Bruce is a decent source of info on them, but he gets weird about it sometimes."

"Yeah, he has this thing about the Company using us because we're raised to help humanity. Like, we're really supposed to believe that never having to think about housing, education, and careers is bad, and there's anything in the civi world as important as policing cryptids? Or as much of a rush?" Jace said.

That got a round of snorts from the other soldiers.

Including from Owen. "Other humans do not understand. They're like cubs, confused and helpless."

"We're only a text or call away," Matteo said, sprawling back on the long seat, arms along the top. "Got any other questions before we knock off tonight?"

Owen had been correct in trusting the rest of Kimi's family-team. They treated Owen as if he was one of them, with respect. Helping him, and not laughing over the many things he didn't know, or becoming angry over his questions.

Checking the darkness, night vision showing him the outlines of animals, he looked around. He'd already established that the others were indoors, Kimi and the old vampire together, him speaking in their second language, and Vee watching her mate in the food area.

Owen still edged closer to the screen, lowering his voice. Trusting his new family-team wouldn't mock him and could help with this as well.

Picking up on his body language as skilled fighters should, they all mimicked him.

"I wish to know about mating, and human customs," he said.

"Mating? Like sex?" Jace rested his elbows on his knees. "Huh. Hadn't thought of that."

"It's a good question, though," his brother added. "Where do you want to start? What questions in particular?"

"I have tried the most important mating cues. Smelling appealing," he nodded at Josh, acknowledging his contribution. "Displaying my large forearms, and gazing into her eyes to touch her soul. Kimi isn't recognizing them. Am I performing them incorrectly?"

Josh made a strangling noise, like a ghoul when Owen wrapped his hands around its throat.

On the screen, his new family-team's eyes grew large.

"Kimi?" Jace said.

"They aren't year mates, so no worries there," Matteo said, then hooted and slapped the chair arm. "You read the *Bros Read Romance* series."

"The first two books only. I consulted others from Kimi's library, though."

"Was that what the kitchen thing was tonight?" Josh turned his stare on Owen.

"Yes, to prepare fancy mate food, and apology food for you."

"Okay. So, Kimi." Jace rubbed his face. Which was very smooth, like his brothers.

So was Owen's, after using the donated bathing supplies.

"Yeah, I can see that. Let's start with what do you know about sex? Uh, mating?" Josh asked.

"That asking is most important."

They all nodded, and encouraged, Owen continued. "To ask about birth control, and disease, and to be honest. I have no disease. I don't understand the birthing control."

"That's any means to prevent pregnancy. I'll show you the most common later," Josh said. "Most female agents have implants that prevent ovulation. Kimi does."

Ovulation Owen understood, the time when females were brought in with males of his kind.

"What else?" Jace took up the conversation.

"That I must bring my mate pleasure first. And that clits are sacred."

Matteo did the hoot again, then grunted as his teammate ground an elbow in his stomach. "C'mon, dude. Business first."

"Right. Sorry," Matteo said. "But yeah, you are completely correct so far."

"I also have questions about other ways of pleasing a mate. And the ways I should tell her what pleases me."

"Do you *know* what you like?" Jace was as intense as his twin had been during the sparring.

"I was never allowed to mate." Heat flushed Owen's face at admitting how defective he was.

"Fuuuck." Jace's eyes grew larger.

This time, Matteo shoved his team-sibling. "No shame there."

From the corner of his eye, Owen dared check Josh's opinion.

"Hey, all true. There was a point where none of us had had sex, either. That's perfectly normal. Some agents aren't into sex at all. I'll get you some books and diagrams, the ones that we were trained with." He gripped Owen's shoulder again.

Relief flooded Owen. Of course there were training images, in order to learn. He understood this type of instruction.

Matteo nodded along. "What he said. Basically, just choose a time when you're both chill, and not stressed, and talk to Kimi. Tell her how you feel. Then, she'll say yes or no. You can't get offended and pushy if she says no, though."

"I will respect her wishes."

"And just because she says yes once—"

"Doesn't mean I can touch her again without asking."

"Exactly. You're doing great." Matteo gave him the thumbs-up, and the other two did the same.

Owen was gratified by his family-team's response. They were also most excellent. Now, they were part of his family-team, and he would kill to defend and aid them as he would Kimi and her sister.

"Dude. You realize what this means, right?" Josh did a happy bounce much like Kimi's.

"Leverage." Jace sounded pleased, understanding his twin.

"Holy sh— uh, shit." Matteo winced, as if he expected to be reprimanded. "We have leverage over Kimi."

"Have you ever investigated the phrase *too stupid to live*?" Vee's mate appeared out of the darkness behind the bench.

Owen tensed, so absorbed in speaking with his new family-team, he hadn't listened for enemies sneaking up. He waited for Bruce to growl again, remembering Josh's words on not responding to the territorial mate.

"Think about it." Josh held up a finger. "Pay back." Then a second finger. "No more freaky marine life sex gifs as surprise screensavers. No more hacking and joining in private text conversations." He held up a final finger. "You will never have to worry about weird glow-in-the-dark underwear birthday gifts again. Ever. This could even extend to your brother, and you never having to explain our sisters' equally weird gifts again. The possibilities are *limitless*."

"Jesus Fucking Christ." Vee's mate shook his head, the outdoor lights glinting off the pieces of glass covering his eyes. "It's like watching evolution in action. And you bunch will not be surviving to contribute your DNA to the next generation."

"Might be worth it."

"It's in all your best interests to think twice before you pull that trigger. Here. You missed dinner thanks to your training-virgins seminar. Movie later." He thumped two plates on the bench between Owen and Josh, then handed Owen utensils. "Stay the fuck out of my kitchen. Convince these idiots they aren't in Kimi's league. They are right about the rest of the sexual advice, though."

CHAPTER 18

imi

I PILED cushions on the couch, including the fuzzy one Owen petted earlier, as he and Josh finally wandered in, Josh extra chill. For the first time, Owen didn't have that hair-trigger watchfulness, like he was primed to fight for his life. Muscles relaxed, he seemed a different kind of confident, replying to one of Josh's comments, corners of his eyes crinkled as he grinned.

He held himself like this was home, and he was hanging out with a friend. Turned out, a happy Owen was as magnetic as the dynamic version that had owned the obstacle course this morning.

Since my brother was a people-person, I'd taken the hands-off approach after the whole kitchen dust-up. I trusted Josh to talk Owen down. He'd perfected his technique on Bruce. First when the cult celebrity figure had landed on a cryptid's hit list and in our ultra-utilitarian under the radar compound, then later when Vee returned as a vampire. My brother was amazing at relating to people in crisis, and offering them ways to deal with the upheaval and stress of adapting to an alien environment.

So when Josh gave me a smug, toothy smile, I made a note to go easy on him after he tried whatever adorable plan he'd hatched to gain revenge on me. Ditto for Jace and Matteo, his co-culprits. Jace's phone log showed the guys had been instrumental in Josh's heart to heart with Owen, though I wasn't sure what the topic had been.

I might even cancel the requisition form where I'd subbed in flannel trapper hats with furry earflaps for Josh's usual sniper baseball caps.

Patting the couch as Owen drifted my way, I scooched to open up more space. He sat beside me, attention bouncing from Vee and Josh's rock-paper-scissors solution to who got to choose tonight's entertainment, to Bruce and Stavros' entrance, Bruce juggling three bowls of movie popcorn.

His version, at least, purple heritage kernels filling the bowl, a dusting of pink salt on their surface.

Bypassing me, he handed Owen one. "This is a snack, extra food between meals if you're hungry. Popcorn, in this case."

Owen cradled the bowl more like its contents were dusted with gold. "Thank you."

Which basically confirmed that Bruce had been privy to at least part of whatever had transpired outside with the guys. His cutting me off at the door when I started to call Owen and Josh in for dinner had been telling, but not conclusive.

His rare patience now was absolute proof.

Stavros took the opposite end of the couch instead of his usual spot in the heavy, formal wingback chair that we'd bought for him, a reproduction of what was popular during his human lifetime. The narrow-eyed look he graced Owen with had me wondering if our papá hadn't also accidentally eavesdropped.

He did his best to maintain our privacy. And probably his sanity. But strong emotions from one of us automatically drew his attention, partially a Master vampire thing, partially a father thing.

The giant flatscreen over the fake gas fireplace blossomed to life.

"We are to see training images?" Owen asked, shifting so we were shoulder to shoulder.

"Nah, these are for fun," Josh said as he sprawled in the other chair, legs taking up an unfair amount of floor space.

The opening strains of a pop tune performed by a chamber orchestra boomed, and a reproduction of a Regency London street blossomed.

"You'll love this, man. Trust me," Josh added.

Josh had won the showdown with Vee, and chosen tonight's viewing. Half of the reason he loved the series was the eerie similarity between him and the first season's extremely attractive lead actor playing the duke. But it was a great show.

Owen had moved to the edge of the couch, almost hanging off. "What is this? I have never seen these uniforms, or vehicles powered by animals before."

Vee caught my eye and mouthed, "Whoa, his first time?"

Because, of course Owen wasn't familiar with movies and shows, anything meant for pleasure, except the stolen books he hoarded.

"This is fiction, something created just for enjoyment. This show is based on life several hundred years ago in England, another country. It follows an imaginary family's life," Vee said. She checked with Stavros. "I'm not sure how historically accurate it is."

Our papá *harrumphed*. One of the most human sounds he'd *ever* uttered. "It is far too generous with regards to city sanitation of the era, and far, far too loose in regards to acceptable behavior tolerated among those not wed before God."

Our adopted father had spent his human life in a stricter culture, a devout Catholic Christian, and had absorbed their unfathomable attitudes about sex. Especially sex between unmarried partners.

He full-on glared at Bruce, which was normal. Though once Bruce proposed to my sister, Stavros had scaled back his growling and pointed remarks every time Vee and Bruce got handsy.

He switched his displeasure to Josh, then to Owen, which *wasn't* normal.

Owen was oblivious, entranced by the actors. I removed the untouched bowl from his hands as it tilted, dribbling kernels on the rug.

I scooted around in my corner, legs folded and knee against Owen's warm thigh, watching him as he watched his first T.V. episode. Every emotion showed, his expression unguarded, another new development. The only time he took his attention off the screen was to check in with me, sharing his wonder and excitement. I couldn't help getting caught up in his mood, seeing the show from his fresh perspective.

The episode ended, and Owen jerked like he'd forgotten where he was. We'd ended up basically leaning against each other, neither of us noticing when we'd inched closer. At my smile, he relaxed again. "This is like a book that moves and speaks."

His enthusiasm was pure and adorable as he angled toward me. "Do you have another of these—"

"Episodes," I signed. "And yes. This is the first of two seasons. A season is similar to a single book."

"Ah. Book one and two."

"Exactly. Do you want to watch another?"

"Yes." In his excitement, he nearly vaulted into my lap. His thigh pressed against mine, and his arm went behind me, along the back of the sofa.

His face was inches from mine, full lips even closer. The ocean and sand notes of one of Josh's body scrubs mixed with the popcorn. Which should've been weird, but suited Owen.

He blinked, long lashes tickling my cheek. All on its own, my hand rose and brushed against his chin. "You smell nice," I mouthed.

He twisted more into me, blocking out the rest of the room. His free hand grazed the corner of my jaw. "I also like the way you smell."

At Stavros' grumble, we both twitched. Owen's face colored and he pulled away.

The screen came back to life as Josh flicked to the next episode.

This whole keeping things platonic with Owen was already more difficult than I'd predicted. I wanted to stay curled up on the couch, with his hands on me. Which meant I needed to be smart, and anyplace other than the couch. I stood, and tucked one of the floor pillows into my spot.

When Owen half rose, question in his eyes, I pressed on his shoulder. Hand staying a beat too long as I enjoyed the hard muscle under my palm. "Stay and watch. I have a couple of things I want to catch up on. Come tell me about the show later."

* * *

210

A KNOCK SOUNDED on my door, and I tapped the one earbud I had in, and stretched enough to open the door.

Josh leaned in. "I'm heading to bed."

I rested my paintbrush on the palette. "Owen?"

"He is most of the way through the first season. I showed him how to work the remote. Stavros already bailed, and Vee and Bruce were behind me."

I pulled my paint splattered smock off, and one-armed, hugged my brother, then signed, "Thank you for big-brothering him."

"I really like the guy. So do Jace and Matteo. Kinda like he was meant to be part of the team from the beginning, and now he's back where he belongs, you know?" He stared at me, like he was trying to project and plant an idea directly into my brain.

As Josh left, I rolled around ideas and opinions. My brother was firmly on Team Owen. In the most unlikely turn of events in history, so was Bruce.

I swirled my brush through the paint, replaying the moment on the couch. Odds were in the ninety-plus percentile that Owen really was attracted to me. I was unambiguously attracted to him.

Sex wasn't the same as a romantic relationship, and was *very* Company. As my sister pointed out, sex could also be therapeutic and healing. The source was different, but we both had ragged emotional wounds. Maybe I was looking at our situation from the wrong perspective.

We all kept underestimating the isolated, empty life Owen had been forced into, like not even thinking that, duh, he hadn't known movies existed, much less had access to them.

Without that kind of exposure we took for granted, Owen had no preexisting ideas about what was and wasn't acceptable or normal. Thus he could be way, way more adaptable to our agent culture than I was giving him credit for, not less. He rolled with everything we'd introduced him to so far, assuming our way was the normal one.

Vee and I had gotten carried away with the fantasy tropes from our favorite books, foisting them off on Owen, when in reality, he was simply unsocialized and unaware of social norms, but ready to absorb ours.

If I showed him that for agents, sex wasn't a commitment, but for fun, a physical connection, and comfort...we could both have what we wanted. There was also a high chance the draw we felt was based on curiosity, and would fade once we satisfied that curiosity.

The unsettling push-pull that nagged me all day settled. Not gone, but back in its corner, and behaving. Creativity reinvigorated, I got lost in my project, paint guiding me to the shape it was meant to be.

I finally dropped my brush in the cleaning jar, and stood back. The first layer wasn't my usual whorls and swirls. This one was jagged, edges sharp and wild. I stretched, the day's bruises twinging, and opened the door. Time for more Tylenol, and arnica gel. Plus checking on Owen before bed. Easing him into our no-strings lifestyle could start in the morning.

He sat on the other side of the hall, back to the wall and a book open. His attention snapped from the page to me.

Again, he surprised me, leaving the streaming series he'd been immersed in, in favor of my boring door and another non-boring novel. I propped my hip against the doorjamb and signed, "You could have knocked."

"You had work. You said to speak with you of the episodes."

"That wasn't an order, plus, you can always knock. If I'm busy, I'll tell you, but asking is *always* permissible."

"I will remember. I am *always* happy to wait for you."

Somehow, I didn't think the statement was a figure of speech. More of Owen's literalness.

"I had a book." He held it up, this one a spicy contemporary. "Josh reported this story was very useful. He is most helpful."

A high-heat story instead of a paranormal worked for me. More sex, less fate. "Did you enjoy more episodes of the show?"

Owen went from Serious Owen to animated, and stood, using his finger as a bookmark. Like his enthusiasm required a physical outlet, the same way my creativity manifested. "It was most excellent. Josh and Vee explained many of the new words and customs, and how to operate the remote device. I watched all of the first season."

"Congratulations on mastering binge watching." Toss up whether Owen's happiness over such a normal activity, or my siblings' drive to include him, brought a warm wash, like a giant mug of Marshall's hot cocoa.

"I will not distract you more." He opened his book, preparing to sit opposite my room again, although his gaze darted to the open door, then dropped like looking was forbidden.

No way was I leaving him sitting alone. "I'm finished painting for now."

"Painting." His forehead scrunched.

Everyone knew my studio was off limits when I was working on a new project. People looking at a partially completed work, commenting or asking questions, ruined my ability to finish. Like their ideas had infected the image, and now it was forever altered and couldn't take the form it was preordained for. I still curled my fingers, inviting Owen, and went back inside.

He was on my heels, only his unearthly reflexes saving him from walking on me. He tucked the book in one of the utility pant's pockets, circling the room like this was a patrol. There were smaller canvasses prepped and stacked on a table, that he seemed to sniff, then bypass.

He squatted by the corner bookshelf, studying the origami attempts at creating a Golden Retriever, scattered down the length of a shelf. He repeated the leaning in and sniffing when he got to the cleaning station, and my linseed oil and solvents. "This is your scent."

I'd never considered that my paints had worked their way into my pores over the years. That Owen recognized the scent, and associated it as mine, was kind of perfect.

He rose, motion all controlled energy, and continued. When he got to the new painting, he stopped fast enough his rubber soles squeaked. His fingers hovered over the canvas as he leaned close.

I moved back into his line of sight, and tapped his elbow, before signing. "Careful. The paint is still wet."

"What is this?"

"An abstract painting. Art."

He cocked his head, waiting for more. "I don't know *art*. What does it do?"

I bumped chaining every Syndicate vampire out in the summer sun to the top of my list. Art was—it was integral to being human.

I stood with him, and attempted to translate a vast concept into words. "Art is another way of expressing yourself. It's meant to make you feel what its creator felt, or represent a moment in time. Often, it's meant to be beautiful and pleasing to look at."

I took his hand, holding it just above the canvas, guiding it along the strokes of paint.

"Ah. Then you are art. You are alpha leader, and brilliant with a great library of excellent books, and a vicious fighter.

You make me feel many things. New things." This close, when he turned his head, his lips grazed my temple.

I shivered, the best kind of goosebumps racing across my skin. Suddenly hyper-aware of the feel of his rough hand in mine, the heat of him where we touched, chest and hip. My nipples pebbled.

His pupils expanded, making his dark eyes seem bottom-less. Deep and unfathomable like the ocean when our year mate Ridge took me out in Galveston, teaching me to surf. So many things going on under the surface that most people never caught a glimpse of.

He inhaled, and angled into me. "I would like to mate-touch you. Have sex. If you would also like to. You can touch me. I have learned tonight the best way to tell you my desires is talking."

Blinking, I processed his speech, heat spinning to life in my core. My sleepiness vanished on a burst of potential. And lust. Definitely lust.

Blunt and direct was pure Company, and I'd been right that he was adaptable. I could totally work with this. "You had trouble communicating something earlier?"

He nodded.

Oooh. The pieces clicked together.

"Is that why you were staring at me in the office?" I understood the frustration of finding a means to communi-cate when other people didn't grasp your intent.

"Yes. I am not accomplished at touching your soul or having desirable forearms as I have no sleeves to roll up, though I am learning to smell uniquely wonderful."

That he'd put such effort into connecting with me...

Lifting my face so he could lip read clearly, I turned his hand upside down, and skimmed my fingers along his arm from his palm to his elbow. His hair rose in a wave. "You have great forearms, and we'll requisition you some long-sleeved shirts. You do indeed smell nice. I find all of you attractive."

"I have no diseases."

"I know. HQ routinely runs a panel of tests along with the DNA verification when agents return from captivity. I checked yours."

Proving again that he was more agent than civilian and that my sexy-times for fun moment of inspiration was a go, instead of protesting about privacy laws, he nodded. "Excellent."

I'd also promised him that I would clarify new concepts, not make assumptions.

I let go of his hand, signing and speaking so there was no mistake. "You understand that you are in control of your body? It doesn't belong to anyone but you, and you choose who can and can't touch it, and when. That is always your choice. You don't owe anyone sexual contact, including me."

"You gave me my freedom. I wish to use it now with you, touching you, and for you to touch me, if you desire." He frowned and shifted an inch away. "Josh is to give me images to study so I do it properly, but I haven't seen them yet."

Oh.

Oh.

My brothers' group conversation had been a sex-ed initiation.

I had considered whether he'd been forced or used. That he'd never had sex, not so much. He'd been taught questions invited punishment, yet I was important enough to him that he'd gone looking for information, putting himself out there in a way no one else ever had.

Then he'd trusted me enough to be honest, and vulnerable, when in his experience, vulnerability equaled weakness, and led to attacks.

I tapped his chin, getting his attention. "I think you're

equally amazing. And while books are invaluable, they are only one way of learning. Hands-on research is also valid."

His attention took on a laser focus. "Like training by doing missions, not watching slides. I also enjoy the hands-on."

My brain threw up image after image of Owen's hands on me. "I prefer more active, sweaty foreplay."

"Foreplay?" He tried out the word.

"The things or moments that make you aroused and interested in sex—in mating. Your performance on the obstacle course? That was sexy."

"Our sparring was also—most sexy."

"Wow, was it. The way you followed me in tai chi, learning as we moved?"

He made a grumbly-growly sound of agreement, pivoting so we were face to face.

"We can explore sex the same way, if you like. Sex is similar to art—different for every person, even from one encounter to the next between the same people, but equally enjoyable."

His voice dropped to a deeper bass. "I will explore with you. I am interested in the kissing."

Me, too, especially with the way he looked at me, like I was glazed in chocolate, his favorite treat. "Tell me if there's anything I do that you don't enjoy, okay?"

"You will also tell me."

We were totally on the same page. And I wanted to experience Naked Owen.

I joined him, skating my hands up his chest to his shoulders. I tilted my head and he bent the fraction to meet me for his first ever kiss. I kept it soft, learning the feel of him while he did the same with me.

Like with our sparring, Owen mirrored me. When I traced his full lips with my tongue, he made another interested grumbly-growl and my breath caught. I nibbled his lower lip, then traced the join. He opened, and our tongues tangled, stroking and exploring. He pressed into me. Then paused, question on his face, asking me if this was okay.

I nudged his thigh, and slid my knee between his legs, as eager to get closer as he was. He cupped my shoulder, pulling me tight, his thumbs running back and forth across my collarbone. Switching, I drew my palms down his chest.

I tugged at his tee, untucking the cotton, and rested the tips of my fingers on his waistband, my turn to ask.

He let go of me long enough to grab my hands, sliding them under his shirt. I touched hot skin, and muscles under my hands clenched. He felt even better than my highly creative brain had imagined. As I mapped out his chest and stomach, over hard abs and raised scars, he took over.

The kiss went from exploratory to scorching, all teeth and tongue. His big hand traveled down my spine, stopping in the small of my back. He pressed lightly, asking me in our developing shorthand.

I wiggled against him, grinding. The room too hot. His groan reverberated through me. Breaking the kiss, I leaned back and touched his shirt, and mouthed, "May I?"

He grabbed the hem, and jerked the tee over his head. "You can look and touch, always."

I took my time, gaze tracking over him, hands following. Fingers bumping over abs so defined he could've been one of those classical sculptures by Bernini or some other Renaissance master. Measuring the width of his chest and shoulders against mine, my breasts ached, ready to be touched the same way.

I kissed the center of his chest, over the healed white line of the scalpel cut. Honoring his wounds and perseverance, and hopefully reclaiming them, building new memories over the old.

"You are better than chocolate and many books. You are better than freedom." His words whispered against my ear, sending goosebumps over my skin.

Not wanting to put enough space between us to speak, I showed him how important he was, dotting kisses on the myriad smaller cuts, punctures, and claw marks.

My lips brushed over his defined pec, by the nipple, and he inhaled, splayed hand dipping lower to cup my ass, fingers strong and possessive. I was okay with possessive tonight, and traced the areola, circling closer. Finally flicking my tongue over the broad, flat bud.

"Yes. This is—more of this," he ask-ordered.

I switched between sides, playing. Enjoying how he responded to me, more completely than any past lover. Also enjoying his obvious pleasure. Slowly, gauging, I drew my hand down, leaving dark skin, skipping to heavy cotton. Finally cupping him.

His hips twitched and he shoved into my hand. I stroked him through the sturdy fabric, and his nostrils flared like it was difficult to breathe, lids dropping to half-mast. "Kimi."

His demand rumbled through me, and silky dampness slicked my core. Popping the tab on his pants, I worked the zipper down in increments, knuckles brushing along his erection.

As for whether he favored boxers or briefs? Neither. A narrow trail of black hair led to his cock in all its considerable glory. I finished unzipping, and it sprang free, as thick and impressive as the rest of Owen.

I circled the base, sliding my hand down the hard, velvety length. Ending with a firm squeeze and tracing around the head and slit. He threw his head back, tendons in his neck standing out.

Then caught my wrist. "I wish to do as we did during the

slow tai chi training. To know what pleases you. For you to touch yourself in this way."

I flexed my hand, and he quickly released me to sign. "The word for self-pleasure is masturbate." I was proud my fingers didn't shake.

"I have done this before."

Thank Stavros' and Bruce's god. The idea of Owen nude and orgasming sent a shot of pure, molten lust straight between my legs. "You have inspired ideas, Owen."

He fingered my sleeve. "I would like to remove your clothing."

I held my arms up, and grinned as a yes. Far more gently than with his own, he hooked his thumbs under the edge of my shirt, making sure his callused palms rasped along my stomach and the edges of my breasts on the way up, pupils expanding at my shiver. He laid the shortie tee on the stool behind me that I occasionally used, then repeated the process with the simple yellow sports bra.

He knelt in front of me, hands spread, fingers tucked under the short's waistband, and brought them down my stomach, over my hips, thumbs converging as he went. Sliding together, and grazing over my mound.

Instead of dropping the shorts, he continued, down my thighs, cupping as he went. Tickling the backs of my knees and calves, the mix of playful and dangerous almost too much. He looked up at me, those thick lashes framing raw desire, and hope.

I stroked over his soft brows, and cheeks. He deserved to know that he was special, and that I saw that and him. And even though it wasn't necessary, used his shoulder as a brace when he lifted each of my feet, removing the shorts. Leaving me in the plain yellow striped boy cut briefs.

"You are the best art." He kissed over my core, breath

heating the thin cotton, and, *wow*. "I wish to paint you." He surveyed the room, brow wrinkling.

I'd indulge Owen's explorations any way open to me. I tipped my head for him to follow, crossing to the short unit tucked beside the window, and pulled out a storage drawer. Bottles of the primary color non-toxic acrylic, fat markers, colored pencils, kid sized brushes, and squares of poster board took up the entire drawer, supplies I kept for when our adopted nieces, Bruce's bio nieces, visited the condo the Company kept downtown for when his family and friends were in town.

Owen fit his hands around my waist. I nodded and he lifted me onto the long metal and wood table holding my cameras and gear, delicately situating me on one of the few clear spots.

I wanted more art, too. As he turned away, I caught a pocket and tugged, then signed, "Pants, please?"

He shucked them, as unselfconscious as any agent, and went back to his original goal, sorting through the art supplies. Muscles rippled in his back, waist narrowing to a stellar ass that I wanted to sink my short nails into.

He returned with bottles of paint, no brushes or paper. He unscrewed lids, staring at me with so much heat I squirmed against the table.

Then he dipped two fingers in a jar, caught and cradled my wrist with his other hand. I should've realized how literal he was in saying he wanted to paint me. He pressed fingertips against my bicep, and slowly drew two parallel red stripes from upper arm to my elbow. My gaze followed the path like I couldn't look away.

He frowned, and wiped fingers on himself. He chose again, but only dipped one finger. This time, he put his empty hand on my forehead, but like he was shading my eyes. Serious, he showed me the blue on his fingertip. "I will not get paint in your hair. Don't touch a heroine's hair, don't get sticky food in it, or dunk it under water is also a rule."

His absolute care with me kept melting away at that barrier inside me.

With the precision of Liv planning a mission, he scooted his hand higher, protecting the baby hairs that had escaped my top knot, then lightly tapped between my brows. He swiped the excess on his chest, paint highlighting ridges and planes, then repeated his process, skating green lines along the top of my dominant hand, and up and over my joints.

He opened the final jar, and drew arches on my chest, over my breasts, not touching even as I sat forward, offering. The pressure of his fingertips, and the cool damp of the paint were almost too much. He finished by rubbing the last low on my ribcage.

He stood back, the same way I did when checking out a painting. "Yes. This is good art for you."

"It is lovely. Thank you," I signed. Wanting more Owen, more of how his mind and creativity had survived, I asked, "Do the colors represent anything, other than being pretty?"

He touched my arm, well away from the wet paint. "This shows you are a vicious fighter-leader.

"This because you are smart, with many plans and books." He brushed my temple.

My hand next. "And you make art, and tiny magic windigos without the stink, and hidden platforms to watch the sky and for enemies."

"This?" I traced above the yellow.

"Freedom. You showed me freedom, and the caring, and this place that Josh calls my home." He frowned at my side. "All of these things must be from the heart, but the heart is easier to access here, between these ribs and up, not from the front like foolish cubs who don't know how to fight."

"We're taught as cadets to stab between those ribs at an

angle, too. Your first time creating art is wonderful. So are you." I spread my knees, and caught his hand, pulling him between them, starving to touch him again.

I rubbed around the streaks and splotches where he'd used himself as a cleaning rag. "You are all of those things. You're also a beautiful work of art, and not because of the paint."

"You enjoy my appearance." His chest puffed, pecs actually popping.

I rolled my lips in, squashing them together so I didn't laugh, and ruin his self-satisfied expression. Which changed as he gazed down at me.

He caught my hip, voice deeper. "Show me what pleases you."

I lifted and he hooked my briefs, pulling them down far faster than his earlier deliberate undressing, and dropped them where he'd tossed his clothing.

"I enjoy kissing, on the lips and all over my body. Nibbling. My neck and ears are especially sensitive." I drew my fingers over my jaw and neck, and cupped my breasts, tweaking and lightly stretching the nipples, his gaze glued to me. Both of us breathing faster. "Breasts."

Propping on my elbows, I let my knees drop to the sides, giving him a clear view. Showing off as much as Owen had. Wanting to affect him the same way he affected me. To make this as special as he was. Switching to one elbow, I glided my hand from under my breasts, down my stomach.

I paused to sign, "You, too. Show me what you want."

He fisted his erection, working it rough and fast. Speeding up as I circled my clit, alternating between swirling and the tapping that worked for me. Slipping a finger in, thumb still tapping. Watching Owen, scarred, covered in primary colors, and his pure belief that everything I did was right.

"You are aroused. Close." He stopped. "There is something I would like to do. From the book." His foot nudged his abandoned pants, and the contemporary he'd stashed in their pocket.

The author was one of my favorites, queen of wall sex. And outdoor sex. And desk sex. This story was her newest and contained some *fun* scenes, involving tongues and flavored oils. I stopped, and mouthed my vigorous agreement, getting that guy chuckle from Owen that they all seemed gifted with once puberty hit.

He closed the space between us, and caught my thighs. "I will not hurt you. Ever."

"I know." I lay flat, excitement building at the sex position he'd chosen. At the evidence of what I was doing to him.

He knelt, and raised my thighs. Hooking an ankle over his shoulder. Keeping eye contact, he took over where my fingers left off. His tongue circling and swirling around and over my clit. Varying the pressure and direction, as if he was hooked directly into my brain.

Heat and excitement spiraled under my navel, pressure building. With Owen's unwavering gaze on me, gauging every twitch, every breath. Stoking me higher, fierce pride in his eyes. I came, hard enough colorful floaters crowded my vision.

He held on, letting the waves crash through me, and allowing me come down on my own. Rubbing his cheek along my thigh, the scruff sending new, smaller sparkles coursing behind the first.

I drew in a deep breath, and sat up, Owen quickly sliding his hands over my hips to the small of my back, helping. This deserved my hands free. "You totally aced giving your partner an orgasm. You're great at it."

He propped his chin on my leg. Seeming content to watch me.

So not happening. "Your turn, please." I motioned for him to stand.

He rose in a smooth burst of power, one second kneeling the other on his feet, his cock bobbing.

I wiggled to the edge of the table, enunciating, "We don't have to rush. No one will disturb us." Or some vampire handler burst in on him, the rough, rushed way he'd touched himself fresh, like he had no privacy and no right to his own body.

Surprise flashed through his eyes, then the kind of pure happiness adults rarely let themselves show.

Wrapping my hand around his thick base, I stroked up, circling the head and catching drops of the pre-cum, slicking it back down his length. With my other hand, I cupped his balls.

He jerked, then stilled like he thought I'd stop. Instead, I increased the pressure, working him in firm strokes. Rolling his balls, watching his face, the way stomach muscles contracted, how his strong thighs clenched.

"What else?" I mouthed clearly. "You can ask. Do you prefer this, or would you like—"

"To be inside you. For us to be closer." He tensed again, expression wary, still expecting to be disciplined.

"Yes." I touched a camera bag, prepared to push everything out of the way.

Owen caught me, lifting me the way I would the camera, effortless. "I would also like my arms around you."

I nuzzled under his jaw, kissing where it met his neck. Hiding, because the simple request for human contact rocked me. I caught his cock, and lined us up, sliding onto it slowly.

His breathing hitched, and I wrapped my legs around his waist, locking my ankles. And my arms around his neck. As he supported my weight, I leaned away enough to catch his eye. To tell him that this was about him, too. That I saw him, and that what he wanted and needed mattered.

Thighs braced, I rose up, then slid down. Showing him. A quiver went through him and I nodded.

Understanding, the same way he had when he went down on me, his hips jerked. Finding a rhythm. Despite it being the first time he had been with someone, not rushing. His strong hips thrusting, arms wrapped around me, face showing no strain. Absolutely silent and intense.

I stretched, kissing him. My tongue matching his thrusts. I drew away, freeing one hand to catch his jaw, needing more contact. Getting lost in him as he did the same.

His motion, the deep, slow rolls, rubbed over my still sensitive clit. That same shimmering pleasure built again. I kept my eyes open, letting them show how much this meant, how much he meant to me.

His pace picked up, arms still steady, holding me like I was breakable. At odds with the raw desire and hunger painting his face. Muscles clenching as he came hard inside me.

I held on as the shudders crested, and slowed.

He shook, almost like he was shaking himself out of a dream.

This was very real. I caught his face, putting all my pride in him into a long, fierce kiss. I mouthed, "You are amazing."

He shifted my weight to one arm, scuffed fingers touching his lips. Then catching the back of my neck, putting us forehead to forehead. His breath tickled my face. "*You* are amazing."

"We are both fucking awesome." I wrapped my arms around him in a half hug.

He nuzzled under my jaw, holding me as the minutes ticked away, arms steady. Which had never really happened before. Not the being held part, but the part where I allowed it. My brain wasn't bored, and ready to find a new project. More importantly, there wasn't the sense of suffocating that popped up after sixty-seconds of such intense contact, the feeling like my partner was presuming more than I wanted to give.

Owen felt different. Here, his heart thumping against mine, breath lifting baby hairs along my temple, felt right. I legit didn't want it to end, but, biology. I kissed the end of his nose as apology, and leaned away to sign, "I need to clean up."

"I can take you to the bathing facility." His arms tightened, tucking me back in, which I also didn't hate.

"My room is fine."

He didn't bother putting me down. Or grabbing clothing, striding down the hall to my door, naked and determined. At least everyone else was already safely in their rooms.

Legs anchored around him, I leaned out and keyed in my code, door disengaging. He entered, pushing it closed behind us.

"This is good."

Like each movement was a fight, he lifted me off him, then set me on my feet. Letting go of me bit by bit. Face forlorn in the muted glow of the moon through my uncurtained window.

"Owen?"

"I want to keep touching. Not for the sex. Is such a thing allowed?"

My heart squeezed. I put myself in the splash of moonlight, and signed, quickly and clearly. "Yes. It's called cuddling. It can be an important part of sex, and relationships." The last word slipped off my fingers naturally.

And again, it felt right. The way a difficult line of code coming together did, or final shading that turned a random assortment of colors and brush strokes into a painting did.

So, the purely sex for fun experiment was an abject failure. My sisters swore my brain formulated plans and made decisions faster than anyone they knew. They were only partially correct.

Mostly, my brain didn't have space or patience for second-guessing. Waffling and second-guessing led to disaster—breaking formation because a cryptid *might* move in a different direction where I *might* intercept it.

In the last—I checked the tablet charging on the night-stand—in the last fifty-ish hours—I had caught feelings. Owen and I were involved, as far more than friends.

And I was great with that, because I wanted him close, where I could touch him, and he could cradle me like I was the most perfect thing he'd ever encountered. Later, I wanted to introduce him to every fun activity and experience I could think of, absorb his wonder and happiness, and watch him discover real freedom.

I cleaned us both up as he patiently watched, like he was learning a new skill, and crawled onto my bed, tossing the Van Gogh Waterlilies print blanket down in invitation.

Owen was in and beside me in another of those flashes of movement. I laid down, and he fit against my back. Curving in and covering me the way he had when protecting my back from the garage's door. Huge arms wrapped me up, his heart thudding against my back.

The top of my head fit under his chin perfectly. Instead of mild claustrophobia, or extreme annoyance at another person crowding me, physically and emotionally, muscles relaxed and I snuggled closer.

"Great at sex. Great at cuddling," I whispered to myself.

"You are also great at the sex and cuddling. Can we stay here until the breakfast meal?"

I stiffened. I hadn't signed. And there was no way Owen could have read my lips from behind me.

"You can hear me." I tested the impossible theory.

He froze, muscles rigid, more like the marble statue I compared him to earlier.

I jerked free, and rolled, straddling him, not bothering with signs, or helpfully leaning into the shaft of moonlight, or enunciating. "You can. You can *totally* hear me."

CHAPTER 19

wen

HE WENT STILL. But heart beating harder than after a batch fight. Being so close to her, the words she said during sex, the way she watched him and only him had captured him. Like falling into the T.V. series or a book, and forgetting he was a soldier, not human, where he was lost in the wonder of another world.

And Kimi was far more wondrous than books and series. More than all the books in her library.

Others couldn't hear her, not her human family-team, or even the ancient vampire. Because hearing her wasn't a human, or human turned vampire, ability. He couldn't lie directly to her, even if it meant she learned he wasn't human, and... he wouldn't consider what came after. "Yes. I have heard you."

"Since when?"

"In the lab, when you whisper-signed."

"The entire time."

He rolled his head to the side. Not brave enough to look his mate in the eye as she rejected him.

A warm hand caught his jaw and she whispered, "Look at me."

He obeyed. Because whatever Kimi wanted, he would always give her.

Head tilted, she examined him, her expression one he hadn't encountered.

"The lab. The experiments—the reprogramming they tried on you." Her hand drifted to the scar on his chest, then to the many on his arms. "This, and your enhanced hearing. Your agility. They did this to you."

He hunched in on himself.

Kimi lay flat on him, forcing him to pay attention, so close her nose hit the tip of his. His eyes threatened to cross, but he looked into hers.

"This isn't your fault. Or bad, or wrong. You had no say in the things they did to you." She rubbed her nose against his. "You were afraid to tell me, because first you didn't know me, or if you could trust me, then—you were afraid it would keep you from fitting in after the misunderstanding with Josh, weren't you?"

The shock was gone from her voice. He detected no aggression, or disgust. No anger. "I am different. I am not human like you."

She rolled off his chest. Clearly, hating him now that he had admitted what he was.

A light clicked on, a strange small one on a stand instead of in the ceiling, shaped like a many-legged sea creature, sitting on another wooden compartment by her bed. Instead of leaving or ordering him to, she scooted back, folding her legs to the side and facing him.

She rested a hand on him. Speaking in her rough-soft

whisper. "What they did to you doesn't make you less. It certainly doesn't make you not human. You're simply— human with a few add-ons.

He puzzled through, hope rising, as she continued, voice excited. "For now, this will be our thing, only between us. I need a bit to formulate the best reveal to the team. They will understand, too. I mean, hello? Vee and papá, and Kit on my sister's team."

Excitement to match her voice and happiness came off Kimi. His mate wasn't rejecting him. His muscles went lax, body understanding there was no longer an emergency

The same satisfaction as when they did the tai chi and sparring rode the air, when her ideas worked. "I assumed that either your diet or the surgical procedures accounted for the oddity in your bloodwork. This makes so much more sense. I should've guessed. That amino acid sequence plays a role in tissue regeneration, so theoretically the higher level is one of the mechanisms that allows your increased performance."

He understood little of what she said, his mate once again proving the smartest leader. All that mattered to him was that he now had a way to not lie, and still remain.

If he aided the family-team well enough, then they would also accept his differences, and his position among them. This truly could be his home. That he wasn't being completely truthful with Kimi, not telling her all the parts he was made of, rubbed at him, like too small boots on an all-night run.

But he would fight, killing many vampires, and do the thing Vee had explained tonight, when the hero in the T.V. had erred, and then corrected his mistake with the heroine. *Redeeming.* He would redeem his lie, doing the task he was created for, but now killing to help his family-team, his mate, and the weak, unprotected human civilians.

He sat, his back against the carved and painted board rising from the fluffy sleeping platform, and lifted Kimi into his lap, not able to stand even the small separation. Reveling in being able to touch and hold her. "I will fight beside you and Josh, and Vee, and Vee's loud mate, and your father-vampire. I will protect what is yours, and make you proud."

He bent, kissing her, memorizing the softness of her lips and skin, her scent that now mixed with his, proclaiming they were mates. "I will make more art, and swim in the tiny not-ocean with you. And bring you many, many more orgasms."

Kimi snort-laughed, and his heart did that funny new thing at having made her happy.

"Deal." She rested against him, head on his shoulder. She rubbed his chest, tracing designs. Not the same as during sex or sparring. Slow. Gentle. This was what the books meant by affection.

Love. This, wishing to spend time together, to make someone laugh, to learn about them, to touch and protect, and for them to do the same—now he understood love as well. He loved Kimi.

Sitting in the warm circle of light cast by an odd sea-creature shaped device, in a compound with vampires who weren't vampires as he'd known them but who instead helped and healed, and filled with the humans he had been taught hated and killed his kind for no reason, holding the leader of the most skilled of all the enemy soldiers, he, a creature made of other creatures and created with no emotions other than rage, was *happy*.

The smaller computer device beside the light chirped. Kimi swiveled, preparing to move off him and reach. He merely needed to lean to grab it, and presented it to her. He was rewarded when she used his chest as her backrest, swiping the screen and reading.

"One of our street informants. A member of their camp disappeared yesterday. Now they saw something climb and cling to the ceiling of a tunnel." She rolled off him. "Mysterious-ish disappearances and physics-defying apparitions. One-hundred-percent our thing."

"We will fight?" He came to his feet, disappointment changing to determination. He wanted more of Kimi and her affection, but this was a chance to begin the redeeming, and fight beside his mate.

Kimi's response was drowned out by pounding on the door, followed by Vee's raised voice. "My street contact just texted. Missing human and probable cryptid sighting. Weapon up."

Helpfully, he bellowed back. "Kimi has already been alerted. I will prepare."

Fingers snapped, and he turned to Kimi. Hairband between her teeth, she resorted to signing, hands moving far faster than usual.

"Kimi also says to cover your eyes," he yelled, opening the door and striding down the hall to his room and uniforms. There was a squeak, and a vampire-fast blur darting down the hall, followed by a door slamming. Later, he would ask Kimi about covering eyes.

Fully dressed, he waited until he heard her familiar footsteps, and fell in beside Kimi. The others joined them, crossing from the house's outdoor area, to the section Owen hadn't visited. They entered the first square metal building, the old vampire already there, laying out weapons.

The members lined up in front of the tall bench, attaching holsters and adding weapons.

"Do you have a specialty?" Josh asked, inspecting a matte black case, one of the long-range rifles inside, then snapping it closed.

"I am trained with all side arms, knives, basic explosives,

234

some surface to air and grenade launchers. I do not have your skill with sniper setups." Careful of how to better aid his new team-family with his abilities without revealing them before Kimi decreed, he said, "Reconnaissance, tracking in all terrain and conditions, and direct combat are my strongest skills."

"You're voting yes on including a non-Company agent on this call-out?" Vee's tone was professional, and she addressed the rest.

Owen caught no anger or deceit. She was truly asking for opinions.

Kimi looked at the old vampire, then at Vee, a brow up.

"Fair point on non-agent inclusion. However, I knew Stavros' capabilities and technique," Vee said. "We had trained and hunted together for over a year."

"Owen is fast, agile, responsive to a partner's position while engaging multiple targets, and understands chain of command," Kimi signed. "HQ sent out the report suggesting the Syndicate had observed enough Company missions to create a facsimile of our style. Having fought beside Owen, I believe the Syndicate has directly acquired a copy of our Academy curriculum. Basically, every guard in our direct escape route from the lab used our exact protocol. The building was almost a replica, down to the position of pinch points that could be sealed. I attribute any deviations to concessions for vampires' avoidance of sunlight, and greater nocturnal social cycle."

Absolute silence held for many heartbeats.

It was his role to support his mate, and leader. "The Syndicate considers your Company their greatest enemy. All training is based on how to defeat you."

Kimi cocked her head, in that sharp expression that he'd discovered meant she'd latched onto an interesting fact.

"This is unfortunate and brings into question how our

protocol was obtained." Stavros' gravelly voice ended the silence, though it took Kimi another heartbeat to return from her thoughts. "However, we knew these demons had adapted and corrupted some of our techniques. Kimora has undoubtedly anticipated this scenario and developed countermeasures, so we are not taken unawares."

Kimi dipped her head, agreeing with the vampire. *Kimora.* His mate had a longer name, because humans had more than one. Some were called by their last name in the books, usually until the hero or heroine admitted to their feelings. Only creatures had designations or single names.

Like him. Even his name wasn't truly his, stolen from another hero.

"Your thoughts on including Owen?" Vee directed the question at the old vampire.

"Kimora has fought beside him. We also know that he has trained with the same methods as you." His eyes changed, the air of a soldier softening. Becoming more human. "You have expended most of your reserves. Were this mission under the noon sun, it would require draining the meager amount of preserved blood in our store. Such a mission would also tax me."

His mate's sister was weakened. Owen would fight harder, and protect her as well.

Vee switched her attention to Owen. Her nostrils fluttered. He put all his desire to aid his mate, and his new sibling-teammate Josh, plus Vee, into his body language for her to read.

"I did promise you we'd kill vampires." A smile blossomed for a moment, then she returned to the serious soldier she was. "Although we have minimal intel on what my contact observed, so we can't make assumptions as to what we'll encounter."

"They may not be present, because vampires are

cowards," he said, unable to keep the growl out of his voice. "But the vampires are behind all new disturbances—ghouls, stinking windigos, their other creatures."

"Aye. The demons are the root of the evil plaguing humanity. We are agreed?" Stavros asked Vee.

She nodded at Owen. "There are extra uniforms intended for nocturnal urban missions in the second locker. Josh will pull weapons for you." She headed for the door, his mate and Stavros joining her. "Let's take a last look at the tunnel and drain schematics."

Kimi joined the conversation, signing. "I've sent a pair of drones ahead, one in a tight formation around the area of the sighting, the second in concentric circles from the outer rim inward. We'll have real time data." Just before the door closed on the trio, she turned and shot Owen a quick look, and did the one eyelid thing. Winking.

Showing her silent belief in him. Happiness rose inside him again.

"I'll grab gear while you change." His new team-sibling pulled Owen back from basking in Kimi's surety, to the business of eliminating all things the Syndicate sent out in an attempt to kill Owen's family-team and happiness.

CHAPTER 20

imi

OWEN EXITED the SUV to stand with me and Josh. In the grayscale camo body armor, and loaded with regulation weapons, he was the image of a Company agent. Except for cold calculation that turned his square-jawed face and piercing eyes from action movie hero handsome to predatory.

Waaay too similar to Vee and Stavros as their eyes turned from brown to the swirling, molten silver of a vampire in hunting mode. They tilted their faces to the night breeze, checking for any evidence of cryptids.

As Josh scanned for suitable spots to set up his rig if needed, I inspected drone images plus infrared. And tested the limits of Owen's ability to hear me. "Do you detect cryptid or vampire traces?"

He turned his back to the group, and slowly signed. "I can detect nothing through the stink of rodents, mold, and canine and human waste."

The drainage tunnel to a nearly dry artificial aqueduct was pungent, both a shelter for coyotes and other urban animals, and the homeless when the weather was rough.

That he was studying and using sign language despite not needing to rely on it pulled a smile free. "Good job."

He edged closer to me, the unsettling feralness replaced with an answering smile. Soaking up the praise he'd never been given.

Okay, praise from me, his—person. His partner. Fate wasn't a quantifiable, scientifically testable phenomenon, and would always get a side-eye from me. The rest was biology, physiology, and psychology, all acceptable. Plus, sexual chemistry. Loads of that.

The brand-new emotion that came to life every time Owen touched me, the way he met me curiosity for curiosity, how he always acted as if everything I did was the right thing, his vow to protect my family, was more than science though. Similar to the startling emotion Stavros had evoked, becoming our parent, something I hadn't known existed or that I wanted until it happened.

Except with Owen there was the added art and orgasms. Art-gasms? He *was* a work of sensual art.

Possibly scenting the effect of my sexy-times memories, his pupils expanded, and he leaned into me.

My tablet vibrated, and I switched from romance to agent. Flicking through the footage and reports, I joined the rest of the team, Owen beside me.

"We aren't picking anything up," Vee said.

"The drones aren't either. No movement larger than a medium-sized dog. The tunnel walls are too thick. The sensors can't pick up heat signatures through the concrete." I employed the tablet's text to voice function. Not the best of reports. But at least there wasn't a battalion of cryptids waiting to converge on us as soon as we entered the tunnel.

Which didn't eliminate the potential for creatures having already invaded the cave-like structure.

Josh stashed his sniper case back in the SUV, and hit the fob to lock it. The vehicle was horribly out of place, the only concealment scrubby grass and darkness. I had alerted HQ, and whatever contacts necessary were activated, hiding our ride from satellites and CCTV. Josh had switched out the regular tag for a government plate, lending credence as a government task force if we did catch local law enforcement's attention.

As soon as Josh pocketed the fob, we drew the nine mils loaded with chem-coated rounds. Vee took point, Stavros a pace behind her. Josh and I in the middle, my focus the ceiling, his the ground. As smoothly as if he had always been part of our team, Owen took the rear, covering our backs and alert for any hostiles who had escaped detection and intended to ambush us and cut off our escape route.

I already knew I could trust him at my back, and after his bonding with my brother and sister, at my family's back as well.

Within a few yards, the only illumination came from the lights mounted on our weapons, harsh white puddles of brightness. The confined space and problem of a teammate's light accidentally blinding another agent prevented us from using the night vision goggles.

Any breeze cut off. Sweat trickled down my spine and settled around my waistband.

The scurry of small, clawed feet and the rats Owen complained about was our only soundtrack. The reek of fishy mud and ammonia covered any other scents.

Josh's light played over debris, some swept in when the water flow was higher, others hinting at the people who were forced to use the tunnel as shelter, water bottles lining the walls, a few alcohol and beer cans scattered in, the occasional pile of stained fabric, too tattered to be of use anymore.

The floor rose subtly. According to the schematics, we were close to a join, where a tunnel from the west intersected the main pipe. The main closed by more metal and concrete since the lake that fed it had dried up.

Moving slower, relying more on their vampire senses, Vee and Stavros approached the intersection, the second pipe an eerie black void to our right. They passed under the join, into the new tunnel. We advanced behind them, Owen last, walking backward, all three of us paying extra attention.

My light passed over the curve of concrete, walls getting lighter, from dirty brown to light gray, the higher they went, not marked by mud or human graffiti.

A dark lump marred the pale concrete, stuck to the ceiling several paces ahead. Too large for a single bat, too solid for a flock of them. A mix of unease and adrenalin skittered along my nerves, my surroundings coming into hyperfocus.

I tapped my earpiece, silently notifying the rest.

As Stavros and Josh turned, silver gleamed in the middle of the lump. Before I could tap out a warning, another set of silver eyes appeared.

Vampires, more like stick figure caricatures, clung to the concrete ceiling. Barely clothed, theirs worse than the trash abandoned by the homeless. Their heads torqued at an impossible angle, even for a vampire. Turned completely backward, staring down at us. Thick yellowed fangs out of proportion to their bodies, in full hunting mode, their skulls barely covered by transparent skin.

With an ugly, piercing *skree*, claws scrabbled against the ceiling, the vampires whipping around. They dropped straight down.

The team split, Vee and Stavros on one end, Josh and Owen with me on the other. The freaky vampires landed on all fours. The concentrated light from our weapons pooled, spotlighting the vampires like they were on a Hollywood stage. Neither stood upright, their legs jointed more like a spider's.

More of the Syndicate's genetic engineering, and objectively, fascinating.

The closest hissed. A viscous fluid dripped from their fangs, too thick and dark for saliva. My fascination flipped straight to unsettled.

I hit the earpiece, keying in the code for venomous, at the same time I spoke, hoping Owen heard and understood.

"Assume they are also venomous." A snarl echoed under his words as he repeated my warning. "Avoid contact with your skin."

Drops of the fluid splatted to the grimy floor. Mud and refuse smoking where it hit, leaving pitted holes in the concrete. Acidic *and* venomous.

Instead of launching at us, the creatures stayed back-to-back. Moving in a dizzying circle, examining us. Too fast, and too close. We couldn't get a shot off without risking hitting teammates on the other side in our crossfire.

Stringy muscles bunched under their mummified skin, their speed increasing. Preparing to use their momentum, and launch for us at the apex of their arc.

Even if we evaded a bite or their grasp, all they had to do was swing their heads, and we'd be covered in the liquid goo that would burn through our body armor faster than it had the concrete.

"Maneuver nine," Vee said from the other side.

A buzz of anticipation settled in my bones. Holding up my left hand, I snapped my fingers to ensure Josh saw. For

Owen, I whispered, "I'm bait," at the same time Josh barked, "Owen, hang back with me."

I got busy antagonizing a mutated vampire. Holstering the useless nine mil, I palmed my throwing knives. Calculating the creatures' rotation. Waiting for the split-second window.

As one creature curved into the arc taking it past us, I threw the knives. Silver whirring. A blade flew past, clanging against the tunnel wall.

The other imbedded low in its throat, where neck met shoulder. Greenish-red blood flew, the color of cryptids, not the red of vampires.

The wounded vampire skidded, shrieking in a high enough register my ears popped. Swiping hard, it jerked the blade free. The guys melted as far into the background as space allowed, and I stomped hard, keeping the monster's attention.

It swung my way, then turned back as its nest mate screamed. Off-color blood covered Stavros' claws where he'd done his version of antagonizing.

I flipped out the blade from my thigh rig, drew it along the heel of my left palm, and then swept my hand wide, flinging blood on my vampire. It whipped around like its body was hinged, and lunged.

Squeezing my hand to leave a trail of drops as further motivation, I raced down the tunnel. Trusting Josh and Owen to keep up with the enraged creature. To be there when I led it far enough out for us to turn and attack it and not risk its nestmate rushing to help it, or shots ricocheting.

Or it getting to the tunnel exit. Vampires shouldn't be able to tolerate the sun, which was close to coming up. But vampires also didn't bleed green-tinged blood, have double jointed extremities, and acid venom. If it took us down, and could tolerate the sun, there was a homeless encampment less than a half-mile away in one direction, the hydro main-tenance office, staffed with clueless civilian workers, in the other.

The snarls and shrieks of the other vampire, and the metallic whistle of Vee and Stavros' chem-coated machetes faded.

The scrape of claws grew louder. First from the ground. Then coming from the right, the thing taking to the walls. Then the left. Ping-ponging back and forth, either herding me or aware of the guys.

I strained, listening for human footfalls. Gauging how close Owen and my brother were, but no reassuring thumps of boots registering.

The fine hairs that escaped my bun tickled my neck, lifted by a puff of air. If I was close enough for a breeze to flow through, I was close enough for a vampire to escape into a public area. The first rays of the rising sun crept in, lighting a potential path to freedom for the monster.

Whether my backup was here or not, I was out of time. With only the the scratch of claws as a guide, I whirled to face the vampire. Knife weaving a defensive pattern.

Silver eyes blinked from the right, barely an arm's length away, and only a few feet above my head. It drew its legs under, and pushed off. Dropping to a knee, I gripped the blade in both hands, and sliced. Then rolled hard to the side, liquid splashing my hand and arm. Blood, not venom.

It squealed, right by my ear, leaving it ringing. I pushed off the wall as the vampire hit the other side, leaping ahead of me. One clawed hand patting at its stomach. A gash ran from mid-chest to navel, grayish-pink of intestines peeking through.

Rushing the vampire, I swiped again, aiming for its face. Trying to get back between it and the exit.

A claw whooshed, missing me. Pain erupted along the

back of my hand, like oil popping off one of Bruce's too hot pans, blisters rising. Burning composite invaded my sinuses as venom burned through the top layer of armor from my wrist to elbow.

Shadows loomed behind the vampire, the guys almost here. But the vampire was even closer to freedom, me and a yard of tunnel the only thing between it and its goal.

It darted left, one hand holding its stomach. The other grabbing for me. Claws locking around the knife blade, not caring that it drove the chem-coated edge deep into its hand. It reared back, claws viced around the metal, snapping the weapon from my grip. Jaws opened, it lunged, aiming for my unprotected throat.

Sunlight danced on metal, leaving an after-image as a knife arced behind the vampire, and it wobbled, the guys finally arriving. Blood splashed and its leg gave, tendon sliced. Another flash, and the other leg buckled. The creature snarled, eyes swirling like a riptide, ready to suck me in, and it swiped, still fast.

A blade slammed through its back, Owen throwing all his weight on the hilt, driving it deep into the muck and pinning the vampire. Josh's knife whistled, and the razor-tipped hand aiming for me dropped, leaving a stump.

My brother rolled across the thrashing creature's shoulders, a swing lopping off the other clawed hand, landing on his feet beside me. The vampire bucked and twisted, venom splashing.

I jerked my gun free, wedged it against the enraged vampire's forehead and squeezed, until the slide locked empty.

Owen grunted, and his blade came free. He slammed it into the vampire's neck and twisted, vertebra crunching and the severed head landing in the mud. Not done, he kicked the skull into the wall, in an explosion of gray matter and bone shards.

Gritting my teeth as blisters popped, I switched the empty gun for the smaller one on my other thigh, and jerked my head toward the way we'd come, and the rest of our team. I bent, dragging my arm through the gunk and mud, the best I could do to dilute, and hopefully neutralize, the acid working its way through skin and armor.

Mud spattered my back, a shadow wavering at the tunnel exit. I twisted around, gun level on the new threat. Josh dropping his knife and his gun coming free of its holster.

Owen blasted past us, grimy blade reversed for another blow that would decapitate whatever had ambushed us.

The sun hit blonde hair, pink and yellow glitter clips holding curls out of our contact's pale face. She froze, eyes huge.

I lurched for Owen. Josh recognized the civi and swore, then yelled, "Stand down. She's one of ours."

The vicious edge of Owen's knife swept toward her exposed throat. Centimeters away, as I grabbed for his arm, knowing I was too late. Visions of him getting lost in his rage at the lab and while sparring with us superimposing themselves over our real-life nightmare scene. His admission that he couldn't stop himself playing on a loop through my head.

The mental film reel altered, a new one taking over. Of his utter restraint as he mastered tai chi, muscles and instinct obeying him instead of falling back into that mindless, violent place the Syndicate tried to drill into him.

"Owen," I whispered, because he heard and understood the way no one else ever had.

The knife reflected the cheery morning light. Resting a hairsbreadth from the girl's skin. I touched his elbow, his arm still and steady. He looked down at me waiting for my orders.

A stiff breeze pulled more hair loose from my knot.

Stavros and Vee flashing by us, Vee shoving her hand between fragile human skin and the knife, curling her claws around the edge and tearing it from Owen, as Stavros pulled the girl into the open.

He put himself in front of the civi, blocking her view, as Vee shoved Owen, knocking him backward with a grunt.

CHAPTER 21

wen

SILVER SHADED the tiny vampire-sister's eyes as she got in Owen's face. "We don't save civis from monsters just to kill them ourselves."

Kimi let go of his arm, and but stayed by his side. He inhaled her calm, trying to understand Vee's anger.

His mate angled, putting herself between him and her team-sister, her hands flying. "He stopped before it ever touched her."

"Would he have if you weren't here? Or would this have been another version of Josh's beatdown, except with a decapitated innocent instead of an agent with broken ribs?"

"Yes." Conviction radiated from Kimi, her signing sure and fast. His mate understood.

"Take a breath." Josh stepped up on Owen's other side. "That was close, but he pulled the blow."

"I was trained not to." Owen refused to add smaller lies

onto his larger one, that he was closer kin to the dead vampire than to the human. He smelled not only the chemicals of the lab surgery table on the vampires, but the base note that his batch carried.

"Man—"

He cut Josh off. "We were trained to leave no evidence, and human lives were irrelevant. Only the training mission mattered, no matter the cost."

Kimi's warm hand wrapped around his wrist. He glanced at her, getting a nod and the tiny smile. Again grasping his intent, believing in him.

"This is a matter best discussed later." The old vampire's voice spread over them, drowning some of the tension.

"He's right. But we need a meeting once we return home." Vee drew in a breath, held it, then let it out. She flipped a phone device from a pocket, and spoke briefly into it.

"I did not harm the civilian human," he said to his mate. Wishing he could tell her the truth, that his reflexes were not *enhanced human*, as she had said. They were cryptid. He had caught the human's scent, the beat of its frightened heart, and stopped immediately, his promise to Kimi clear, his promise to Josh and his other team-brothers, Jace and Matteo, equally clear.

But he had no way to explain the human had been safe, his blade halted long before. He hadn't brought it away and down because he heard his mate as she touched him, and did not want to risk bumping her, with her already wounded from the venom-acid, yet still directing her team-family.

Kimi's hand slid down, wrapping around his and squeezing, before letting go to sign, "I know. You did great."

She left to crouch by the vampire's carcass, then by the head, one of her clever hidden-in-her-boot knives in her hand, tip digging into crushed bone and brain even as blisters on her hand popped. Pulling something out, and wrapping it in white gauze, before sealing it in a bag. She repeated the process, slicing the handless arm and peeling skin back. Digging something out from it as well.

She drew the tip of the blade through the venom pooled by the head. Metal sizzled, and she frowned, wiping the knife through the mud, then tap-tapping the damaged tip against her boot, her thinking face on.

He moved deeper into the tunnel, finding Josh just past the bend, standing over the torn apart remnants of the second vampire. "I would not have killed the human cub."

His team-brother clapped him on the shoulder. "I know. Kimi will convince Vee and Stavros. I think Vee gets wound up because of having to learn control when she got infected. Stavros was way harsh on her, but it was all he understood to do back then, you know?"

His team-brother's words soothed Owen. But he did not want to cause unhappiness between Josh and Kimi, and the rest of the family-team. "I will aid you in disposing of the bodies."

"Nah. We get a pass on that. Our Cleaners are nearly here. These are heading straight to the Lab division. Because this?" He toed a double-jointed leg, separated from the torso, claw marks on the bone stump. "This is freaky times a thousand. They'll be thrilled getting these samples. A live one would've been better, but, acid spit and all."

The whir of a motor filtered in, distorted by the tunnel. Moments after Owen isolated the noise, Josh leaned out of the connecter, then back. "Sounds like the Cleaners. Come on. We can watch them lose their shit over these. They'll act like it's their birthday."

Owen followed his team-brother, who was not upset with him, in time to shield his face from flying grit as a helicopter like those he had learned to leap from, landed in the cleared space behind the team's vehicle. Humans piled out, in different uniforms, fancier black jackets and pants, two pulling wheeled cases, also carrying concealed weapons.

He didn't know *birthday*. The new humans stopped by Kimi, and as she signed, gave off whiffs of disbelief, then excitement, snapping the cases open. When his mate finished, the fancy humans divided, half staying with Kimi's kill, the other half stopping in front of him and Josh.

"Josh, Mister Owen." The one in the lead, a shorter, intense woman nodded to him."Kimi says there's a second specimen."

"We'll show you." When Josh strode away, Owen stayed to the rear of the group.

The leader-human walked fast enough that Josh had to hurry. She broke into a jog when they turned the corner and she spotted the mangled vampire. Kneeling like she didn't notice the mud, she pulled on gloves and poked at the head, using an odd pinching tool. "This is gene splicing on a level the Lab hadn't even guessed at. R and D, and Medical, may want samples, too. A live specimen would've been better. If you encounter another, do your best not to kill it." She rocked back on her heels, tone dry as she addressed Josh.

Who nodded and made strange non-word noises. When she was no longer looking, he rolled his eyes at Owen, and mouthed *"See?"*

If this human knew what Owen was, she would not have greeted him by name and as an equal.

The lab. Samples. A live one. To experiment on. As Owen was experimented on. He would not go back to a torture room and cell. He couldn't tell his mate and family-team what he was, or why the human had been safe from his weapon, to reassure Vee and make her happy with his mate once more. Body feeling heavy, as if ghouls were piled on top, he headed for Kimi, who was still carving into a specimen that shared parts with Owen.

* * *

Owen took his time cleaning and replacing the team-family's weapons, a job he had volunteered for. Josh had watched him break down and detail several, then gave Owen a thumbs up and left for the bathing areas in the house.

Alone, the memories of Vee's anger and the old vampire's hesitation, and the fancy Cleaner-humans enthusiasm at having creatures to slice up and study, circled non-stop through his head.

After the fancy agents left, Stavros had smeared his special blood over Kimi's hands, healing the acid-venom burns. Kimi had once again sat with Owen in the vehicle as they returned to the compound, her hand resting on his. Josh sat in front of them, arms folded and staring at the backs of the family-vampires' heads, like he was defending Owen. The ride back hadn't felt like when the family-team left for the mission, all seeing Owen as part of their group.

He returned the last weapon to its spot in the locker, and forced himself to continue on to the house. Food smells had met them when they arrived, Vee's mate returned, but for the first time, Owen felt no desire for a meal. He circled, entering through the side into the laundering room, where Vee's mate had instructed them all to leave their boots *or else*.

Voices floated from the office room to Owen as he quietly closed the door, looking for the place to shed his mud and gore crusted boots. Bruce was now also part of Owen's family-team, after bringing Owen extra food and supporting Owen's learning to please Kimi.

"You gotta admit the guy fit in today like he'd trained with us since he was a kid." Josh's calm voice came through easily. "He didn't need explanations of plans and signals, took orders with no push-back, and stayed tight with me, instead of being a ball hog and rushing ahead."

"I'm not arguing he isn't highly effective. He is a fighting machine," Vee's more measured tone cut him off. "Like, literally a machine. Because his lack of restraint? It's kind of chilling."

His mate was also in the room, her heartbeat clear, faster than normal. Without thinking, Owen found himself in the hall outside the office-room and the door that had not completely closed. He crept sideways until he could see Kimi.

She signed, hands moving almost too quickly for him. "Owen has made huge strides. After only a few days here, he grasps what teams and family mean. He is constantly absorbing and processing rules, and what it means to be treated as a real person, and live and interact with humans."

"He almost killed someone." The tiny vampire's check dented in, like she was biting the inside. Apology changed her body language. "A civi. We nearly killed our own street contact, and she did not deserve to be treated that way after all she deals with on the daily, plus aiding us."

His mate jumped back in. "Agreed, even though she blew us off about staying far away from the site until we messaged her the area was safe again. But Owen learns with astounding speed. You aren't giving him enough credit. The split-second he saw she was a human, not another vampire, he stood down. His completely grasping Company policy and values is only a matter of time and continued coaching." She turned to Stavros, hope on her face.

The old vampire's gravelly voice held an undercurrent of regret. "The team and the humans we protect may not have that time to spare. The demons view humans as their rightful food, and take joy in corrupting and ruining God's creations, valuing only their own petty desires and inflicting pain and evil. The boy means no harm. Yet he was also brought up under vampire indoctrination. I am less sure of his ability to differentiate and restrain himself than you."

"Papá—"

The vampire dipped his head to Kimi, and spoke more gently. "He will not intend breaking our laws. The results will be the same, intentional or accidental. If he kills a human during a mission it will be the end of us all."

A tangled web of emotions came from the room, too many and too complex for him to pick apart and match to a person. Other than his mate's surprise, and hurt.

He backed away as silently as he'd approached, choking on the conflict and doubt. Then bolted through the cleaning room and into the open, running until he cleared the buildings, and track, and tree platform. Away, where he didn't risk anyone with his frustration. He would do the *taking a beat*.

His body fell into a rhythm that could carry him for many miles. He couldn't outrun facts. Half of the family-team believed he would fail. That he was defective. His mate was upset.

The shine of metal drew his attention. The section where the fence was looser, the point where the compound was bounded by sheer rock. Which he hadn't yet remembered to tell Kimi, another error on his part.

His head pounding from the ideas spinning inside, he let his body take over. Climbing over, burrowing under, or touching the fence set off alarms inside. Once he had backed far enough away from the fence to gather momentum, he ran all-out for the rock face. Pushing off, he grabbed for the nearly invisible cracks and protruding sections.

Slipping inches, boot soles a breath from the fence, he dug his fingers in, catching his balance. Hauling himself sideways, a toe found purchase. Inch by inch, arm and thigh muscles burning, he moved away from the fence, further and further until he was on the opposite side of the compound, outside even the secondary fence.

Sweat dotted his face as he descended into the barren

valley slowly, fighting for every finger-hold. As his hands threatened to cramp and lock, he dropped the last twenty feet to the ground, landing in a crouch, fist against the sandy dirt steadying him.

He wiped sweat away and rose, flexing his fingers until they obeyed, then stretching arms and legs. Staring up the way he'd come from, he huffed out a breath. Again, his instincts had won out, instead of his brain. He hadn't considered the fact he'd have to climb back up, his only way in without setting off alarms. Then Kimi would be forced to tell her family-team what she knew of his abilities before she finished her plan.

Frustration worse than before he'd run, he paced away from the outcropping. Breeze drying his sweat, he prowled, hoping for a stretch of rock with real ledges and cracks to use on the trip up.

The wind brought a chemical tang and his lip curled off his teeth. Lifting his head and inhaling with his mouth open, he matched it to scent memories. This was the one he'd encountered many miles away when he first came to the compound. The same scent-taste pattern as the strange tunnel vampires. Like his but not.

This one was a threat. Owen would not allow threats to his family-team, no matter how angry they were at him.

He changed course, tracking the scent, scrub grass and stunted plants flashing by, going the way he'd intended to in his search for an easier way into the compound. Fur under his skin ruffled and stood up. Something Syndicate was here. Close

Hugging the rock wall, carefully picking his way through noisy fallen pebbles, he slunk until he was nearly on top of the scent. He moved out and around an outcropping. Coming face to face with his prey.

A growl trickled out. The creature whirled around. In the

same dark training tee and BDU's Owen once wore, with the same holster and Syndicate .45 and blacked-out combat knife, head shaved. Another like him, but from a strange batch, the like but not edge that had confused Owen when he encountered the smell.

Owen rose to his full height, balanced on the balls of his feet, showing his dominance. He didn't carry even basic weapons, fleeing from the compound without thinking.

The other batch-person stared, inhaling the same as Owen had, classifying what it faced. The face narrower and paler than his twisted into a snarl. "We have heard of the defective one who *ran*. So weak that he lives among our prey."

It moved and Owen mirrored it. Circling each other, testing.

Its nostrils fluttered again, and it spit on the sandy ground. "You *mate* with our prey? Your batch-mates should have torn you apart as a cub, and chewed on your bones. Traitor, you—"

Owen launched while it was distracted with insulting him. Fist smashing into the scout's face, staggering it. The other recovered, staying on its feet, hammering a punch to the side of Owen's head. Owen took the hits, pressing the other hard, not giving it time to reach for gun or knife.

Feinting, it pretended to come at Owen. Then took the opening, boot lashing out into the side of Owen's thigh.

Owen's turn to stagger, and fall into a half crouch. The enemy jerked the gun free, barrel rising. Owen launched, staying low, ramming into his opponent's stomach. Picking the other up and slamming it against the rock face. Grabbing the hand with the gun, smashing it against the cliff, bones cracking. Gun falling from broken fingers.

The pop of a sheath snapping open was nearly lost under their snarls and grunts. Warned, Owen shoved away, off the other soldier and its knife. The black blade whistled by, snagging Owen's shirt but missed gutting him.

Owen blocked the next swing, catching the other's knife arm between his. Muscles straining, fighting exhaustion, pitted against the other soldier's which weren't tired from a climb. On a desperate burst of energy, Owen ducked and twisted, his enemy's arm still in his grip, wrenching it behind the other's back. Popping the shoulder from the socket. Slamming the limp arm against the rock, crushing the hand with the knife. It clattered to the ground.

From behind, Owen wrapped his right arm around the soldier's throat. Owen's left hand gripping his right wrist for leverage. Forearm pressed against his enemy's throat, choking him. The Syndicate soldier bucked and heaved, trying to shake Owen loose. Crashing backward to grind Owen into the cliff.

Finally, the soldier faltered, movements weaker, wheezing, unable to get air in through his crushed throat. He went limp. Owen held on another minute, ensuring this wasn't a trick. Then adjusted his grip, snapping his foe's head to the side, breaking his neck.

Owen let go, the body falling. Snatched the knife at his feet, and kicked the soldier to his back. Then stabbed the knife hilt-deep in the Syndicate soldier, not caring about ruined knives, taking no chances on the enemy healing, throwing his weight on the hilt, bone giving and ramming through into the heart.

On his knees, Owen sucked in air, waiting for his damaged rib and knee to start healing, enough for him to move again. After too many minutes, he stood, knee throbbing but usable. He spit on the dead batch-soldier the way it had spit at him, all it deserved for intruding into Owen and his mate's territory and happiness.

Stripping the holster off the enemy, Owen buckled the

straps in place, finding and holstering the gun. He jerked the knife free, wiping it off on the hated black training tee, and snapping it in the sheath. Searching, he found no communication devices on the soldier. This one had been sent to search and report back in person, handlers probably wary of Company devices detecting any attempt at communicating, and ruining the mission.

There would be other batch soldiers, prepared to act on the scout's intel, trained the same as Owen's batch. Aside from too little cover in this remote area, if the Syndicate had known the compound was here, they would have already attacked. There was no estimating how long the soldier had been exploring on his own, though when Owen had searched for devices, the water pouch attached to the holster was close to empty, and all of the food bars eaten, the packets stuffed into a pocket.

He dragged the enemy against the cliff base, gathering rocks to cover and hide the body, to gain time for Owen to think.

He retraced his route to the point he'd jumped down, climbing and brain scrambling for a way to warn Kimi and her family of the new danger they were in, a reconnaissance scout almost at their door.

* * *

HE'D COME up with nothing by the time he dropped from the rock face and back into the compound, other than telling Kimi what he really was. He didn't want to return to a lab, and not because of the experiments, but because he couldn't be separated from her. That part, he wouldn't survive. Yet far worse, eclipsing even losing his mate, was Kimi being blamed for rescuing him and bringing a not-human into the compound, around other Company humans, then along on a mission and near the weak civilians.

As the sun dipped behind the horizon, moon visible, he entered the house through the laundering room, his boots and Bruce's anger not seeming a problem compared with what waited for them outside of the compound.

From the food area, many voices competed against each other, loud and laughing. This would make taking Kimi away to explain more difficult.

As he stepped through the doorway, Vee pulled up, in his path. Carrying a cup filled with a bright pink juice, though it also held the sharpness of the red juice the scientist had preferred. "Kimi was about to go looking for you. You've been gone a while."

"I am sorry." He kept his gaze on the floor.

Bare feet appeared in his line of sight, toes with color on the tips, the same shade as her drink. "Hey, O."

He stiffened his spine and met Kimi's team-sister's gaze.

"I am sorry about this morning, and my accusations. Sometimes, I get the vampire kind of overprotective, not just the C.O. kind." Her cheek did that dented in thing. No anger or distrust came off her.

"As am I." This, her doing the apologizing, should have calmed his worry. But the knowledge of the scout's incursion and its purpose prevented calmness.

"We do need to work on overcoming your conditioning, and replacing it with our way of ensuring civis aren't injured. I mean, I get it. It's crazy-difficult to overcome instinct." She sighed. "I was at fault for not insisting you weren't mission-ready yet. I can also admit I was low on blood, and hyped over discovering hey, the bad guys whipped up an even worse kind of vampire, something I didn't think was possible. Plus, we couldn't even feed from them, since who knows what else their blood carries." She wrinkled her nose, as if smelling the vampires and their acid-venom again.

"I will never hurt a human. I will stay here, and train as much and as long as the family-team and Kimi order. No matter how long you require."

"We'll work on that tomorrow. Tonight is for celebrating," she said, as a burst of laughter rose. To high-pitched for anyone here, and too many voices.

"There are strangers here." The scout—could another have already snuck in, pretending to be human the way Owen was?

At a touch on his arm, he twitched.

"Hey, just me." Vee took a careful step away. "Liv's team passed the Assessor inspection while we were all out discovering gross new mutants. After the Syndicate facility revelation, nearby Division teams are being pulled in here. Liv's assessment was accidentally hands-on, thanks to an emergency call-out. It was close to us, at the edge of her Division, so they just finished up and got here ahead of most of the others."

"Kimi's other team-sister? And Jace and Matteo?" Perhaps his new team-brothers would again support him, this time when he told Kimi the truth. He moved back beside Vee, an apology for reacting as if she was dangerous when she touched his arm.

"The whole crew. You haven't met Liv, Marshall, and Kit yet." She hesitated, laying a hand cool from the drink on top of his. "Kit isn't human. He's a cryptid, but non-predatory. Plus, he's only a kid."

"I understand." Many of the lesser cryptids, those who didn't kill, had been taken by the lab and scientists. Some used as bait to train the silent psi-creatures and teams of ghouls and stinking windigos.

"And Jamison, the Assessor, from the video call at the

cabin. He's already a fan of yours, since Josh shared your part in dealing with today's mission." She set her drink away on a laundering machine, and took both of Owen's hands, doing the happy-bounce. "Oh! I almost forgot. Jamison got a notification as they all arrived. Another group of captives like you escaped from a smaller facility. They've been picked up and are on their way to our California HQ—the population in this state is so large, we have our own."

"Like me?" Dread icier than Vee's drink wrapped around Owen.

Still holding his hands, she tugged him along. "Yes. All humans the Syndicate was trying to turn into daytime soldiers, like you. We're guessing the vampires are in disarray after losing a main facility, thanks to you and Kimi, and this group took the opportunity to run. They knew about the Company the same way you did, so searched for a team to ask for help. O, they might be some of your siblings or friends."

Horror choked him the way he had the Syndicate scout. There were no others like him. His batch, all batches, were taught enough to appear human. To get close to unsuspecting victims, the entire reason his kind was created.

This though, this was different. An entire group, who had requested admission to one of the Company's center sites, when Syndicate training emphasized only one or two batch-soldiers approaching at a time, to reduce the chances of suspicion.

As Vee had said, vampires were territorial, and unaccustomed to being defied. Owen also knew them to be arrogant and vicious, to taunt and torment for fun.

His instincts told him this wasn't true infiltration, to gain information. This group of batch-soldiers were sent for revenge and destruction. They would gain admittance as taught, then destroy the site's systems to slow the Company down, the way the attack on the site had the Syndicate. The group would kill every human in the site.

His escape had led to this. No group had been considered ready for such an attack, not considered smart enough to differentiate between useful information and equipment to retrieve for the Syndicate, and useless devices and papers. Until he had seemed smart enough to escape and join the Company.

He wasn't smart. Kimi was. He had only been lucky, that she considered him as a mate, and planned the escape and took him with her.

Lying to his mate had put Kimi and his family-team in a lethal situation. He had to talk to her, now, and explain. Even if she was angry with him and sent him away. She would make another smart plan, to save the other family-teams, and hers.

He rushed, taking Vee along as she squeaked in surprise. Stopping fast at Bruce's territory, the giant food area filled with humans. He scanned, over his family-team, and Jace and Matteo. Past a female, one who looked like Kimi and Vee, though taller. Another large human male with red-brown hair brighter than the streaks in Kimi's stood beside her tall team-sister. In a bright blue shirt instead of team uniforms, his arm was over her shoulders, the two angled towards each other instead of the group. Another mated pair.

Finally, he found Stavros and Kimi, by the cold food device. His mate pretending not to smile, though her body language did.

Owen would never allow hurt to come to her.

A human cub with bright hair, also not in their uniform, argued with Kimi about training headphones and colors. A mix of many different citrus-foods came off him. Kimi didn't sign, only whisper-spoke to the other. Who therefore wasn't a human, but the cryptid cub Vee told Owen of.

Owen let go of her, and circled the food counter, the fastest way to get to Kimi.

His movement caught her attention, and she did the happy-bounce, motioning for him. She whisper-spoke to the cub. "Kit, this is Owen."

The cryptid-cub paid no attention, still arguing. "But they'll get delivered *there*, and I'm *here*. Then what if we lose because I don't have the good headphones?"

Bruce rested against the counter, arms folded. "You don't need another pair. If you did, you would've finished and turned in your assignment."

Guilt crossed the cub's expressive face. "I *would* have finished. It's not my fault there was a call-out, and we *all* had to go, and then come here after."

Bruce snorted. "You negotiated for paid Asset status and space on the team. You knew what that meant, and the responsibilities. Nice try, though. There are functional tablets and laptops in that truck you spent hours in, getting from there to here, and online access to the Academy library. You goofed around instead of working. There are also tablets aplenty in this house that you can use. Start now, and you'll be finished well before this all-out gaming battle."

"All true. Use the largest tablet on the top right shelf in the sitting area. We'll hit a shop in the city tomorrow that had the model of headphone you want in green," Kimi whisper-signed.

The last human, the male agent one from the cabin video call who wanted Owen to leave Kimi and go to HQ, watched the conversation, attention jumping back and forth between the team-family.

"Fine. If I'm too exhausted to play this weekend and we lose, not my fault." Shoulders drooping, the small cryptid squeezed between Bruce and the agent human, exiting the food area, almost running over Owen.

Large eyes half hidden by hair flopping over them widened. The cub spun and bolted behind Bruce, as fast as only a cryptid or one of Owen's kind could, its voice shrill. "It's one of them!"

Owen stopped, his plans and hopes shattering.

Vee joined her mate, voice soft and soothing. "That's Owen. He was a prisoner of the Syndicate vampires. That's why he smells like those creatures. That's all."

"Kit—" The human male in blue left his mate's side.

"It is!" The cub abandoned Bruce, darting behind the much larger human, tugging on his sleeve. "Marshall, it's like the Franken-non. When my flock disappeared, its scent was *everywhere*." The small cryptid's voice rose higher and higher, enough that Vee and the old vampire winced.

Bruce frowned and left his spot at the counter, kneeling by the cub. The rest switched from talking, to crowding around, offering the cub comfort.

Except Kimi. She looked from Kit to Owen, brows drawing together

Owen saw the moment his mate understood. That the cub heard her because he was a cryptid. That Owen heard her not from experiments, that the cub recognized Owen's smell not because Syndicate vampire scent had rubbed off on him, but because he was also a cryptid. One created to obey vampires, and kill humans and other cryptids.

Kimi understood that the cub was truthful. That Owen hadn't been.

He had never hunted the cub's kind, though others of the batch must have, but the fact wouldn't matter. Only that Owen wasn't human mattered.

Her face turned lighter, and she grabbed the cold unit's door as if to stay erect. Hands covering her mouth, saltiness carried on the chilly air, the dark eyes Owen loved now red-rimmed and watery.

He backed away, waiting for her to warn the family-teams, the one he no longer belonged with, his heart and chest aching. She didn't move or sign, the liquid overflowing her eyes and dripping down her cheeks.

He had lost Kimi's trust, and would his family-team's as soon as they realized. Because he had been wrong to lie, they would never believe him now, that he wasn't an infiltrator. That although he had lied about everything else, he wasn't lying about the danger they were in, or his love for his mate.

The vampires, his batch-mates, the scout, the frightened cub, they were all correct in rejecting him. He was too defective and broken to belong anywhere. He was the kind of damaged that would get his family-team, all the family-teams in the Company site, killed.

His mate was in danger from the batch now, and if she survived, would also be from her family-team and Company for trusting Owen, all because of his cowardice.

Owen had also been wrong about part of the scout's purpose. The soldier hadn't cared about the compound. He was a true infiltrator, and had been sent to find a way for his group to appear as humans, and ask the family-team to take him in. Without a communication device, he hadn't known another batch had already made contact.

There was only one way to correct what Owen had caused. On his own, he couldn't intercept the batch already on their way. But he could follow the scout's trail, and discover if there was a hidden group waiting for their batch-mate to report back with a way to walk in and then destroy the Company.

If the group existed, and if he could fool them, convince them he had been a scout sent by the Syndicate the entire time, he could sneak in among them, use their intel on the other group to intercept it himself, to destroy them all, himself included, before they breached the Company site's security.

The family-team crowded around the cub, as Owen broke free of the food room, Kimi's gaze still locked on him. His last glimpse of his mate was of her shock and betrayal, as he turned and ran, out of the house, out of the compound.

CHAPTER 22

 imi

HEART CRACKING INTO PIECES, in more pain than when the ghoul had clawed half my throat out, I considered curling into a ball the way Kit was. The kid was inconsolable, shoulders shaking, drowning in snot and tears despite Marshall putting himself between Kit and where Owen had stood. Marshall hugged the terrified boy, repeating nonsense reassurance, Liv, Jace, and Matteo encircling the two and offering their own comfort.

I didn't get to curl up and hide, though. I also didn't deserve reassurances and hugs.

I had brought a Syndicate hybrid, a product of manipulating genetic material from who knew how many cryptids and then camouflaging the twisted results inside a human-seeming disguise, into our *home,* among my family. I'd allowed him access, not bothering with supervision, while he harvested an unknown amount of sensitive information from us.

I also hadn't been able to force myself to move or sign, and report what Owen really was, letting him bolt, a stupid, stupid sliver of my heart still attempting to convince me I'd misunderstood. Because no way would he betray me, or ever purposely hurt me. The way he'd fought alongside me in the lab, his open joy at finding out I liked reading, half the contents of the library on his bed, how he had met and matched me in sparring and sex, moving like we were connected, how he'd tucked me in and wrapped around me on learning that cuddling was a thing...it had felt *real*.

Frozen now, I watched Kit's heartbreak at reliving the loss of his family, if not at Owen's hands, then at the hands of other hybrids like him. Because Owen caring had been nothing but a flawlessly executed ploy to gain information that would provide our worst enemy the means to destroy everything I loved.

It had taken years, but I'd finally screwed up again, the way everyone had feared. Instead of getting a teammate killed, I was potentially responsible for the death of hundreds of agents.

At a tap on my shoulder, I swiped at my face, scrubbing away tears I had no right to.

"I'm not exactly clear on what's happening here. I assume Kit detected traces of that damn Syndicate lab on Owen, and not understanding Owen was only another victim, it triggered the poor kid's PTSD. It was good of Owen to remove himself from Kit's view until Marshall can help the boy calm down and understand. Is there anything I can do to reassure Kit?" Jamison's forehead was a mass of wrinkles.

"No, but thank you," I signed, instead of immediately spitting out the truth. That he called Kit by name, and obviously meant the offer, should've made me feel better, but selfishly didn't.

My brain was a whirling mass of confusion, kind of like the spinning screen icon when a file wouldn't load or an operating system glitched, grabbing for the words to convince our Oversight handler that my family wasn't culpable for this breach. That the chips in my siblings and father shouldn't be detonated and Bruce forced to watch the other half of his soul die. That I was the only one responsible and deserving of punishment.

"Poor kid. It's flat out amazing how he survived alone for so long. I'm glad he found Liv's team. Nobody could see him now and ever again doubt he didn't feel and hurt the way we do. No one is that accomplished of an actor."

The comment tickled at the back of my redlining brain, the part that collated data with no seeming similarity, and turned it into code, or a painting, or a solid practical joke on my brothers.

Oblivious, Jamison moved closer and lowered his voice. "I hate to ask at a moment like this, but can you come with me to the office and the secured C.O. uplinks? I've tried to get in touch with Aida, then to my Oversight link, with no avail. Same result when I try to contact the team transporting the humans, who were rendezvousing with one of your HQ team escorts."

The spinning icon heralding a system failure disappeared, as disparate snippets, conversations, and theories snapped together. My brain tickle processed and finished, spitting out one solid conclusion.

Maybe.

From a purely scientific standpoint, my theory was ridiculous, a last-ditch attempt at justifying emotions over reality.

Logic said Owen was a Syndicate spy, and the mission

where I'd been captured the kind of long-game setup vampires loved creating. That he'd been taught to play on human emotions, and use our psychology against us. I was the target of choice, because, hey, my sisters fell for wounded civi guys, and thus it was statistically probable I would, too. Same for carting wayward non-agents home with us. Owen's whole story about being seen as defective was text-book perfect, meant to cause me to identify with him and defend him.

An unsocialized, abused super soldier with a penchant for romance books conveniently in a cell beside mine? That should've been a glaring *WTH* moment, too scripted to ever be real.

Those were all observable and quantifiable facts. Running one-hundred simulations would return a one-hundred-percent probability that Owen used me, and I'd again overestimated my ability, and failed my team.

This once, no amount of calculations and data were more accurate than my absolute certainty Owen was real, and that what we had was pure, and that for him, I was his fated mate. And that for me, I was his person.

Now I needed enough facts to make an argument for not only removing Owen from the traitor category, but also not calling in a strike team to end us.

Instead of wasting time coaxing Jamison to understand, I pulled in backup. No matter our titles and disagreements, my sister would listen. "Get Vee. Meet me in her office."

Well trained, or smart enough to trust me, Jamison left, threading through our extended team unit, after my sister.

By the time they arrived, plus Liv and Josh, my facial recognition scan had pinged.

"Hear me out," I signed, half-queasy on fear and hope at the same time. "Kit wasn't wrong in associating Owen and the Syndicate. Owen isn't a Franken-non, but he is a human-cryptid hybrid."

The silence built, heading for an explosion. Liv and Vee's faces going pale and ashy.

"Where is he," Jamison rapped out.

"He ran when Kit outed him."

I winced as the room erupted, which brought everyone but Marshall and Kit to clog the office doorway. Snapping my fingers was useless, lost among the noise, no one noticing.

Josh stepped in, scanning the room, focus resting on me.

"Enough. Kimi isn't finished." His voice boomed, quieting everyone.

Mostly.

"Explain. And then elucidate on how this breach is associated with my inability to reach anyone." Jamison's voice was professional, face expressionless.

All Very Bad Signs.

"Look," I signed, then flipped the laptop around, re-started the CCTV recording my program had hit on.

Multiple Company SUV's were parked in a circle in an otherwise empty commercial lot in a not great part of town, headlights on. Perfectly highlighting Owen striding into the center, and interrupting the other enormous, shaved-headed non-Company soldiers gathered in the circle. More soldiers clustered at the edge of camera range behind Owen, a few with ripped shirts and bloody faces, like they'd already been in a fight.

There was no sound, but it wasn't necessary. Body language spoke clearly, several soldiers intercepting Owen, and Owen snarling at them, backing them off. He spoke to the group for a few minutes, and the hostile body language eased. Until he faced what had to be the leader, a hulking figure who easily outweighed Owen.

I pressed my hand to my stomach, easing the burn of Owen fighting for his life.

Neither spoke, launching at each other throat-tighteningly fast. The fight was brutal, each intent on ending the other, blood spraying. The blows that connected pulled gasps from everyone in the room, the way it had me when I first watched.

Owen dodged a rush from the other soldier, pivoting and coming up behind him. Pulling the other soldier's knife free and driving it into its owner's throat, slicing deep enough blood sprayed on the closest watchers. Then jerking another blade from a holster rig we hadn't supplied, hurling the blade to lodge in the eye of a soldier inching close, looking to take out Owen since he was weakened, and steal the upgrade in status. The usurper swatted at the blade, retreating but none of the group offering to help him.

Owen finished by picking the dying soldier up, and slamming him over Owen's raised knee, breaking the ex-leader's back. Tossing the dead alpha to the asphalt, Owen stared at the soldiers, one by one, until they all dropped their eyes. Acknowledging him as their new leader.

The smaller pack of soldiers that had arrived with Owen but been off-camera now joined the main unit.

Jamison swore, more proficient than I would have ever guessed. "Those are the rescue teams' and HQ team's trucks." He leaned closer, stiffening as he made out the tangle of bodies off to the side, the murdered agents dumped like garbage.

I put myself in front of him as he spun, possibly to try contacting Oversight by another means, definitely to head to the HQ.

"Look," I signed.

The soldiers piled into the trucks, the drivers in uniforms they had scavenged from the dead agents, including the phones and onboard computers allowing automatic access to HQ.

All except Owen. His back to the trucks, he looked up at the camera. And did his best to sign.

"Why the hell are we watching this spy mock us in some fucked up parody of Company ASL, instead of immediately contacting HQ, and opening the secured line in here for me to reach Oversight?" Jamison backed away, giving himself room to fight. The suspicion he'd first approached us with when Vee mysteriously returned was back in full force.

"Owen didn't see all of the code when I signed to the parking garage camera the day we escaped and I checked in. He is trying to recreate the agent requesting backup message," I signed.

Behind me, someone rewound the recording. When I checked, the very end played, Liv, Vee, and Josh glued to the screen.

"That's—it isn't. Is it?" Liv looked between us.

Josh stabbed a finger at the screen, the laptop sliding and only Vee's reflexes keeping it from hitting the floor. "It is. Owen didn't go darkside. Check it out."

Jamison's jaw clenched, but he looked. Slowly translating. "You're my heart—"

"Heroine," Liv finished for him, giving me a nod of sisterly solidarity. "He's telling Kimi that she's the heroine of his heart, and that he loves her."

"Which proves nothing."

"It proves everything." Josh got in Jamison's face. I'd never loved my brother more.

Liv and I slid between them before Josh did anything unforgivable.

I signed, maybe too fast, since Vee added a vocal translation. "Owen isn't a spy or plant. He honestly hates vampires, and the Syndicate. He tried to tell me—I mean Kimi—he wasn't human, but I misunderstood. He isn't like the rest of the hybrids. He was in that lab cage because he refused to obey orders to hurt humans, instead repeatedly attacking the vampires around him." He had said it—that he wasn't human. I had made an assumption yet again, instead of taking into account how literal he was.

"Meaning? What is his endgame?"

I signed and relied on Vee to translate, all my nervous energy flowing to my hands. We *had* to bring Jamison around to our side. "Some sacrificial book hero gesture. He intends to stop the others. I can't say *unequivocally*, but can with ninety-percent accuracy, that he either intends to alert the guards as the SUVs stop for admittance into HQ, thus drawing HQ's fire, or to lead the hybrids into the sanitizing breezeway, then alert the guards, who will lock it down. The Syndicate facility was a mirror image of Company HQ plans."

I dropped the worst part on Jamison, and my family. "Those are Owen's only options, because after accessing this video, I can't get back out for calls, messages, emails to other team leaders, signing on to another uplink for the Office or Lab divisions at our HQ or at the Southwestern HQ. None of my backdoors work. HQ, Oversight, phones, comms, all are a no-go. The Syndicate has done a total blackout, meaning Owen also can't use the SUV systems to contact and alert HQ." Either of the last-ditch plans would end with Owen dead, the occupants of the truck bombed, or security sealing the entrance and exit of the sanitizing room, and sending in crack security teams, killing the hybrids trapped inside.

Jamison still tried the laptops and Vee's C.O. line himself, as my pulse hammered, each tap marking how much closer I was to losing Owen.

"Oh my god. He looked *so* sad," Vee said. "Like—"

"Like he didn't think we would care, even if we got his

message," Liv finished for her. "The CCTV thing was smart. Kind of disturbingly martyr-ish, but smart."

Bruce's snort carried all the way across the office.

"Right? And dang, has he learned quickly. Martyr-level heroics are the complete opposite of what he was taught." I didn't bother attempting to hide my pride and admiration.

Giving up, and accepting the blackout was real, Jamison faced us. "How certain are you that Kimi's interpretation is sound? Obviously, there are some emotions involved on her and this hybrid's part, which could cloud her judgement."

"His name is Owen," Josh said, pushing into the center of the room "If Kimi says it's true, then it is. She is never wrong with mission details, and she'd never risk us, or the Company."

I stared at my brother. Almost asking him to repeat himself, because Josh was the worst actor and liar in the history of ever, and right now, he sounded like he was as sure of what he'd uttered as he was of his love for his autographed Kobe jersey.

"Agreed. Kimi doesn't make mistakes," Liv said, lining up with Josh.

Vee joined them. "I would put my team's lives, that of civilians, as well as the Company, Academy, and every agent, cadet, and instructor, in Kimi's hands. She's that good. You already know that from memorizing her record and files."

The room wavered. *I* knew I wasn't making a mistake with Owen. But that my family believed it, had truly believed in me along... "Really?" I signed, facing Josh.

Jace pushed through, looping an arm around me, kissing the top of my head.

Josh took my other side, arm over my shoulders. "For someone so brilliant, sometimes you aren't very smart."

In true Bruce fashion, Bruce bulldozed through the crowd, not giving a damn about rank and rules, getting nose to nose with Jamison. Arms crossed, he dared the Assistant AIC to disagree.

"Fucking hell. All right, what's our play? Let me in on whatever plan you're already hatching to warn HQ and Oversight, and end this with minimal bloodshed," Jamison said.

Taking pity on him, I didn't let on that it wasn't so much *hatching*, as already fully *hatched*. Instead, I signed, "Can you get in touch via mundane civilian means with any nearby Assets with helicopter access? Say, one of the Maintenance crew from the Sheriff's department aviation hangar? Tell them we need a ride. Wait, two would be better."

I handed him the sticky note containing the Asset's name, the hanger number, and the Asset's personal phone number, as one of my brothers snickered, then grunted as Liv or Vee elbowed them.

CHAPTER 23

imi

"WHERE DID YOU GET A FUNCTIONING PHONE?" Jamison yelled, leaning as far as the webbing strapping us in allowed, the helicopter loud even with our coms units in.

One-handed I tapped out a text-to-voice message on my otherwise useless phone, too busy swiping through feeds on the civi one to sign. "I borrowed it from one of the lockers in the hangar." I couldn't access anything Company with a civilian phone, but I *could* hack into traffic cams.

"Borrowed from who? Our Asset was the only person there."

"Whoever had locker seven." Super-cute as his naivete was, I let Vee answer the rest of his questions, tuning him out to concentrate on finding four black SUVs amid Los Angeles County's mass of traffic. Not even Company vehicles and hybrid soldiers had an edge navigating the annoyance of an overburdened highway system.

We *couldn't* be too late, Owen already sacrificing himself while we were busy doubting him.

Catching a large black blob on a cam outside a bank, I zoomed in, getting a grainy view of the stolen trucks. That wonderful-awful mashup of relief and fear spiked through me. They were well ahead of us, and I calculated drive arrival time versus air arrival time.

The answer wasn't in our favor.

Propping the live feed on my knee, part of my attention on it, part on Jamison and Vee, I signed, "It is going to be close. Right now, we are at least six-minutes behind."

"The pilot is doing his best. So will we once we touch down," Josh said from his seat opposite ours.

Beside him, in atypical fashion, Bruce didn't comment. He hadn't said anything since the argument with Vee and Liv, which he won by weaponing up and buckling into the helicopter seat.

I got Vee and Liv's protest. Especially Liv's. His behavior was way too similar to his spiral when we thought Vee was dead, Bruce defying all of us, joining us on missions as driver and agent.

He wasn't courting an ugly end out of heartbreak this time. He also wasn't here so much because HQ was at risk, as because Vee was. She and Stavros had drained their emergency blood stash, but they weren't close to fully powered up. Bruce lived daily with the possibility that they would accidentally reveal what they were. Doing so in front of Company agents was a death sentence.

We all lived with that fear, but for the first time, I truly saw it from his perspective. I hadn't worked out how to save Owen from the Company, supposing we all survived the coming fight. Owen was freaking impressive. Twenty-plus Owen's, who had one goal and no restraint? That was...I squashed the disloyal thought that even he couldn't beat those odds.

The trucks vanished from the phone screen, replaced by a bland looped feed showing only regular traffic and birds. The convoy had hit the dead zone around HQ. I tossed the phone aside, getting a look from Vee. I fought to get back to my usual slightly detached place, where mission parameters, probabilities, and formulating multiple contingency plans took up too much space to allow emotions in.

A complete no-go.

HQ came into view, the sprawling campus and buildings that posed as a private group of research and development companies large enough to have its own homes and school. The copter banked over the outer fence and guard shack. Both looked the same as every time we'd visited, aside from no one manning the gates.

The illusion shattered as we cleared the public-facing section. Something had gone wrong.

Smoke billowed from overturned vehicles, and a hole gaped in the inner security point that directly accessed the parking garage and main building, full of offices, and labs. Chunks of reinforced siding and safety glass littered the entry, bodies in Company uniforms forming a semi-circle where agents had intercepted the intruders. I strained to see as the copter's nose dipped. Counting only two non-agents among the slain. Owen wasn't one of them.

That there wasn't a phalanx of agents outside after what had to have been at least one pitched battle meant there was still a communication block in place, and the main buildings hadn't seen or heard what was really happening, lulled by some other looped all-is-well false videos.

"Decontamination," I signed, and got nods all around, adrenalin cresting. Once Owen got into the sealed unit, he was trapped. Stavros crossed himself, a major breach since he was always utterly contained and controlled going into a mission.

His concern fed mine, my knee jumping and fingers tapping a nonsense rhythm, my body needing to *move*.

We touched down, and poured out as soon as the Asset piloting us signaled the all-clear. Behind us, the second copter did the same, Liv's team joining us.

On the ground the carnage was worse. Forms moved ahead of us, crossing the garage, shaved heads visible under the cranked-up UV lights meant to deter vampires.

"We're on their heels." Vee's voice came through our earpieces.

We stayed in formation, using the Company rides as cover, until we hit the end of the parking and the open area leading to the decontamination breezeway.

We had to get to the narrow corridor before Owen was sealed into it with a pack of hybrids who would shred him once he purposely tripped the alarm. Vee and Stavros surged forward, and we fanned out to the sides, surrounding the hybrids, who were forced to slow to get through the pinch point of the doors. Through the clear safety glass, I picked out Owen in the lead, nearly to the breezeway.

Huge machetes out, Vee and Stavros reached the hybrids, speeding to block the entry. Their blades flashed, biting into a hybrid. Instead of falling, the blocky soldier turned, a backhanded blow sending Vee reeling.

As I pivoted to grab her, she rebounded, tag-teaming the bleeding opponent who showed no signs of pain.

I tapped out a warning, and we paired up, Liv joining me, Josh with Bruce, and Jace, Matteo, and Jamison forming a three-pronged group.

Another four hybrids went through the entry. A soldier almost Owen's twin tried bypassing his cornered teammate, but the vampires and their target whirled back and forth, trading blows as they went, knocking him off course.

Liv and I caught up with him, Liv getting a shot off, and the hybrid's knee buckling. Without pausing, he had his gun out, sighted on my sister. Closer, I charged, then dropped to my knees, favorite knife in each hand, both raised over my head. Sliding under the soldier's upraised arm.

I spun on one knee, pivoting back. His hand hung by tendons, sliced nearly through. The gun dropped from his useless hand. He snatched it with his other hand, in a blur of movement, barrel rising again.

Rolling, I aimed for the backs of his legs, slicing along the calf, too high to hit his Achilles. He bobbled enough that his shot whistled by Liv's cheek as she bent to the side. Whipping back, she fired, hitting his chest, and blood soaking his shirt.

She stumbled, Bruce bouncing off her where his and Josh's hybrid had shoved them. Bruce's gun skittered over the floor and out of reach.

My soon to be brother cussed, grabbing Liv's elbow and stabilizing her. Then charged back at his target, pulling his backup weapon as he did.

Liv's gun barked, and more blood ran from the hybrid's chest, but he didn't falter. Going for another drive by, I rose and sprinted, aiming for his arm. As I passed, his elbow slammed back, catching me in the stomach.

Air whooshed out and I doubled over, wheezing but on my feet, right behind him. Not able to hit him without risking me, Liv traded gun for a long knife almost cryptid-fast. Feinting right as a distraction.

The hybrid moved with her. Hand viced tighter, textured hilts of my knives pressing designs into my palms, I jumped, landing on the soldier's back. Wrapping my legs around his waist, slamming one knife deep to help anchor me, stabbing in and out with the other.

He kept up the freaky silence, not crying out or growling. Not willing to give up his gun, he reversed, running backward, aiming for the unyielding safety glass to smash me against.

I let go, leaving one knife in him, slicing the other down his bicep as he clamped down with his elbow, pinning my leg against him. Twisting, I swung my other leg free, bringing it around to the same side. Bracing it against his ribs, and twisting. Shoving my blade under his chin.

He finally bellowed, grip disappearing as he grabbed the knife.

Liv did her own drive-by, leaving her knife jammed in his eye.

I shoved free as he spun, dropping to my feet. Liv appeared beside me. We pulled guns out, bullets peppering the hybrid's face, then his skull, then face again, as he whirled, searching for an out.

He finally fell to his knees, and we split, angling out of each other's way, and both of us adding final shots until his body toppled sideways and he quit moving.

We went back-to-back, searching for hybrids. One corpse slumped against the wall, Jamison and Matteo stood on another, hybrid down but thrashing. Jace knelt on its chest, barrel against its forehead, and blew gray matter over the floor.

In unison, Vee and Stavros stepped away from a hybrid. Or at least its torso, the head smacking against the wall and stopping.

Bruce had their hybrid backed against the safety glass of the breezeway, Bruce steadily firing into its chest, Josh dropping a used magazine and slamming a new one in its place. We all sprinted to join them.

As Vee ducked around Bruce, her machete sliding through his opponent's heart and twisting, the last hybrid crossed into the breezeway, a compressor whirring on as the process began. Far too many of the freaking nearly indestructible soldiers already inside.

At the head of the group, Owen stood watching. I hit the glass, hands out to stop myself. Owen stared over the others' heads. Heartbreaking surprise crossed his face, eye bruised and lip split, leftovers from his fight for leadership. Then he hit the raised emergency panel by the door. Blue and white lights strobed, a warning blaring, as the breezeway doors sealed, trapping the hybrids and Owen.

No, no, no.

One of the hybrids unholstered his forty-five, firing at the door. The bullet ricocheted, hybrids ducking, hitting one in the side.

I grabbed Jamison's arm, getting his attention, and signed, "What's the protocol here? How do they neutralize hostile incursions from the breezeway?"

He frowned, taking a beat as he probably mentally pulled up this HQ's information, the information all Assessors had to memorize. "Water. They'll flood the chamber."

A body hit the glass inches from us inside the breezeway, neck twisted, and slid down. Inside, hybrids mobbed something.

Owen. His back to the wall to prevent a hybrid coming at him from behind, he fought against the pack. The narrow walkway at least only allowed two people to stand shoulder to shoulder. Most of the hybrids were like Owen, too big for two to stand together and still have the freedom to fight. They had at least learned from the other hybrid's futile try at shooting out the glass, and left guns holstered. Knives took the other weapons' place, one in every soldier's hand. A spiky horde, all after one target.

Owen took a blow to the face, skin splitting on his cheek-bone. He knocked the knife out of the attacking hybrid's grip and returned the blow, spinning, kick taking the soldier down for a moment. Owen put the dazed opponent in a headlock, and wrenched, breaking his neck.

He was beautiful and deadly, and so alone. A band clenched around my chest, threatening to suffocate me.

I shoved the useless panic aside, as Owen kicked the body away, another hybrid hurtling over it, head-butting Owen, ramming him into the wall, knife aiming for Owen's unprotected side.

Shifting fast, and the knife burying in the wall, Owen brought his joined hands down on the hybrid, knocking it flat, then stomped viciously, caving its skull in. He heaved the dead soldier at the others.

Spouts opened all along the floor, water pouring in, and my hand spasmed on my pistol hilt.

"You have to get in touch with the Director here," Vee said.

"It'll take overriding the blackout. I'm open to ideas," Jamison answered, staring as Owen took down another opponent. His shirt was ripped over his stomach, blood flowing slowly.

The HQ and Company blackout had hit right after the parking lot dominance fight, the moment when all of the hybrids entered the cars. Like, immediately. No call from a hybrid could've gone through, and the order been implemented that fast, even by vampires. There was always providing verification of identity, and passing the order down the line, typical safety protocols since the Syndicate mimicked Company structure and rules.

Meaning whatever was causing the blackout was on a soldier, or in one of the SUVs. I bet on inside the trucks, not only as an extra safeguard, but because having an official uplink into HQ would've been a must-have to implement the virus or blocker. But leaving Owen here, struggling to survive, while I played guess-the-device-location...

The water kept rising, at knee height now, Owen holding another hybrid's head under. With a last look, I turned and bolted for the parking entrance.

Doors stood open on all of the stolen SUVs. I dove in the first, pulling out the folding keyboard and waking the built-in screen. Searching for a code or virus entry. Finding nothing, I started at the driver's side, feeling around along the frame, under the seats, in the console between the seats for a device, working my way back.

Exiting out of the hatch, I hit the next truck. Then the third, all with the same results. Refusing to think about rising water, and a horde of monstrously strong hybrids turning Owen into shredded meat, I slid into the last truck. Repeating the pat down, my fingers slid over the dash. And skipped, hitting a raised area. I pulled the small boot knife out, and wedged in between dash and window. Placing the tip under the raised area, I applied pressure. An oblong piece of plastic, the same color as the dash, popped free.

Breaking it might end the lockdown. Or it might not, leaving us with no option to reach the agents inside and beg to have the water turned off. Much more carefully, I inserted the knife tip into a groove, gently twisting. The back clicked up, exposing circuits and wiring. I positioned the device under the interior light.

"Kimi, now's the time to work your magic." A panting Jace braced on the door frame, leaning in. "Vee, Stavros, and Matteo and Josh are doing their damnedest to force a door open, at least enough for water to drain, but it's not looking good."

"Leave her the fuck alone and go help your brother." Bruce shoved Jace out of the way, then crossed to the other side of the truck, climbing into the passenger seat. He pulled his phone out, turned the flashlight on, and directed the beam at the blocker for me, careful to angle it so there were no shadows.

He stayed quiet, sitting with me the way I had with him during the worst of the chemo treatments. Offering silent support, no matter the outcome as I navigated the complex motherboard, reverse engineering to understand what would shut it off as opposed to ruining it, my heart hammering, sweat or tears or both dripping from the tip of my nose and splatting against the truck upholstery.

My finger hovering over the circuit I thought was the answer to the problem, I froze. Josh had confidence in me. But I'd been so wrong before and what if—

"Follow your instincts." Bruce let loose the patience and love that only a few ever got to see, voice steady. "You already know the answer, so don't start questioning yourself. You're too damn good to let doubt fuck you over."

With his grumpy-reassuring pep talk, I ignored the dire voice in my head listing the ways I might've miscalculated, used the edge of my nail and eased the mechanism slide to the left, the direction an outer trigger slide went to break the connection.

From one of my BDU pockets, my phone chimed, then an almost non-stop number of alarms pinged, one on the heels of the other, the Company system back online. I tossed it to Bruce, signing, "Call HQ, give your code, and explain. Call Southwestern HQ and do the same. Tell them to run a complete systems check, and be alert."

Then I gave in and bolted for the building, swallowing but failing to get rid of the metallic taste of fear. I skidded to a stop by Jamison, but my eyes on the breezeway. Bodies floated and bumped against the glass like some macabre aquarium. The pink-tinted water was over Owen's lips, more red seeping from him in too many spots as he grappled with the last hybrid.

My family was tearing at the door seam, Vee and Stavros' claws out and digging at the weld. All trying to save Owen.

Jamison had gotten through to someone, and was talking fast. He looked at me, shaking his head and cut the call. "Director here doesn't trust that I haven't been compromised. There's no hiding he isn't human. And your sister…"

"Please," I signed and spoke.

"Fuck it." He punched in a number, then a long set of numeric code. Whoever picked up, he barked, "This is Jamison. Situation critical. Put me through to the Five, immediately."

I grabbed his sleeve jerking him along to the breezeway. The water was over Owen's head now. Within an inch of the ceiling. He was moving slow, exhausted. Diving, he pushed the hybrid's head down. Holding it against the floor, drowning the soldier. And himself. I hammered on the glass.

Jamison stood beside me. "Yes. The last—the last hybrid is dead. No ma'am. Yes, ma'am, there is still one heartbeat registering, but he is ours. Another Asset."

Owen let go of his drowned opponent. And swam to the glass.

"Go up. There's an air pocket," I signed. "Hurry, please."

He looked up, then back at me. Water met the ceiling, the pocket gone, and my gut bottomed out. I splayed my hand on the glass, and Owen opened his, placing it against mine from his side as Jamison lost his unflappable Assessor cool.

"Look." He turned his phone to the tank. "That is a soldier dying to protect a Company HQ. No, he isn't an Asset. He is the damn definition of an *agent*. This is what we've been after."

Owen pressed his whole body to the glass. I matched him, stupid tears dripping. "I'm so sorry." I spoke, our thing. "I didn't listen when you told me you weren't human. I don't care though. I love you exactly the way you are."

Shock, then joy transformed Owen's face. Then it went slack, life gone from his eyes.

Slapping the unbreakable barrier, I screamed, even though the only person who could hear me was dead.

Gears creaked and whirred. Water began to drain out. Too slow, though. I spun to Jamison and signed, "The doors. Break the seal." Then abandoned him for the entry, where my family was still trying, refusing to give up.

I wasn't either, jamming my fingers in the door seam beside Liv and Vee's, and pulling. My focus narrowed to the breezeway entrance, hands knotted tight enough my joints popped in protest. *Please, please, please.*

The door retracted, and water surged out, force and dead hybrids knocking us off our feet. I grabbed, first Stavros who had hung onto the frame with vampire strength, hauling myself up his side and closer. Then the door frame, and pushed against the water, wading in, searching for Owen.

An arm bumped my leg. Blue and yellow paint stained under its nails and around the cuticles. I knelt, terror giving me strength to flip Owen over as easily as flipping a page. Running through the drown victim drill, I put my lips over his, exhaling two deep breaths, straight from my soul into him. Then leaned on his chest, starting compressions, switching and repeating again. Pushing in a demand to live, not to abandon me.

Stavros and Vee crouched next to us, wrists flipped over to expose the softer inside and the tracery of veins, ready to dose Owen, trying their best to help. Hands rested on my shoulders, my sister and brothers offering support and comfort, as I switched back and forth between compression, and breathing for Owen, breathing my hope and apology into him with every exhale.

Hands wrapped around mine, lifting mine away. I snapped my elbows back, hitting a warm body, and grabbed for a hand and fingers or a wrist to break. Fighting to get back to my mate.

Instead, the long arms tightened, trapping mine, and shook me.

"Kimi, look. Look, okay?" Josh said, like he'd been repeating it for a while.

Everything blurry, I stopped. Taking a last look at the face I loved, something I hadn't thought I wanted, and had been careless with, and now it was gone.

Air whistled from between Owen's lips. His lashes fluttered. I grabbed his shoulders, hauling him to his side, my chest aching like I was the one drowning. His throat convulsed, and water and bile spewed out. I held him, whispering encouragement and apologies, until it stopped.

Owen coughed, then jerked, fighting to get away. Still battling imaginary hybrid enemies. I could still lose him, because a berserker Owen would undercut Jamison's play, looking like a raging monster instead of a human.

I pushed Owen back, straddling him, and hands knotted in his tattered shirt. Putting my forehead against his so he inhaled my scent, and felt my touch. "It's Kimi. I'm here. And you have to listen to me," I said. "Stop fighting."

Owen stilled, only his chest rising, and lashes fluttering. His eyes opened, staring at me, recognition coming back. He mouthed my name, and I nodded, mouthing back, "Don't move yet, okay?"

Boots thumped, and agents poured in like the water had. Weapons aimed at Owen, and by extension, us. I rolled off Owen, my weapons all gone but standing over him protectively. Even if I'd been weaponed up with everything in the armory, it wouldn't have mattered though, red laser dots from multiple guns clustered on each of our heads and chests.

"Let me handle this, Kantor." Jamison stepped past Bruce, who was between us and the HQ agents, bristling like an angry hedgehog.

Jamison recited his name, position, and code. He eyeballed a redhead with the bearing of a C.O. "Director."

"Stand down, Assessor Jamison. I didn't authorize venting the breezeway, and no one in the control room initiated the release sequence. Our systems were taken over again, and these—whatever they are released."

His steely calm back, Jamison stayed put. "No, Director. Oversight utilized their access and drained the chamber. The Five have a message for you." He held up his phone. Multiple panes opened, five blacked out. Only Jamison's partner, the Assessor in Charge of our case, was visible.

I had known she was important—all Assessors reported directly to Oversight and only Oversight—but this was next level. She had to be the actual Assessor in Charge of *all* other Assessors, and the right hand of this Five group. Annoyance at not having extrapolated the relationship, from Jamison always being our in-person Assessor after the first encounter with Vee and Stavros despite the fact he was supposedly the junior member of the pair, Assessor Swift's deciding we all got to live, decreeing our team would act as an Oversight shadow team and rattling off rules without contacting Oversight first, and the—relative —leniency in allowing both our teams to add unconventional members.

The Company had a contingency plan to cover cryptids being discovered, or our being outed, that only C.O.'s and above were briefed on. Oversight had a web of plans within plans that even HQ's upper echelon didn't have a clue about.

"Director. AIC Aida Swift here. I am charged with

speaking for The Five." She wasn't any more warm and fuzzy with the Director than with us.

Owen attempted to stand, and I squatted, rubbing soothing circles on chest, his heart thumping in a reassuringly steady rhythm under my palm. No way had we come this far to lose him and my family. I whispered, "Not quite yet, okay?" as I thought of then discarded alternative escape ideas.

"Assessor. Board of Five." The Director came to full attention, like a cadet confronted by an Instructor. Her agents traded *WTF* looks, but kept their weapons on us, too well trained to falter.

I stored away the whole Board of Five designation, obviously a title, the fact that the members were ghosts, and that HQ Directors knew more than I'd thought. And whether that meant they knew what my sister and papá were, and potential repercussions.

"Make your case, AIC Jamison." His partner leaned back in a chair, the room background blurred. Waaay too at ease, given the whole *blackout, mystery super soldiers attack, and two not strictly human teams she was tasked with policing* thing.

"I formally submit the recommendation that Mister Owen be designated a full agent, and added to Commander Ruiz's team at this time." The words rolled off Jamison's tongue smoothly enough that he *had* to have rehearsed them. I awarded him a bonus thousand points for his high-quality subterfuge, not even pinging my radar.

"You cannot be serious. That isn't human," the Director broke in, hand tightening on her weapon, finger flexing like she wanted to pull the trigger.

"Director." The AIC's tone dropped to a fascinatingly frosty level, as Owen's rough hand curled around mine.

Color climbed the Director's pale face, the same neon as Marshall's, clearly a redhead trait. "Apologies."

"Continue, AIC Jamison."

"Mister Owen is what can best be described as a genetically modified human, a completely new category. He isn't a cryptid nor a vampire. Therefore, no rules bar my submission from consideration."

This time, there was audible whispering from the HQ team.

Owen got an arm under him, and pushed up, rolling to his knees, his fingers trailing across my hand like they didn't want to let go. But they finally did. The tension in the room spiked.

He laced his hands on top of his head, facing me. Voice even rougher, he spoke to the officials, but his eyes stayed glued on me. "I am not human, and am defective. It is your right to dispose of me. Kimi and her family-team did not know. I tricked them. They do not require punishment, or modification."

No. Not happening. I popped up, standing over him again, putting all of my conviction and belief into my voice and hands, signs exaggerated and passionate. Owen was done being regarded as lesser, and done thinking that of himself. "You are the ideal Owen. Brave, resourceful under pressure, loyal enough to die for us and the Company, protector of clueless civilians, smart, with stellar taste in reading material, and my mate."

"Exactly what Agent Albisu said." Jamison didn't hide his kinda exasperated amusement. He got serious again. "You have examined tonight's video. Commander Ramirez's and Commander Muñez's teams are what the Company strives for. Assessor, honored Board of Five members, do I have your permission?"

The screen muted, and the AIC's fuzzed as my heart thundered hard enough it felt like my sternum should be visibly bouncing with each beat. A moment later, the AIC's screen cleared. "The Five are in agreement. Proceed."

"Directors. Oh, this is being sent to *all* HQ Directors, and Commanding Officers," he said, a gleam in his eye hinting at how much he enjoyed his role, as he steadied his phone screen. "It's time you all see what we, and Ramirez's and Muñez's teams, have dealt with the past four years. It's past time you're brought in on what's really out there, how wide-spread the influence the entity behind the cryptid upheaval and appearance of non-native and lab-created creatures is, and how outnumbered we, as in the entire Company, are. It's also time to introduce the pilot programs Oversight has been running as a viable counter-measure."

I tuned out the movie-style gasps, and confusion as he gave a rundown of the Syndicate, their creations, what Kit was, and his and the other non-predatory cryptids' recent contributions. Nothing about Vee and Stavros. Yet.

Brushing the back of my hand over Owen's battered cheek, mine aching in sympathy, I spoke just for him. "Vee and Stavros would be happy to heal you, the way they healed me. Oh, you can stand up. If you feel like it."

Plastic tapped my elbow, and when I glanced over, Bruce handed me a water bottle he'd magicked-up from who knew where. I cracked it open and passed it to Owen who rinsed his mouth, likely getting rid of the taste of blood and nearly getting drowned, then emptied it, wary eyes on me the entire time.

"What is happening? I don't understand." Voice clearer now, his suspicion was heartbreaking, and my heart was already plenty beat up today.

"The human-cryptid alliance timetable just got fast-forwarded. Also, welcome to the team." I offered him my hand.

After a long beat, he accepted and I helped pull him up.

Guess I wasn't the only one recalling my reaction in the kitchen to figuring out what he was, then standing there like I was rejecting him. I hadn't stopped him, to hear his side, letting him leave thinking I hated him.

"I lied to you, and your family-team. I was a coward." He dropped my hand, muscle in his jaw clenching.

"Tell me why you lied?" I signed gently, barely keeping myself from grabbing his arm and pulling him closer again.

"At first, I did not want to be sent back to a lab to be tortured." His voice dropped to an agonized whisper. "But then I saw you were my fated mate, and I did not want to be separated from you. Josh treated me as a person, and team-brother. I searched for ways to aid you in fighting, to be worthy and allowed to stay even though I am not human or Were-human. Instead, I have put you and the family-team in great danger."

I caught his chin and made him look at me, and spoke, fresh tears sliding down my face. "I understand. It must have been awful for you. I am sorry that I led you to believe I wouldn't love you if you weren't a certain way. To me, you are perfect."

"I am still your mate?" Wounded, beat to heck, and with broken ribs from my CPR, he straightened and his shoulders squared up. The same delight as when he discovered our library perked him up.

"You are," I promised him. I could have Bruce go on another renovation spree, tearing out walls, and creating a suite combining my room, my studio, and Owen's. Plus a private library

"I will stay with you, and my team-brother Josh, and team-sister Vee and her mate who is territorial but shares excellent food, and your very growly team-father?"

I was making sure he never had to question where his home was, and who would always have his back, ever again.

Resting my hand low on his ribs for a beat, the fastest route to a heart, I spoke and signed. "You are staying. You're part of the family-team now. You are one-hundred-percent my mate, and I'm one-hundred-percent yours. And just ignore our papá—he gets growly on the regular."

Owen grabbed my waist, fingers cupping my hips, head tilted in question.

"Yes, please." I linked my arms around his neck, ready to get closer even with C.O.s, Assessors, mystery Oversight leaders, and deeply confused agents watching.

In spite of his injuries, Owen lifted me so I didn't have to raise on my tiptoes, hands cupping my ass and supporting me. His lips covered mine, employing all he'd learned. And *dang*, was he a great student. A-plus-plus.

Our papá grumble-growled, as the rest of my family oohed and squealed, Josh the loudest.

Also a good student, laughter clear in his voice, Jamison said, "This is what cross-species partnership looks like."

He was so getting added to our gamer group. I called dibs on him for my team.

CHAPTER 24

wen

"Read the entire list." Bruce shoved the many pages of paper across the food area counter, at Owen

"I require snacks." Owen had discovered snacks, excellent fancy-tasty food. Some were in the food area shelves and cabinets, some in the cold food device. He approved of the good cereal, hidden in the tall, narrow cupboard. The one too tall for Vee's mate to reach easily. Not too tall for Owen. He gave his family-team brother a smile showing teeth.

Bruce glared, suspicious, then rattled the paper. "Read first, or no snacks."

"Seriously, man?" Josh sat on the backless chair at the counter, facing out, and popped a handful of the snack, dried citrus food, and more importantly, chocolate, in his mouth. Matteo and Jace sat on the other side, also with the snack.

"You signed it, and Owen damn well will too." Bruce

flicked a pen to roll next to the papers. "Do you need a refresher?"

"No." Josh slumped, and repeated words. "Bruce isn't our cleaning service. If Bruce is at a pop-up and we have a mission I call as soon as we hit the truck seat afterward, on pain of losing my Kobe jersey, which again, is overly harsh. Closed doors are closed for a reason."

"And?" Bruce crossed his arms, his colorful skin art not matching his rumbling and yelling.

"No shit junk food, including sports drinks, which I still argue should be exempt."

"It says sports in the name," Matteo said. "Right on the bottle. That ought to earn a free pass."

"Seconded." Jace held up his hand.

This was a rule Owen's team-brothers didn't obey, though the extra tasty snacks of tiny doughnuts with chocolate were hidden, as Owen once hid books. He very much liked that he knew this, and Vee's mate didn't. Owen smiled with teeth again.

As if he knew Owen's mind, from behind Bruce, Jace made slashing motions across his throat, shaking his head.

"I don't make people sign stuff at our compound." Marshall, also now Owen's team-brother, who made excellent food *and* never yelled, pulled out fruit and a knife. He also never yelled about people touching his knives. "Just saying."

Bruce transferred his glare to Liv's mate, who ignored him. The one earbud in Marshall's ear wasn't for missions, but for the phone device he always had in a pocket. Today, the swoosh of ocean waves came from it.

Owen did want the snacks already here, though. Beside him but sitting on the counter, not in a backless chair, Kimi nudged Owen's thigh with her bare toe, the nail a blue like the sky, the color Owen liked best. He had already promised his mate he would put his name on the papers. As well as never tell Bruce of the secret snack places.

Kimi pulled the papers closer, and ran her finger down the numbers with rules alongside. She flipped pages, then stopped, brow up at Bruce, and tapped.

"Yes, you two get new rules. Do you know why? Because instead of teaching him socially appropriate conduct, you're teaching him more bad habits."

Kimi's smile didn't have teeth. It meant the same as Owen's anyway. She still nudged the paper closer to him.

Owen did as she silently asked, reading the words aloud. "No nudity in shared areas of the compound. This means the pool and tree house, too. Sex equals nudity, even if one or both of you are partially clothed. Don't touch my knives, even if a horde of windigos and ghouls rampage through the kitchen. Don't touch anything with a motor, batteries, heating element, cooling element, or blade, period."

There was still room on the paper and Owen pointed at the empty spot. "You must sign *my* rule."

Owen's team-brothers made choking noises, though when he checked to see if they required assistance, there seemed to be no snacks stuck in their throats.

"Let's hear your damn rule," Bruce said.

Owen wrote it and held the paper for Bruce to read. "You must say it out loud."

His mate made the scratchy snicker-laugh. Owen liked those almost as much as a full laugh.

"For fucks sake." Bruce snatched the sheet and obeyed. "Owen is not food. Owen also is not hyperbole food."

Owen had researched and learned to spell hyperbole.

Instead of more yelling, Bruce made his name on the paper, and tossed it down. "Your turn. Quit stalling."

"Perfect timing. Once you've signed that, and I'm not even asking what *that* is, you can sign the Company contract we talked about earlier." Jamison, the leader-agent who told other agents what to do walked in from the office room with Vee and Liv. There had been many talks with him and Owen's team-sisters in the office room, and with other leader-agents appearing on device screens, in the weeks since Owen killed the Syndicate soldiers.

The leader-agent had also done the apologizing to Josh, Vee, and the old vampire for putting bombs in them, though Owen may not have understood correctly. All explosives he had been taught to use would not fit inside a human.

Owen took his time, writing out his name on the paper, since he read faster and better than he wrote.

Jamison glanced at the paper, scooting it away and laying a device and pencil-stick used on screens in front of Owen, and pointed at a line. "Sign here. It requires your first and last name."

Owen didn't touch the device. He had no second name to write out. Kimi said it didn't matter to her or the family-team that he was a different type of human. Owen believed her. He liked being stronger, and faster, and able to hear her speak, things he was able to do because he was different. But sometimes the differences mattered to *him*, reminding him he might not ever truly belong.

"Albisu."

Confused, he twisted to his mate at the single word, spoken but not signed, so meant only for him. "This is your second name. Kimora Albisu."

She butt-hopped across the counter until her knee rested against his hip, her heat spreading through him. She leaned for a kiss Owen was happy to give. Rubbing her nose against his, she sat back. "It's also yours, if you want it."

Even more carefully, Owen wrote his name and new second name on the device.

"You're officially an agent. Congratulations." Jamison offered his hand.

Owen closed the leader-agent's hand into a fist, the way Kimi taught him, and bumped knuckles. "I am also officially Kimi's mate. Include that in your device paper."

CHAPTER 25

*L*aying flat on top of Owen, the noise and contained chaos of having my whole family under one roof, or at least around one outdoor kitchen and pool, filtered in through my open window.

Whatever religious-adjacent phrase Bruce had just used to warn Matteo not to touch the pizza still in the wood fired oven, our papá's, "Can you not refrain from blasphemy for one day?" carried clearly, and I snicker-laughed.

Okay, I was a little giddy, but the relief of having Oversight's sword no longer hovering over our collective necks, and of no longer stressing over how to explain Owen to my team, was major.

There were plenty of new dangers ahead. So far, all team C.O.'s knew about Owen's hybrid status, and about Kit and his ancestry. Kinda impossible to keep the California HQ attack and loss of their agents, plus the loss of the team originally escorting the hybrids, quiet.

There was also plenty of chatter about the attack, and ensuing revelations. I'd sorted all my feeds, and divided names into those who were curious but reserving judgement, those who were cautiously optimistic, and those who full-on hated the idea. There were far fewer of the latter than I'd predicted.

Part of the goodwill was from it being our team used for the test. We'd been popular before, and our success rate had gone up exponentially since Vee returning and Stavros joining us. We were constantly in the Company public eye too, thanks to our mandatory monthly testing, proving we hadn't been infected. Most of those visits also included bringing in live cryptids and vampires for study and questioning, so, our legend was firmly established.

The other half was from the footage of us, mostly featuring Owen, defending California HQ. His dedication, and sheer ability, were impossible to ignore. The footage highlighted his performance. It was also strategically edited.

The section where Vee and Stavros had pulled on their abilities, claws and vampire strength directed at trying to open the breezeway chamber door as Owen drowned, had been deleted, including from the Cali HQ's recording. Vee and Stavros being basically half-starved and not able to go full-vampire had been a strange plus in the end. Quicksilver eyes, skull faces, and inhuman speed were difficult to digitally manipulate and hide. Whereas disappearing claws buried in a door seam, surrounded by multiple human hands doing the same, was a gimme.

So far, only Oversight and the Company's central governing group knew what my sister and father were. That reveal… not something I wanted to contemplate. Accepting infected agents, while fighting one of our most hated threats, now an organized, high-tech group, at the same time, was going to be a harder sell.

Owen's scarred hands slid down my back, then up again, carefully shifting my hair to one side. The contrast between the accomplished, deadly soldier on the video, and the bookish, devoted, and slightly nerdy hottie in our bed made our relationship even more special.

He peered at the phone in my hand. "Putting songs about baby shark-cubs on Josh's device is doing the pranking?"

I finished replacing all of my brother's ringtones, alarms, and notifications with the song, adding an image of the cartoon shark in question as his screen saver. Laying the phone to the side, I said, "Yes. And thank you for distracting him so I could borrow it."

"I will do the distracting again so that you may un-borrow it back into his pocket."

Leaning in, I gave him a quick kiss that he returned enthusiastically.

"I require a snack." His statement rumbled from his chest through my entire body, pulling a shiver of excitement free.

But, Stavros was directly below us, and we'd leaked enough emotional goo over our papá for the day. Further sexy-times could wait until later. "Dinner is nearly ready. Pizza. An all meat one for you." Owen had taken to our pizza addiction nicely.

"Snacks are ready now."

"Good point."

He sat up, bringing me with him, lifting me and setting me on my feet. "You must wear clothes."

He'd also taken to Bruce's rules. Mostly.

By the time I'd rounded up my clothes from wherever they'd landed earlier, both of us in a hurry to get naked, Owen was back in tactical pants and a tee, holding the door for me.

We raced each other for the kitchen. When Owen jerked to a stop, I bounced off his back. He caught me, but turned his body at an angle to the kitchen, shoulders dropping to seem smaller.

Kit was in my preferred spot on the eat-in, a picked over

bowl of fruit beside him, metallic green headphones on and lost in a video or game.

I moved in front so that the first thing Kit saw was me.

When he either felt the vibration of footsteps, or his high-frequency hearing picked up our heartbeats over the explosions on the tablet, he glanced up. An only slightly toned-down version of the fear that had taken him when he first scented Owen hit, and his gaze darted around the room, searching for the closest escape.

The tablet fell from his frozen hands.

In a flash Owen was there, catching the new tablet before it hit the tile floor and cracked.

Kit shoved away, back hitting the wall.

Owen crouched so that his head was lower than Kits, gaze on the floor. "I am sorry. I only meant to save the device you use often." Owen's voice was soft enough I strained to hear it.

He had tiptoed around the poor kid the last two weeks, while Jamison, Vee, and Liv held non-stop meetings and calls, that I'd saved to review later. Owen had also commandeered Jace and Matteo, making trips into the city. Piles of every fruit grown or shipped into California appeared after each, left in spots Kit favored. The same for new air pods, tees with gaming characters, and graphic novels.

"I did not mean to scare you," Owen said to the patch of tile he was staring at.

"Well, you did anyway." Kit's voice quavered, but he didn't hit the sonic range that brought on nosebleeds for anyone in the vicinity. "You're stupid-big, and you smell bad, and you probably eat us Lesser Nons."

"I do not eat Nons. I would not eat my—my batch-mate cryptid relatives." He cut his eye at me, checking to see if he'd used the right term.

I gave him a double thumbs up, heart hurting for him and for Kit.

"You're *not* my family," Kit squeaked.

"I am not human or vampire. I am from many different —Nons."

"Are not."

"I can catch scents and understand them like windigos, though I don't stink like one. I can track across any distance like the large lizard creatures, though I do not have their mind-venom. When needed, I can dig like the chupacabras. I can do this." He pursed his lips like he was whistling, but no sound emerged.

Kit bolted upright, narrowly avoiding cracking his head on the cabinets he'd hidden under. He jumped off and I prepared for him to run away. Instead, he zoomed around the room, venting excitement or nerves.

When he stopped, it was in front of Owen, fists clenched. "Do that again."

Owen complied, emitting what had to be one of the many frequencies outside human audio range.

He hunched, as if he could ever make himself smaller than the kid. I loved him for his attempt at reassuring Kit. "I believe you when you say you smelled those from a batch near where your flock disappeared. We all share a base scent. But it was not the batch I was born into. I also have never hunted or harmed your kind. My handlers ordered training exercises. I have killed many ghouls and windigos and vampires. And others like me. I do not kill cubs, or the weak."

Kit stood, thin chest heaving while I made myself not rush over and hug him. He was way worse than I'd ever been concerning what he viewed as being coddled and suffocated. The kid had survived by acting tough.

"You're like me. Only a little, because you're still stupid-big. But whatever." Kit folded his skinny arms, a credible imitation of Bruce.

Owen raised his eyes to the kid's. "The jerk Syndicate vampires keep many cry—many Nons. Some of your flock may be alive. I vow I will help you, and search for them on every mission. Kimi will help me make plans."

Kit stared at him for a beat, hair moving as the mostly humanish ears underneath twitched. "Why aren't you on our team?"

"I am. I am official."

"Not the team-team." Kit gave a truly epic huff. "Our *gaming* team. I'm going to have to teach you, like, *everything*, so I hope you aren't totally dumb."

"Kimi says I am not."

Kit ordering Owen around was officially the best thing ever. Owen and I were breaking the rule about clothes and the pool later, after everyone else went to bed. Bruce could get over it.

I left them to bond, and closed the office door. Rear-ranging the desk to clear a space for my butt, I settled in, reviewing some of the calls and meetings I'd saved.

Midway through Terrance, another Southwestern C.O., complaining about Vee and Liv not telling him, their closest non-family friend, about their newest team additions, a notification popped up.

I closed out the video, and swiped to open the program I'd had running, decrypting all the stolen data from the skeleton key program I'd turned loose in the Syndicate lab computer what seemed like years ago, instead of weeks.

Files opened, and I scanned. Then slowed, and *really* looked. Aside from info on shell companies and laundered funds, local companies popped up. The Syndicate had people in a lot of entertainment groups. The movie industry, and all the streaming services we subscribed to. News groups, fringe and mainstream. Publishing houses. The Syndicate had a *major* presence in Hollywood. Actor's guilds, directors, writers, among investors.

The Syndicate having a facility smack in downtown L.A. wasn't a coincidence, or an attempt to monitor us. They were this close to Hollywood and soundstages for the same reason every other actor or media insider was.

I bailed, jerking the door open and running for the outdoor room. Attracted to the wild beat of my pulse, thanks to their shared DNA, Owen and Kit were a stride behind.

Matteo caught me in a beefy arm, saving me from crashing into the center table and bowls of hummus. "Whoa, carnala. Don't stress. I'm protecting your share of the pizza."

I tossed the tablet at Vee to read, and signed, "Guys, we are about to have a problem."

"We are fighting? I will gather our gear and your knives," Owen rumbled.

I pinpointed my media savvy future-brother-in law, happier than ever to have him on our side, and signed, "Bruce, this is more your kind of fight."

ACKNOWLEDGMENTS

All my gratitude to the amazing Anne Raven of Black Bird Book Covers, as well as to the incredible PR teams at Psst Promotions and Let's Talk! Promotions.

Big, big, HUGE appreciation to editor extraordinaire Dawn of Dawn Alexander Books, for translating my whining into actual plot points, and making Kimi shine.

Props to my fabulous ARC team—the Advance Cryptid Recon Agents—for their enthusiasm, creativity, keen eyes, and cute critter videos. Y'all are the best.

A huge thank you to all the readers who have fallen as hard for the Region Two crew as I have.

Finally, all my love to Mr. WW for his patience, those hours sitting in E.R. vet clinics, and buying the good coffee.

ABOUT THE AUTHOR

Janet Walden-West lives in the Southeast with a pack of show dogs, a couple of kids, and a husband who didn't read the fine print.

She writes intersectional sexy-times romance and boss-girl fantasy heroines.

A PitchWars Mentee/Mentor alum and RWA Golden Heart finalist, she's the author of the contemporary romance series, SALT + STILETTOS: South Beach Romances, and the Region Two Urban Fantasy series. Her Urban Fantasy short stories are available in multiple anthologies.

She is represented by Eva Scalzo of Speilburg Literary Agency.

Visit and sign up for her newsletter to be the first to hear about giveaways, bonus content, and new releases!

Janet Walden-West Home

Janet Walden-West's Advance Cryptid Recon Agents

ALSO BY JANET WALDEN-WEST

If you enjoyed Kimi and Owen's story and want more of Region Two's cryptids, snark, and steam, check out the rest of the series.

Book Five out in Spring 2024.

THE REGION TWO SERIES

Agent Alone: Region Two Series Prequel Novella .5

Agent Zero: Region Two Series Book One

Agent Down: Region Two Series Book Two

Agent of Chaos: Region Two Series Book Three

Agent of Change: Region Two Series Book Four

Visit and sign up for my newsletter to be the first to hear about exclusive content and new releases!

Janet Walden-West Home

Agent Alone Is a FREE Bonus to Newsletter Subscribers

Urban Fantasy Short Stories

"Road Trip" in Chasing the Light Anthology

"Stalking Horse" in Witches, Warriors, and Wise Women

"Glass Ceilings" in Predators in Petticoats Anthology

Contemporary Romance

SALT+STILETTOS